Ursula Hegi

Intrusions

Scribner Paperback Fiction
Published by Simon & Schuster
New York London Toronto Sydney Tokyo Singapore

SCRIBNER PAPERBACK FICTION
Simon & Schuster Inc.
Rockefeller Center
1230 Avenue of the Americas
New York, NY 10020

First Scribner Paperback Fiction Edition 1995

SCRIBNER PAPERBACK FICTION and design are trademarks
of Simon & Schuster Inc.

Manufactured in the United States of America

1   2   3   4   5   6   7   8   9   10

Library of Congress Cataloging-in-Publication Data
Hegi, Ursula.
Intrusions / Ursula Hegi. — 1st Scribner Paperback Fiction ed.
p.   cm.
I. Title.
PR9110.9.H43I5   1996
823—dc20   95-16112
CIP
ISBN: 0-684-80136-1

Grateful acknowledgment is made to the following for permission to reprint
copyrighted material:
General Mills, Inc.: Recipe for "Brains" adapted from *Betty Crocker's Cookbook*,
1978. Used by permission.
Prentice-Hall, Inc.: Selections from *Going Bananas* by Charles Keller. Copy-
right © 1975 by Charles Keller. Used by permission.

For Eric and Adam

*Special thanks to Jean Kennard,
Donald Murray, Rebecca Rule, Susan
Wheeler, and John Yount for their
advice and encouragement.*

Intrusions

1

Megan Stone was walking along the deserted beach.

You will probably ask, Why another book about another woman walking along another beach? Another deserted beach, to be more specific. And you will sigh impatiently, wondering how soon Megan is going to arrive at some monumental insight which will liberate her dramatically from her husband, the demands of her children, and the eighty or ninety Christmas cards she feels obligated to send every year—an insight which will leave her alone in an open-ended situation that could lead anywhere, not excluding nowhere.

Or you might scan the horizon of the plot, waiting for the appearance of a prospective lover, quite likely younger than Megan's forty-one years, who will introduce her to multiple orgasms and fellatio (in neither my *Webster's Collegiate* nor my *Funk & Wagnalls Standard Desk Dictionary*), not to mention various imaginative positions, some of them slightly uncomfortable, and who will serve as a catalyst to free her from her marriage. Naturally, you will expect Megan to sooner or later leave the younger lover (hereafter also referred to as Y.L.), in order to demonstrate her ability to make independent decisions.

Perhaps you imagine their bodies entangled in one of those small harbors of safety among the dunes, those little alcoves away from the ocean where the tall blades of grass protect them from being seen, where the fine sand is soft and white. You can follow the course of Y.L.'s suntanned hands as they explore Megan's body. She arches her back, moaning, as he parts her thighs with his bearded chin, his face nuzzling against the warm softness, his agile tongue circling and probing. She locks her fingers into his thick black hair. Y.L. comes up for air and gets sand up his nose, while Megan, sitting up as she hears him cough and sneeze, gets sand up her . . .

There! Nothing like having your fantasy disrupted by the probabilities of reality. Of course you could have prevented this by including a blanket, one of those woven, striped Indian affairs in rich earthy colors: terra-cotta, Sahara beige, harvest yellow, tobacco brown. Or their position could be entirely different, precluding the possibility of sand obstructing the course of events.

Perhaps you don't want to imagine Megan in the traditionally submissive position, yielding only to those sensations that Y.L. chooses to expose her to. Yours might be a more aggressive, a more independent approach: Y.L. on his back, his knees bent, the only slightly callused soles of his feet digging into the warm sand, the muscles in his thighs trembling with what soon will be ecstasy, as Megan mounts the erection she created, lowering herself, slowly rotating while guiding Y.L.'s right hand to her clitoris (we'll do without worn terms such as surging, throbbing, sliding, etc.), then abandoning herself in a wild ride that would leave Attila the Hun in a cloud of dust, her long, wheat-blond hair whipping the salty breeze like a victorious banner.

2

You could go on to other possibilities, but in reality (the reality within this novel) Megan Stone's hair is short, and not blond but rather a sort of red, too light to be called auburn, the kind of red that usually goes with sunburned skin. She is only twenty-nine, and she has never had a lover, neither younger nor older, not even before she married Nick Stone.

While her as-yet-unknown-to-her husband-to-be was actively researching intimate behavior in Japan, Vietnam, California, Connecticut, and Walsenburg, Colorado, Megan was actively defending herself from becoming the research project of a lifeguard on the Cape who was two inches shorter than she; a ski instructor from Hoboken with a phony Austrian accent; and a history major from the University of Hartford who talked a lot about integrity in politics and opted for graduate school in a failing effort to evade the draft.

Later, when she had been married several years, she found herself cautiously wondering what it would have been like, mildly resenting the disadvantage of not having any basis for comparison. It made her uncomfortable to realize that she still harbored the old but well-worn double standard, that it was all right for a boy but not for a girl. Eight years ago, when she had married Nick, she had actually been glad that he had gathered experience, while she had been in a condition referred to by her Aunt Judy as: clean.

Aunt Judy was not aware of Nick's power of persuasion.

Aunt Judy also had very concrete ideas of what was and was not suitable for a young girl, and, in the fifteen years that Megan had lived with her, Aunt Judy had tried her best to mold her into the role of a NICE GIRL.

Roles. Sometimes it is extremely difficult to shed the roles others expect to see us in, because they obstruct our selves. Perhaps you would like to see me in the role of a writer who does not interrupt, who presents a *slice of life* without interferences, without calling attention to the fact that this is a story.

I won't accept that role.

After all, this is made up, written and revised in many small installments while my youngest son is taking his naps and his brother is in school, after my husband and sons are asleep, during the hours when I should be cooking, cleaning, or studying for a graduate seminar. Part of it is written to the tune of "Sesame Street." (I owe you much, Big Bird and Cookie Monster.) There are sections that won't be written, because at the time I think of them I'll be skiing, pushing a shopping cart, teaching my Freshman English class, or swimming my three-quarters of a mile. All this affects the writing of a novel. I'd expect it to be very different if I lived alone or if both children were in school, if I were not constantly on call. At times I fantasize what—

"No, you may not have another cookie."

My oldest son is standing in the half-open door of my study. "But I'm still hungry." He'd eat all day if I let him. Yet he is skinny. Tall and skinny.

"Why don't you eat an apple?"

He comes closer and picks up the pages I just revised. "What are you doing?" Brown eyes, too inquisitive, start reading.

Standing on my head. Can't you see? But of course I don't say that to him. Instead I answer: "Writing," and take the pages from him. For a second-grader he reads only too well.

"What is it about?" His straight blond hair covers his eyebrows, his ears.

"Why don't you color or play until your brother wakes up?"

"Is it like *Star Wars?*"

"No." Where was I? Megan . . . Aunt Judy . . . Roles . . . What am I going to make for dinner?

"Can I have one of your pencils?"

"Here." I hand him one of my carefully hoarded #1 EX-SOFT pencils. "But it's the last time. If you chew the eraser off this one again, I won't—"

3

When Megan tried to figure out what had motivated her to defend her virginity so staunchly, thereby breaking up several beautiful friendships and free skiing lessons, she could only come up with two reasons: Aunt Judy and the Ten Commandments. And at this point it would have been too costly to find a basis for comparison, even though Nick, during one of their *What if . . . ?* conversations, had indicated that he had no objections if she wanted to do some comparing.

She didn't believe he really meant it.

He sincerely believed he meant it, armed with the slightly superior suspicion that she would never go through with it because of her affliction.

It was not that she was an albino.

Neither was she retarded, spastic, diabetic, arthritic, big-nosed, nymphomaniac, deaf, or claustrophobic. What Megan thought of as an affliction also had nothing to do with her height of six feet plus one and a half inches.

Megan's affliction was rather an absolutely unreasonable sense of guilt, an amount of guilt sufficient to cripple the population of a medium-sized town, a force of guilt powerful enough to stop a mismatched army of Foreign Legionnaires.

It's difficult to trace an affliction like this back to its origin, but it certainly was nurtured by her guardians' reaction to Megan's confessions:

"I broke a window. Afterwards I helped a blind man across the street."

"I threw mud at Benji Steckler. I learned how to count to one thousand."

"I had to stand in the corner because I didn't listen to the teacher. I was the first one finished with the spelling test."

You might argue here that this was merely an early and rather clumsy attempt at diplomacy, a sly effort to lessen the predictable punishment by padding the bad news with an absorbent layer of good. I don't think so. Chances are that Aunt Judy and Uncle Vincent would never have found out about the majority of Megan's *sins*. But she told them, voluntarily, feeling compelled to confess before she could even bring herself to talk about anything else. Strict disciplinarians, her guardians would punish her for what she had done wrong, thereby absolving her. Afterwards they would express their satisfaction about her honesty, and she'd feel new and clean and good. Until the next *sin*.

Megan attracted guilt the instant she committed something even remotely resembling a prospective *sin*. While other children her age had to strain in order to search their souls, had to sweat while working up the lather of guilt with the bristles of regret (indispensable for the cleansing of above souls), Megan held stock in SOAP. She was the chairperson of the board, the one who called the mergers, the virtuoso and the ascetic. Even contemplating a *sin* produced guilt. But since she also was an extremely stubborn child who refused to defer to the wisdom of those who considered themselves wiser—thereby exposing herself to a lifetime of ITOLDYOUSOS—pre-action guilt rarely kept her from doing something she really wanted to do. She carried the tortures of guilt with the stoicism of an Indian.

4

"Indians don't cry," her Austrian grandfather had told her. He had emigrated to Manhattan when he was nineteen and had lived there in a narrow brownstone with his wife, Dagmar, until he died the year before Megan's parents and brother were buried.

She would have liked to be an Indian. Crying filled her with shame and fury. She saw it as a sign of weakness and never even cried during a funeral service.

"She is such a cold little girl," Aunt Judy told Mrs. Edwards.

"She will be tall like her father," Aunt Judy told Uncle Vincent.

It didn't matter that there were no Indians in Austria and that in 1626, three centuries before Megan's grandfather came to *Manahatin,* the Indians sold their hill island to Peter Minuit, the director general of the Dutch colony, for sixty guilders.

They were paid in goods.

NO REFUNDS.

Indians don't cry.

5

But I'm wandering off, leaving Megan all by herself on the deserted Nantucket beach. So let's get back to the first sentence of Chapter 1:

Megan Stone was walking along the deserted beach.

There was nobody but she—no husband, no Y.L., no Indian, no lifeguard, no mad-killer-rapist (or is it mad-rapist-killer?), no Good-Humor-person. But there was a building, a lighthouse: the Great Point Light.

It looked deceptively close.

If somebody had walked up to Megan with a microphone—say, a reporter from the Boston *Globe* or the Hartford *Times*, perhaps even from the Laconia *Evening Citizen*—a reporter who would have asked her to define what was most important to her, Megan would quite likely have replied: *solitude*, to be completely alone without even the slightest possibility of an interruption, without even the slightest probability of the possibility of an interruption.

Two hours later, her feet bleeding, her priorities would have changed considerably.

But while walking toward the Great Point Light, only about halfway on the five-mile stretch between Wauwinet House and the light, she would have opted for solitude. Being Megan, she probably would have added that she considered walking along a deserted beach one of the most romantic things in the world. Walking barefoot, that is.

You have to take into consideration that, prior to the disillusioning walk on this specific Nantucket beach, Megan had never been able to find a deserted beach, and that although she had pretended to be walking along deserted beaches in Connecticut, Maine, New Hampshire, and New Jersey, while picking her path through toddlers, sand castles, pet chihuahuas, plastic shovels, and other elements associated with tourism, she had never quite succeeded in convincing herself that these beaches were deserted.

So let's dismiss the reporter, who is merely another figment of your imagination, and let's follow Megan on her solitary walk along the beach, stepping into the imprints of her bare feet just before they fill with water that seeps in minute bubbles from the wet sand, foamy bubbles, making her footprints indistinguishable from those areas she never touched.

Solitude.

This was the year when Megan's children were two and

four, when she always felt surrounded by their needs even when she was not with them (which was very seldom), when ninety percent of her conversations hovered on the level of a two- or four-year-old, when she began to doubt if she had ever possessed any intelligence and, if so, worried that it was evaporating like fumes from an open can of cleaning fluid.

(—Wait. I just remembered a critic who wrote that women writers tend to use metaphors connected to their houses. Maybe I should change the cleaning fluid to paint thinner, moving at least into the garage area of metaphors.)

6

The year?

Let's make it 1976, also the year that Megan became aware that the unhappiness she felt from time to time was not caused by her husband, was not caused by her children, was not caused by Aunt Judy, was not caused by her neighbors, was not caused by her friends, but—(we'll start out here with the insight and go back to the causes of the insight later, although this is highly irregular)—was caused by her expectations.

There. Insight: Megan became aware of the painful clashes between her expectations and reality. Sometimes those clashes were mere frost bumps in the road, easily absorbed by her present means of transportation. At other times they were collisions that shattered her perspective. The most painful ones were the falls like the one when, nine years old, she practiced to be a tightrope walker for the circus to which she was going to run away when it came the next time. For weeks she rehearsed on top of the narrow metal fence in back of her friend Karen's house.

It became easy.

She became confident.

The only difference would be the height.

But they had nets.

She'd wear a white skirt, a short white skirt.

She'd learn to juggle oranges.

She would not carry one of those frilly umbrellas.

When she slipped, the metal rod stopped her fall by slamming against her crotch. She limped home, afraid to tell Aunt Judy and ashamed to examine her bruises, which brings a lengthy deliberation on clashes between expectations and reality back to where it began. Sometimes, unless it was one of the metal rod/fear/shame variety, Megan would collect the shattered fragments of her expectations, salvage them and embroider them into the semblance of more realistic expectations.

7

I can hear him breathing on the other side of my door, can hear his body move as he curls up against the door, can hear the clicking sound his tongue makes when he sucks his left index finger. What kind of mother could keep on writing while her youngest is pressing his body against the other side of the closed door? I certainly can't. Noise I can handle, fights between the boys, chicken pox, even the continuous: *I'm hungry, Mommy.* But not this. It's the third time he's doing it; the other days I stopped typing immediately, opened the door, asked him what the matter was, watched him grin at me, then played and read with him for the next few hours.

Maybe he'll go away if I don't pay attention.

But the carpet in the hall is soft. Comfortable.

I don't want him to catch on that his breathing under the door is more effective than loud complaints about not having enough of my time. It's effective because it makes me feel guilty about writing instead of spending time with him and his brother, makes me worry that something might happen to them while I'm behind the closed door of my study.

How much time is enough time?

clickclickclickclick

I can't stand this.

As I open the door, he's lying there, waiting, trying not to grin. His fine white hair is messy. It always looks messy, even minutes after brushing. His eyes are blue, his eyebrows almost black. My child of contrasts. Not only in looks. Little-boy toughness and wanting to be held.

"Why are you doing this to me?" Did I really end the question with *to me*? The all-time guilt-producing ending of a question? The ending I consciously never, or almost never, use because I don't want my children to grow up with a guilt complex.

How I wish I were somewhere else, alone, walking.

8

Megan's feet did not begin to bleed until she was almost halfway back to Wauwinet. While walking toward the light, which, consistently, looked a mere few hundred yards away, there had been a certain stubborn motivation that made her set one foot in front of the other, even after she stopped enjoying it. She never thought of going back before getting there, just as she would never consider not finishing a book after investing several hours in it.

The lighthouse was empty and boarded up, the door crudely nailed shut. A faded, printed sign threatened prospective intruders with fines and/or imprisonment.

Megan, who had pictured a winding wrought-iron staircase, an unspoiled view of the island from above, serenity, and untamed cries of silver-bodied seagulls, sat down on a rock next to the door of the Great Point Light, right in a tamed, silver-white glob of seagull shit.

Walking back was total misery.

Two Jeeps passed her, whipping up the sand, while Megan felt as though she were treading in place. They were heading in the wrong direction, toward the lighthouse. Both had fishing poles in back. What if she motioned the second Jeep down and asked, no, begged the driver to take her back to Wauwinet? Before she could decide if it was safe and if he would be insulted if she offered to pay him and what Nick might say, the Jeep had passed her. And it was only then that she remembered she hadn't any money with her. Nick had dropped her off in the parking area next to Wauwinet House, and she had left her wallet in the side pocket of the canvas beach bag. Although Nick sometimes did not share her dreams—in other words, thought it ludicrous to walk barefoot across ten miles of sand but didn't quite come out and say so—he usually was moderately cooperative in helping her to achieve them. He wouldn't be back until two, five hours after leaving her off.

She could picture him on the old blue quilt, lying on his stomach, his face turned toward the ocean, watching Tim and Nicole. Nick preferred the children's beach: there were barely any waves. Instead there were bathrooms, a snack bar, and play equipment.

She began to meditate on the luxury of lying on a quilt among oodles of oiled bodies, on the pleasure of watching Timmy erect a sand hill and telling Nicole not to destroy her brother's artwork. Naturally, Nicole eventually would manage to step into her brother's castle, and he would have to be reminded that it wasn't right to mug one's sister.

How she missed them!

She stopped and sat down, feeling hot and perspired. Her shoulders tingled. After she'd walked for an hour, the lighthouse looked as though she had left it minutes ago.

It would be nice to take a quick—

"Yes, I'll be out in a minute. Just let me finish this

chapter. I know it's hot. We'll go to the lake in half . . . Why don't you get your bathing suit on? Help your brother find his. No, I don't know where it is. Just a—"

9

It would be nice to take a quick swim.

Staring at the expanse of sand and ocean, Megan was blinded by the combination of shifting slate and monotonous beige. Yesterday, Timmy had whined her into buying him one of those rubber shark atrocities, modeled after the mechanical shark partly responsible for the commercial success of *Jaws*, a grayish-white and blue, soft-bellied, double-toothed, red-tongued, green-eyed, flat-skulled, sick-to-the-touch tourist snag. It was ridiculous to even think of that; no self-respecting shark would be caught dead or alive looking like what Timmy lovingly called his "Jaws."

She couldn't bring herself to walk into the water.

It would be different if someone were around, at least a witness to her disappearance, just in case she got pulled out by the undertow or was attacked (and this was too absurd to even consider, but she considered it twice) by something resembling the model for Tim's rubber shark.

She could picture the headlines:

CONNECTICUT HOUSEWIFE disappears without trace from Nantucket . . . the young children, vulnerable in their innocent grief [good grief] . . . too young to fully comprehend . . . huddled closely to the hairy legs of their tall, handsome father. . . . His grief-stricken words: "Even if she hated to make breakfast, I still loved her." . . . A statement from the victim's mother-in-law: "I was always suspicious of a wife and mother unable to find pleasure in cooking eggs and bacon every morning. Although we gave her every chance to make her way into our hearts—and I mean, *every chance*—I just knew she would come to a bad end. . . ."

Nick's mother would click her tongue—tuttuttut—and shake her Florida-styled hair with the light hue of blue. She'd lose no time finding a proper wife for her son, a local girl from a good West Hartford family, a girl who'd have to sign an affidavit prior to the wedding, swearing to cook a four-course breakfast every morning.

"Poor children," Nick's second wife would sigh when visiting her new in-laws twice a month in their brick colonial. "Poor darlings, they were actually surprised to get eggs and bacon every day. Well, not just eggs and bacon, I do bring some variety into their half-orphaned lives with French toast or waffles and sausages. But the poor, sweet dears thought that a decent breakfast was a special treat reserved for birthdays, Christmas, Easter, and Father's Day."

"It was probably all for the better," Nick's mother would say. "How I admire you young mothers. I don't know how you do it."

The second Mrs. Nick Stone would probably be a blonde. A blonde with lovely legs. Megan had never felt self-conscious about her straight legs until Nick had told her, once, after five Harvey Wallbangers, that he was basically a leg man, as opposed to a tit or ass man.

"Then you married the wrong person," Megan had replied.

Nick had assured her that he had married her for her brains.

Brains were a soft, gray, and not very appetizing mass; although some people seemed to consider them a delicacy. Megan had never eaten them. On one of her rare excursions through *Betty Crocker's Cookbook*, which Nick's mother had given her a couple of months after the wedding, she had come across a recipe for brains, right next to the page announcing the fish and seafood section, with a color photo of a dead-looking, scaly fish with glassy eyes, laid out on a bed of ice. With a mixture of fascination and repulsion, she had read the recipe:

BRAINS

Brains are soft in consistency, very tender and have a delicate flavor. They should be cooked immediately. Precooking makes them firm, then they can be broiled, fried, braised, creamed or served in a sauce. Precooked brains can be served in the following ways: broken into small pieces and scrambled with eggs; reheated in a rich cream or well-seasoned tomato sauce; dipped into slightly beaten egg, then into crumbs and fried in a small amount of shortening or in deep fat until a delicate golden brown; in croquettes; in salads.

Following the precooking instructions were detailed suggestions for surgery, so intricate and full of finesse that only a brain surgeon could have performed them: drain (drain the brain?); plunge into cold water; with sharp knife remove membrane . . .

One thing she could be certain of: whenever Nick thought of her brains (and she didn't know how he pictured them) they certainly would not appear in a vision of broken small pieces scrambled with eggs.

Yes, the second Mrs. Stone would have very nice legs.

The second Mrs. Stone would also be very domestic, extremely domestic, a former home economics major, baking pies and Lemon-Pledging previously unPledged furniture, an expert in cake decorating.

Instead of T-shirts, the second Mrs. Stone would be wearing see-through nightgowns to bed. She'd read the social announcements in the local paper, and she would not only go to but also give Tupperware parties, serving cupcakes from plates-so-shiny-you-can-see-yourself. Lovely. She would join all the organizations whose invitations

Megan, politely, had rejected, including the Create-a-Recipe-Group, the Green Thumbs, the Mothers-of-Toddlers, and the West Hartford Coupon Swappers.

Once a week she'd have her hair done at the Saucy Scissors Sunshine Salon. Her face she'd do herself, twice a day, to get that natural look. Lovely. Before Nick came home in the evening, the second Mrs. Stone would slip into something-more-comfortable, and on weekends—

No.

Megan could believe the breakfast part, perhaps. But the rest? Nick would die of boredom.

Of course he would.

Did he really know how many attempts she had made to fulfill that part of wife-ness that meant so much to him, dragging herself to handle pans, eggs, bacon, dishes, obligations, butter, jam, and various other things she couldn't get herself to face in the morning, trying to look cheerful while watching Nick and the children stuff their faces with the harvest of her guilt, wishing to crawl into her favorite corner of the sofa with a cup of coffee and a book until sufficiently awake to officially start the day? She didn't mind stirring hot cereal and pouring juice for everybody, even making hot chocolate before withdrawing to her corner and book; but the barbaric preparation of runny egg whites and globby yolks filled her with resentment. Facing streaked dishes and scrubbing the pan afterwards didn't help to entice her into repetitions of the ordeal.

The longest she had ever lasted in uninterrupted breakfast making was six days.

Still, Nick would die of boredom with the second Mrs. Stone, with her painted, perky sexiness, her artificial naturalness, her lemon-scented personality.

10

Would he?

Megan got up and brushed off the fine warm sand that clung to the back of her damp thighs. Cautiously and against her better judgment she walked into the ocean to where the waves broke just above her knees. As she stopped, she felt the water rush back out, taking the particles of sand from beneath her toes, making her feel as though she were being washed out with the sand, sliding into the ocean, even though she hadn't moved. Another wave covered her kneecaps and rushed out from under her. She dug her toes into the wet sand, trying to hold on to it, but the waves continued to wash the sand from beneath her feet, from between her curled toes, making her sink deeper into her own imprints.

After walking another ten or fifteen minutes, her feet hurt more than before. Softened by the water, they were swollen. Particles of sand rubbed sharply against her skin.

CONNECTICUT HOUSEWIFE felled by sore feet . . .

She had never thought of herself as a housewife until last fall when she had to take Freshman English at the University of Hartford. After years of enrolling in one course each semester, slowly working toward her B.A. in humanities, she didn't find out until she was a senior that she should have taken Freshman English a long time ago, that she couldn't graduate without it. By then her original adviser was teaching at the University of Arkansas, while her new adviser assumed she had already taken Freshman English.

She was the oldest in the class; even the instructor, a five-foot-one Ph.D. candidate who dressed in velour jackets and jeans, was younger than she. Three weeks into the semester the students were asked to interview each other. Megan's partner was Daniel, a green-eyed, fat-chinned freshman from Bristol, whose last name either started with an F or an M, and who confessed to such areas of interest as motorcycles, the church he attended, snow-mobiles, and TV. He enjoyed reading science fiction and motorcycle magazines, admired and held in highest regard the 1974 winner of the National Motorcycle Races, and had ambitions of becoming either a disc jockey, a mission-ary, or a motorcycle racer.

Revising and editing her interview at home while Nicole napped and Timmy played next door, Megan spent hours straining her understanding and insight, trying to credit Daniel with sensibilities foreign to his nature. She didn't write about his breath, a stale combination of chocolate and onions. She even left out his skimpy mustache of unidentifiable color, the kind of mustache that would always look skimpy and ratty. Instead she created an image of such intelligence and premature wisdom that it would have brought tears of gratitude to his mother's eyes.

The following week they exchanged their interviews.

The title of Daniel's paper ran three lines:

How a thirty-year-old housewife manages to go back to colledge and still fufill her duties for her husbant, children and house.

And that was the best part of the paper. The rest was downhill. By the time Megan had deciphered his sixteen lines, she felt middle-aged. Twenty-eight or thirty, what difference did it make? She might as well have been from another generation, another planet.

Daniel's write-up of her possible disappearance would probably run something like this:

CONNECTICUT HOUSEWIFE, mother of two, apducted from Namtucket beach. No traces. Eyewittneses report the apearance of a gigantic white wahle of mythycal proportions. After spouting around for a wihle, he rode off into the sunsset, carryng upon his back a tall redhaired Connectucut Housewive . . .

11

To justify my intrusions into this manuscript, I might have pretended to have found a diary somewhere, not necessarily on a deserted Nantucket beach, but perhaps in an attic room my aunt rented to a stranger.

Or I could have told you that I came upon this story when I went through the records of, say, some government official at the customs house, that I'm tracing the lives of those committed to black ink in his stiff handwriting, that I'm trying to make sense of their experience, separating that which is of value from that which is not, ordering, patterning.

What if I had begun with the headlines from a murder trial, drawing upon the court stenographer's notes, accounts from witnesses, gossip from the exterminator and from the man at the poodle parlor, significant information that could lend an aura of credibility to this story?

All these devices would excuse the intrusion of the "I."

But I've never gone through the records of a government official at the customs house, and there is no diary, murder trial, or poodle in sight.

Perhaps you expect that I'm using the "I" as a screen, that I'll identify myself in the last chapter as Megan, jumping out of the six-foot-one-and-a-half disguise, shouting: *Surprise!* leaving you with the rewarding feeling of having guessed it all along.

But I'm not Megan.

I'm only writing about her; making her up; imagining a

childhood, husband, friends, even children for her; changing words, sentences, paragraphs with each revision;
adding details, lovers, dreams, and fears; taking out
scuba-diving lessons, lovers, semicolons, a demented
milkman, entire chapters.

12

Nick didn't say: "I told you so."

She wasn't surprised. She had known all along he
wouldn't say that.

He showed neither an excessive nor a mild amount of
sympathy which would have proven extremely beneficial
to her crushed state of mind and her sore and blistered
state of body.

Instead he said: "I hope you remembered to pack the
Solarcaine."

He looked well rested, evenly tanned, while Megan's
arms and shoulders were burning—a hot, tingling sensation which she knew from experience to be only the early
stage of what would be a fierce, throbbing (acceptable,
except in previous and subsequent sex scenes) burn by
evening, a burn that would keep her out of the sun and in
the shade for the rest of the vacation, a burn that would
ensure her celibacy for at least three days, a burn that
would ultimately leave her with torn shreds of peeling
skin.

"Yes. It's on the shelf in the bathroom."

"I'll put some on you when we get to the cottage."

The children were asleep on the backseat: Nicole with
her thumb about to slip out of her chocolate-smeared
mouth, her pale curls frizzy from the salt water; Timmy clutching "Jaws" against his terry-cloth jacket, his
reddish-brown hair still damp from swimming.

"Did you have a nice morning?" Megan asked into the
silence.

He nodded.

"I hope you weren't too worried about me," she tried.

He shook his head.

She believed him.

"What if I hadn't been back in time?"

"But you were," he said without taking his eyes off the road.

Why did so many of their conversations have question marks behind her sentences and shrugs or nods instead of his sentences? Why did he have to be so infuriatingly uncommunicative? Although she knew that he didn't like to talk a lot while driving, his silence annoyed her. It also annoyed her that he never seemed to have any doubts that she could take care of herself. While she worried about him, worried about the children, worried about what might or might not happen in one or ten years, Nick never seemed to worry about anything, least of all about her, even when she was alone in ten miles of treacherous sand where anything could have happened. He didn't even know how lucky he was that nothing had happened. He probably wasn't even aware of all that could possibly have happened to her out there.

Sometimes she thought he didn't care about her at all.

Sometimes (and this was not one of those times) she thought he must love her very much to not interfere in her decisions.

Sometimes she wished he would try to talk her out of a decision.

There are conversations and there are conversations. Some of them are not so ideal. Others are.

For Megan, on August 19, 1976, the ideal conversation would have run something like this:

NICK: I wish I had come with you. You must have felt miserable out there, all alone.

MEGAN *leans her head against* NICK's *shoulder.*

NICK: I was terribly worried about you. Anything could have happened to you out there all alone.

MEGAN *nods, rubbing her left cheek against his bare shoulder.*

NICK: I couldn't live without you.

BACKGROUND: *the sound of violins.*

AUDIENCE: *gets sick and/or walks out.*

13

This chapter belongs to my husband, who is taking our sons to Burger King so I can write.

"Who is Nick?" he asks as he is leaving.

"Nick?"

He nods. "Nick." His dark brown hair looks shorter than usual; I wonder if he had it cut today.

"I'm hungry." Our four-year-old is tugging his father's hand, trying to pull him out of my study.

"You were talking in your sleep again last night," my husband says.

"In English?" Most of the time when I talk in my sleep, it's in German. That's what my husband tells me in the morning. I take his word for it, although it surprises me, since I think in English by now.

"I'm not sure. I couldn't understand a word except for 'Nick.' That you repeated several times."

"He's just one of the characters in the novel." I wish I could decide what Nick looks like. So far I've avoided a physical description. I know he's tall and a good tennis player. A demon at the net. Should I give him dark curly hair and glasses? Or is he blond? Maybe I'll give him blue eyes and blond hair, straight and thick, covering the tops of his ears. Yes, I can picture him with straight hair. He'd push it back once a while with his hand. Which hand? It would be out of habit rather than necessity, because it isn't long enough to hang into his eyes. His eyes could be blue, a very dark blue. If I decide to make his hair dark, his eyes could be hazel. I'll give him monogrammed shirts. His mother buys him three every Christmas. He wears them because he doesn't care enough about clothes not to wear them. Would that make sense? The first time Megan sees him, she—

"You want us to bring you anything?" my husband asks.

"No. Thanks. Are you sure you don't mind taking them out again?"

He shakes his head, as I hoped he would, and by the time he closes the door, I'm already typing.

Sometimes our oldest son sits at the desk in his room and writes stories in the blue books I buy for him. Already he has written four sequels of *Star Kids*. His fiction is better known than mine: his teacher encourages him to read his stories to the other second-graders. I admire my son's confidence. To him the dedications are almost as important as the stories. All his blue books are dedicated to us, except for one, which reads:

> For the boy I was—
> the book I could not find.

When I first saw it, I felt shaken. Awed. How could he conceive something like that? I must have failed him. *The boy I was.* Did he feel his childhood was over at seven? How much had my writing intruded on my children's lives? How often had I asked them to play quietly and not to interrupt me?

"Why did you write that?" I asked.

"Because I wanted to."

That night I barely slept. Not only had I deprived my son of his childhood, but I had also neglected to find the right books for him. My husband assured me there must be a logical explanation. I thought he was heartless to be able to sleep.

To concentrate on my writing was impossible the next morning. Instead I read Dr. Spock. But Dr. Spock did not offer a chapter on the dedications of seven-year-old writers.

When my son came home from school, I sat down with him in the living room, prepared to spend the rest of the day in a long conversation to reassure him his childhood was not over yet.

Very carefully I began, "What made you think of writing this dedication?"

He shrugged.

"You can tell me." I put one arm around his shoulders.

"It's in front of that book with step-by-step animal drawings. The one you gave me for my birthday. It's neat. Can I have a snack now?"

14

Perhaps I should have started this novel with the beginning of Megan's life. But chronological time is not necessarily instrumental in influencing present experience. Fantasies, dreams, wishes, and half-forgotten memories all become part of it. Megan, faced with a decision, might narrow the alternatives by applying logic, drawing upon her knowledge and experience. After limiting the options to the best one, weighing the consequences, considering their effect on Nick, Tim, Nicole, a dozen or more other people, and, maybe, herself, she might suddenly find herself doing something completely different from what she decided, something perhaps motivated by a memory that surfaced, such as catching her reflection in the gym window when, at twelve, she was more than a head taller than the other girls in the class; or falling down right in front of Norm Vallencourt just because he smiled at her from a distance, and she got so confused that she stumbled over her own feet; or dreaming almost every night that there would be a knock at the front door and her parents would be standing there with her brother, Michael; or having her hair braided by Aunt Judy and hearing her say: "Your mother had pretty gray eyes, just like you."

Megan's first conscious memory was that of a room with the curtains drawn.

Whenever she tried to remember beyond that day when she was three and had to play in her bed, although it was still light outside, her mind stopped at the same image: the low railing in front of her bed, white, with small toothmarks.

In the next room her mother cried.

Once, her mother screamed.

Then there was another sound.

Most of all she remembered the hand. It smelled of soap. It was a square hand with black hair on it. Curly hair. It looked very dark and big and it held two white things.

She took them.

"Stop crying, Meg."

The booties were soft and fuzzy.

In the next room her father laughed.

"Remember me, Meg? I'm Dr. Hamilton. I just brought you a surprise. Listen."

The other sound in the next room was a baby crying.

"That's your new brother, Michael. You can play with his booties."

So they came with booties. Her mother said the stork brought them. Dr. Hamilton said he brought them. Storks liked sugar. Sometimes she put sugar cubes on the windowsill in the evening. They were always gone in the morning.

Maybe the stork had bitten her mother.

15

She remembered her mother as always smiling.

Two days before they all were to fly to California for a vacation, the left side of Megan's neck began to hurt whenever she chewed or swallowed. The following morning her mother found a swelling under Megan's left ear, a hard swelling that covered part of the jawbone and pushed up her earlobe.

"Mumps," said Dr. Hamilton.

"I'll take care of her," said Aunt Judy. "No need for you to cancel your vacation. You've planned it for so long. Besides, it's only for a week. She'll be fine with me."

"I'll miss you," said Megan's mother. "I'll call you every evening."

When they told Megan, she was drinking apple juice. The plane had crashed ten minutes after taking off, killing everybody.

Indians don't cry.

"Megan is such a cold little girl," said Aunt Judy to Mrs. Edwards, the mother of Megan's best friend, Maureen. "I worry about her."

Megan could never tolerate the taste of apple juice again.

She tried not to think about them at all.

When you're six years old and your parents tell you that they'll be back in a week, that they'll call you every evening and then go away and take your brother with them, but not you, when they never call you as they promised and never come back, but just die, you learn a powerful lesson. You learn that someone you love can just leave. And if you think about it, think about it for a long time, you suddenly know that it's much safer not to love. If you don't love anybody, you can't be hurt; nobody can walk off with part of you and leave.

And when they make you stay with an aunt you knew from Sunday dinners, an aunt who smells nice like pine needles but has a loud voice and wet kisses that you used to squirm away from when she visited, when they leave you with this aunt who won't let you forget because she says:

"Blue was your mother's favorite color too," or
"Your father would be proud of you," or
"I know how much you miss your parents,"
you might find that, sometimes, you even hate your mother and father for breaking their promises.

As an adult her memories of them would be identical to the black-and-white photos in the beige album her mother had kept in the form of a diary. She would remember only those occasions her mother had chosen to enter in blue ink, never certain if she remembered them from the album or from her own experience.

10–12–50
Megan started nursery school last month. Today she ran away from there for the third time. She rejects any kind of constraint. Her teacher suggests keeping her home until she is four. It worries me. In a few years she'll have to accept structure.

Prior to this entry were others which she didn't remember, entries which seemed to support Aunt Judy's opinion that she had been a difficult child.

7–14–49
Although she likes to go for walks, Megan always asks first: "Hold hand?" If I answer: "Yes, you have to hold my hand," she refuses to go, and there isn't anything that can entice her to come along. I've tried to persuade her that it's safer to hold my hand because of the traffic. We've punished her, even tried to bribe her with caramels. Nothing seems to work. I wish I knew what to do about her stubbornness.

There was a chart of Megan's height and weight, first on a weekly, then on a monthly, later on a yearly basis. Below the photos her mother had written little captions.

LEARNING TO WALK. Bowlegged, clinging to a hand extended to her from above, Megan squinted into the camera. She wore a light-colored dress with ruffles. Next to her was a very shapely pair of legs, covered to below the knee with a dark skirt. Nick would have appreciated those legs. She wondered if they belonged to her mother.

HER FAVORITE BEAR. Megan at three, holding a dark, limp shape. She was sitting on her mother's knees. Her mother's hair fell to her shoulders and she was smiling. Her mother's name reminded her of the sound a brook makes: Barbara.

There were other pictures, taken after her brother was born, with her mother holding both of them and smiling, or Michael sitting on her mother's lap while Megan stood by her side. Michael's hair was light like her mother's.

12–25–52
They get along so well, maybe because they are very different. Megan sees everything as a problem, requiring an immediate solution. Sometimes I wish she were less serious. Michael is satisfied to let things follow their natural course. He loves to listen to the stories Megan makes up for him, and she answers every one of his many questions.

Only a few pictures of her father were in the album; he must have been the photographer. He always wore a suit and tie and looked very tall and thin. His glasses were square with dark frames, and he smiled with his lips closed.

SHE LIKES TO TAKE CARE OF THE RABBIT. Megan, four or five, holding a rabbit and sitting with her grandmother on the back steps. What ever became of the rabbit? Aunt Judy said she'd never seen the rabbit and that she didn't know whose rabbit it was. After the accident Megan had wondered if perhaps the rabbit too had been on the plane.

16

The characters have moved in. They follow me around, even crowd my family at the dinner table. There isn't enough room for all of us. I can barely move. Nobody but me is aware of them.

"My name isn't Nicole," my youngest son complains when I ask him to wipe his mouth.

It could be worse.

I might have to cook for them.

But they seem to require no nourishment, and I don't know who folds their laundry.

17

After the blue writing stopped, Aunt Judy kept up the album. One of the first photos was taken on Megan's seventh birthday, sitting at the kitchen table with Maureen, Uncle Vincent, and her grandmother, Dagmar, who had come from New York for a visit. Sometimes she wished she could live with Dagmar. She pronounced it Doug-meh, the way her grandmother had taught her to. Aunt Judy said New York wasn't a good place for a child to grow up in. Megan liked the stories Dagmar told her, stories about her mother, Barbara, when she was a little girl. Her favorite was the story of when her mother was a baby, two months old, and her grandparents came over with her on a big ship, all the way from Europe. Aunt Judy was born three years after they settled in Manhattan.

Aunt Judy never told stories; she read aloud already-made stories from books she bought for Megan. For her birthday she gave Megan two books, a dress, a red bicycle, and soap: three pieces of soap shaped like ducks in blue, yellow, and green. When Megan took them into the tub that evening, they sank to the bottom instead of floating like ducks should. They were pointy and hardly made any foam.

From the living room she could hear Aunt Judy's voice: "I wish you wouldn't let her call you by your first name, Mother."

"Not again, Judy. We've been through this before."

"What's wrong with calling you 'Grandmother'?"

"She's called me Dagmar since she learned to talk. Don't you think there have been enough changes for her this year?"

"If you ask me . . ."

"I'm not. So don't tell me what to do."

Megan thought of the other day Dagmar had told Aunt Judy not to tell her what to do. That day it had rained. Wearing a dark blue skirt that felt itchy against her thighs, she had sat between Dagmar and her aunt on a hard bench, listening to the voice of the minister without understanding what he was saying. Close to the minister were three coffins. She knew they were called coffins because she'd seen coffins in monster cartoons. Two were brown and large; the other small and white. She knew who was in them. She knew. And if she pressed her fingers against her left cheek, it still hurt. But only if she pressed hard.

"Don't," Aunt Judy said and took Megan's hand into hers. Aunt Judy was wearing black gloves.

Afterwards she drove Megan to the duplex and left her with Maureen Edwards's mother, who brought out cookie cutters and six slices of white bread. Megan and Maureen cut out soft shapes: stars and dogs and bears, brushed them with melted butter, and sprinkled them with sugar and cinnamon. When Megan dropped the sugar bowl and it broke, Mrs. Edwards told her it didn't matter and got out the dustpan and broom.

They baked the bread shapes on two round cookie sheets; the whole kitchen smelled of cinnamon.

Everybody else was at the place where the coffins got

buried. Dead people got buried. Everybody knew that. But where? What if nobody ever told her where?

Maureen ate all the warm cinnamon bread because Megan wasn't hungry. When Aunt Judy came to pick Megan up, her eyes looked puffy, and she wouldn't say where they had taken Megan's Mom and Dad and Michael.

"Hush now," Aunt Judy said. "You don't want to be thinking about that."

Through the backyard they walked to the kitchen door. It wasn't raining anymore, but the grass was still wet, and Megan stepped into the shallow puddle next to the back steps. Aunt Judy looked at her but didn't say anything. Dagmar was in the living room with Uncle Vincent and some other people whose names Megan didn't know, all of them wearing black clothes like Aunt Judy. On the coffee table was a glass vase with white flowers, a cake, and a plate with small sandwiches.

"I want to go there." Megan looked at her grandmother.

"Where?"

"Where they're buried."

"Be a sensible girl now," Aunt Judy said.

Uncle Vincent got up to look out of the window. The back of his suit jacket had a long crease in it.

"How about some nice hot chocolate?" Aunt Judy asked.

She'd never find them again. She wouldn't know where to look for them because . . . Because . . . "I'll never find them."

Dagmar got up, reaching for her handbag. "Have you seen my car keys, Judy?"

"Now, Mother," Aunt Judy said. "She's far too young to—"

"Don't tell me what to do, Judy," Dagmar said.

They left the car next to a gray pillar by a wide hedge with a straight top. Holding her grandmother's hand, Megan walked with her on the wide dirt path between graves. That's what they were called, Dagmar said, graves.

Most of them had flowers and bushes and tall rocks on them. Headstones, Dagmar said. The one where her parents and Michael were didn't have a headstone. Not yet, Dagmar said. But it had been ordered and would have their names on it. Now there was only a mound of wet brown dirt. No weeds or grass on it like on the dirt pile in back of the house where she and Michael used to dig tunnels for their cars.

And then she knew where they were.

Walking back down the path, Dagmar's hand felt cold. They drove to a restaurant where grown-ups were drinking coffee and tea at small round tables. Just grown-ups. No kids. A waiter in a red jacket brought a tray with two pots of tea, slices of lemon, wrapped sugar cubes, and four little square cakes with pink and white icing. Megan ate three cakes; the tea was sweet and lemony. Then she slipped off her chair. Just like that. It wasn't the slipping she remembered—she didn't even know she was slipping —just the sudden sitting on the floor and looking at the curved metal legs of the table. A half-burned match was lying on the floor. Dagmar helped her up, and Megan ate the last cake, white with a pink flower.

When they got home, Aunt Judy's eyes still looked puffy, and she didn't yell. Twice that night, when Megan woke up, Aunt Judy got up from the blue chair by the window and bent over her bed. Once she brought her a glass of water. In the morning she was still sitting in the chair, asleep, wearing the black dress, her head and shoulders slumped sideways, her mouth a little open.

18

There were other photos in the album, some of them showing Megan alone, standing in front of a door or a tree with her hands behind her back, her shoulders pulled forward so she wouldn't look so tall. She didn't like being the tallest in class. In a few of the pictures Maureen Edwards was standing next to her. Most of the photos were taken during vacations. Aunt Judy would approach strangers, explaining to them how to use the square camera she usually carried tied to the handle of her light brown handbag. There were snapshots of Aunt Judy, Uncle Vincent, and Megan in London, Venice, Heidelberg, Budapest, Zurich, and Washington, always in front of a church or fountain easily identified with that city. In all of them Megan stood between her legal guardians.

And then came the pictures of Megan and Aunt Judy without Uncle Vincent, visiting many of the same places again. Uncle Vincent and Maureen Edwards disappeared from the beige album within the same page. The last photo of them was taken Easter 1961 in the garden behind the duplex. Mrs. Edwards and Aunt Judy stood in the front row, wearing their new spring dresses. They were framed by the Edwards twins, Butch and Oliver, both in brown suits with short pants and knee socks. Behind them stood Uncle Vincent, Mr. Edwards, Megan, and Maureen, even though Aunt Judy wanted the girls to sit in front of her and Mrs. Edwards.

The picture was taken after dinner in the Edwardses' side of the duplex. Mrs. Edwards had stuffed a turkey and baked a ham, while Aunt Judy contributed creations from the gourmet class she was taking that spring in the basement of a retired chef from the Bronx, Calvin Bennodrillo, who was compiling a volume of his own recipes entitled: *How to Cook for Forty-seven Years without Repeating a Single Recipe*. Aunt Judy served Flaming Brussels Sprouts, Wine-Soaked Crescent Rolls à la Mode, Mozzarella Pie with Sweet-Sour Carrot Filling, and—a creation she took the greatest pride in—Easter Egg–Cauliflower Hash au Gratin.

Soon after this memorable dinner (which is not to

suggest that it happened because of this memorable dinner) Uncle Vincent began spending time in the wrong side of the duplex. As an insurance salesman it was easy for him to disappear for hours without leaving a forwarding address. He would park his tan Ford in the parking lot behind the West Hartford Stores, which gave him any number of possible excuses if Aunt Judy should see his car there and ask where he had been.

Mrs. Edwards would pick him up behind Sage-Allen or the tobacco shop. Hidden under the mustard plaid blanket, Uncle Vincent would lie crouched on the floor between the seats while she maneuvered her little red VW home, parked it in the garage, pulled down the garage door, and made certain nobody was around. Then she would let Uncle Vincent out.

Megan liked Mrs. Edwards. One always knew what to expect from her. She was patient and easy to be with. Perhaps Uncle Vincent liked Mrs. Edwards for the same reasons.

While Megan and the Edwards children were in school, while Mr. Edwards was dissecting frogs or impaling butterflies with sixth-graders, while Aunt Judy was attending one of her meetings or gourmet cooking classes, Uncle Vincent and Mrs. Edwards undressed in the master bedroom which shared a wall with the bedroom where he would put on his pajamas that night. They made love in the full-size bed which was less than a foot from the king-size bed that Aunt Judy covered every morning with the orange and yellow flowered spread that matched the drapes she had bought at the last G. Fox white sale for $38.50 off the regular price. In a kitchen that backed his own kitchen, Uncle Vincent later would relax with a cup of Salada tea, made with water that came from the same 216-foot artesian well as the water that Aunt Judy filled the tub with at night and pine-scented with green crystals from a plastic jar. He used the bathroom that shared the plumbing with his own bathroom, thereby eliminating his bodily wastes down the same channels (which is not to imply at all that, ultimately, it didn't make any difference).

Years later, when Megan was to see a deodorant commercial of a man opening the medicine cabinet in his bathroom and looking into the face of his neighbor, she broke up laughing, picturing her uncle opening the Edwardses' cabinet and staring into Aunt Judy's face. (Would you please hand me the Trojans, dearest?) In repetition the commercial lost some of its appeal, but it never ceased to remind her of Uncle Vincent's questionable talents for short-distance travel.

19

How did Aunt Judy ever find out?

Not until Megan's third date with Ted Woodard (who was nearly as tall as she) and her talk with Aunt Judy in which she was cautioned against all men, regardless what age ("They're all after the same thing"), did Aunt Judy, only to make a point, tell Megan about the cooking class that had been canceled two years ago. All in the mood to create a recipe, she'd come home and had begun to whip up something special. Halfway through her preparations, with the oven preheating, she had discovered that she was fresh out of arrowroot. Wiping her hands on her apron, she had stepped out of the kitchen door, walked through the backyard to the Edwardses' kitchen door, and, her hand raised to knock against the upper glass section, had seen her Vincent drinking Salada tea and holding the back of Mrs. Edwards's right hand pressed against his left cheek. Almost eagerly he had confessed, details too, while Mrs. Edwards didn't even have the decency to look embarrassed.

But I'm getting too far ahead. Let's stay in 1961 for a while, when Megan did not understand why she was forbidden to talk to Maureen Edwards in the weeks before the Edwardses moved to Farmington and Uncle Vincent took an apartment in East Hartford. From fragments of an argument she had overheard between her legal guardians, Megan guessed it had something to do with her uncle and Maureen Edwards's mother. Aunt Judy told her not to ask any impertinent questions and rented the other half of the duplex to an elderly couple with two cats that never went outdoors but sat on the back of the plastic-covered sofa all day, looking out of the window.

Megan wished she knew what had happened.

20

The first draft of this chapter was written with eight interruptions. It ended up disjointed, disarranged, disabled, disenchanting, diseased, disconnected, dismembered, dismantled, and displaced.

I answered a call from the school nurse, picked up my oldest son and his temperature from class, tucked him into his bed with juice and books, obeyed the Perma-press bell from the dryer, didn't open the door to two religious fanatics peddling their fanaticism, made lunch for the children, hung up on a speed-talking aluminum-siding salesman allegedly calling long distance, and was beaten at Chutes and Ladders by my youngest son.

Disappointed because after twenty-seven revisions this chapter still fails to display any sense at all, I disqualify it from participating in this manuscript and dismiss it.

21

Perhaps you find it difficult to believe that a fourteen-year-old girl could be so ignorant about sex. Although Megan had abandoned her early impression that the stork brought babies and knew that they grew inside a woman, in a place called a uterus, she didn't have the slightest notion how they got started in there.

It had something to do with kissing and with dancing. "It's her own fault," Aunt Judy said to Mrs. Chadwick when the girl at the bakery started looking big under her white apron. "With dancing every weekend, what do you expect? It's shameful."

The two books about human reproduction in the library of her parochial school showed black-and-white drawings of embryos in various stages of development. They did not explain how the embryos had begun.

In movies Megan had seen men and women kissing. In the next scene there would be a baby. Trying to imagine how babies got started led to impure and confused thoughts which had to be confessed before the next communion. "Father, I was thinking impure thoughts three times last Wednesday and once on the way to church today" (without coming to a conclusion).

Periods had something to do with it. Babies were made from the blood of periods that didn't come. Everybody knew that. Megan's fourth period didn't come on time. She knew why. She had been thinking about Norm Vallencourt, wondering if she'd let him kiss her, should he try. That's why her period hadn't come. Aunt Judy would be terribly upset if she found out about the baby.

How she wished Maureen were still living in the duplex.

At night she lay awake. Her belly did not feel big. Not yet. Shameful, Aunt Judy would say.

She finally asked Mrs. Chadwick, the cleaning woman who came every Thursday afternoon.

"How do I know for sure, I mean if . . . I, you know?"

Mrs. Chadwick stopped cleaning the bathtub and sat on the heels of her red sneakers. "Know what?"

"Oh, about babies. I mean . . . how they get started and all that."

"You don't know that?"

"I don't think so. But . . . I think I am. I think."

"What in heaven's name are you talking about, girl?"

"My period." Megan swallowed. "It didn't come."

Mrs. Chadwick got up and closed the lid of the toilet. Sitting down on top of it, she crossed her arms in front of her yellow sweatshirt.

"What if I am . . . you know . . . pregnant, I mean?"

"What makes you think that?"

"I've been thinking a lot about somebody. A boy at school."

"And?"

Megan began chewing her left thumbnail. "Nothing. Just my period. It didn't come."

"That aunt of yours." Mrs. Chadwick shook her head. "Have you told her about this?"

"Don't tell her. Please. Promise you won't tell. She'll say I talked dirty."

22

"I'm surprised you ever managed to have a normal sexual relationship," Nick said when Megan first told him about her imaginary pregnancy and subsequent enlightenment by Mrs. Chadwick.

They were lying on their sides, facing each other, after making love.

"You call this normal?" She grimaced. "Just normal?"

He bent his neck and ran his tongue around her left nipple. "Mmmh. Let me think. How about a healthy relationship?"

"Sounds almost as bad as wholesome."

"Too average-sounding for you?"

She shrugged.

"And there's nothing quite as horrid as being average, right?"

"You're learning."

"What about fantastic? Tasty? . . . Stop that. What are you doing?"

"Just checking."

"I think we used it all up."

"That's a cliché."

He turned on his stomach. "I have to go to work in the morning."

"And it would be like running another mile and a half, right? I thought you like it when I make the first move."

"But this is the second move."

"So?" She laughed and rolled over, resting her right cheek on her hands and looking into Nick's face.

"Let's just talk," he said.

"About what?"

"Mrs. Chadwick. I've always been fascinated by women who wear red sneakers."

"Nut."

"I'm serious. In second grade I had a big crush on Veronica Smith. She sat in front of me. I don't remember the color of her hair or eyes, but I'll never forget those sneakers. Bright red."

"I don't think Mrs. Chadwick realized how little I knew about sex. When she told me, I couldn't believe people actually did something like that. I thought God should have come up with a nicer way for getting babies, elbow contact or something like that."

"Nobody would dare ride the subway."

"It made me sick to think I got started that way."

"Didn't you ever discuss sex with other girls?"

Megan shook her head. "Not really. Maureen was my only close friend; after the Edwardses left I just kept to myself. The teachers certainly didn't volunteer information like that. Even after Mrs. Chadwick told me, I was still confused. I didn't know what a man's genitals looked like. Stop grinning." She pulled his hair. "I remember finding myself staring at men's zippers against my will and then looking away quickly. It was awful. Embarrassing. I must have seen my father and brother when I was small, but that was too long ago."

"I'm so glad I was able to contribute to your education."

"So am I, even if you are conceited."

"Conceited?"

She laughed.

"I don't think that's funny," Nick said.

"It isn't. I was just thinking of Uncle Vincent. I once saw him in his underwear, streaking through the hallway to get to the bathroom."

"That must have been a rather forgettable experience."

"You should have heard Aunt Judy."

"What did she do? Read him the Ten Commandments?"

"Something like that. She had a few of her own."

23

Have I mentioned that I am a closet writer?

Are you sure you're using the right expression? my husband asks as I try this line out on him. He thinks that coming out of the closet means something entirely different.

What I'm trying to say is that I write secretly. Aside from my family, my students, and a few friends nobody knows I write. I keep it hidden like a bad habit, a bad habit which is growing into a six-hours-a-day bad habit.

You don't write in a closet, my husband tells me, you've taken over the study. You've taken over my desk. I remind him that he volunteered his desk to get my typewriter and manuscripts off the kitchen counter, so that the kitchen counter could be used for space on which to prepare wholesome and nourishing meals. He asks: What meals?

As to my habit remaining a secret, my oldest son is changing this very quickly. He brought this drawing home from school yesterday. The children were asked to draw one of their parents at work.

I love him for drawing me this skinny.

I would love to be this skinny.

My husband puts on his reading glasses and asks if that's a bug behind the typewriter, one of the bugs that'll be running around my typewriter pretty soon if I don't get back to writing only three hours a day. When he sees my face he quickly says he was only kidding.

At times my husband's sense of humor is very twisted.

My sons bend over the picture, their blond heads touching, the older boy's hair several shades darker. The younger declares with authority that the little thing behind the typewriter is a frog, that anyone can see it's a frog. He also is the child who insists Big Bird comes through in yellow on our black-and-white TV.

To me, the little thing behind the typewriter looks like inspiration walking off my desk.

My younger son wants to know what inspiration is.

Our older son tells us that, of course, it's a frog, that even a four-year-old can see it's a frog.

24

The marriage?

Well, they did not get married because they had to. Megan didn't experience pregnancy symptoms until they were married one year, and then it was the one Nick would call Houdini, since it got away in spite of the maternal feelings Megan was beginning to develop. Her period was merely two weeks late; she felt a peculiar sense of loss.

They neither got married because they searched for security, nor was their union the result of parental coercion, fear of loneliness, or the desire to fit into the roles designed for them by tradition.

Actually, Megan didn't want to get married until—and this is the way she thought of it—until she'd be quite old: at least twenty-five. But that was before she knew Nick. When she met him, or, as Nick would say, when she beat him, she was twenty, a liberal-arts major in her junior year at the University of Hartford, where she also worked part-time in the library. No, she did not beat him with a broom handle, a broken exhaust pipe, a whip, a baseball bat, a desk lamp, piano, or spatula, nor did she beat him at tennis, polo, long-distance swimming or watermelon eating. Instead she beat him in chess, as she had beaten every opponent since she was fifteen.

She had made the semifinals at the university tournament and was playing against Dominic Cassara, a graduate student in mathematics. During the last half hour of the game she became aware of someone tall and thin watching her moves. He looked a few years older than the other students and he was leaning against the green wall about five feet across from her. His blond hair was thick and straight and kept falling over his forehead. Several times he pushed it back with his left hand, more out of habit, it seemed, than necessity: it wasn't long enough to fall into his eyes. He wore a light blue shirt, open at the collar, sleeves rolled up loosely to below his elbow. Occasionally he squinted and shook his head. She wished he'd go somewhere else; she didn't want to be distracted. Twice he nodded, more to himself than to her. He left five minutes before she checkmated Dominic's king.

When she went to get her coat, he was leaning against the Coke machine in the hall. She wondered if he could stand straight without leaning against something.

"You gambled when you sacrificed your bishop," he said as she walked past him.

"I knew what I was doing." She noticed the initials NCS on his shirt pocket. An ex-preppie, she thought, definitely an ex-preppie.

"You were good," he said. "You set him up beautifully. But I would have seen through it." He loosened himself from the Coke machine and miraculously stood on his own. He was about an inch taller than she. From this close his eyes were a very dark blue. "If your opponent hadn't fallen for it, you would never have gotten his queen so quickly. All he had to do was—"

"It's always so easy in retrospect, isn't it?"

Her sarcasm seemed to be lost on him. "You got half an hour?" he asked, turning on a little-boy grin that didn't affect her at all.

"Why? Is that all you'd need to beat me?"

"No." He pushed his hair from his forehead. "Twenty minutes would be more than enough for that. But it would also give me time to introduce myself." He extended his right hand. "Nick Stone."

His hand felt dry and firm. She wondered if the initial C stood for conceited.

For the first time in years she had to abandon her favorite opening, the one that often gave her the game in five moves, and had to work on her defense. It was a close game, lasting six hours and forty-three minutes. She beat him by a narrow margin, him, who had felled his opponents at Princeton and Harvard and who had become bored by the lack of challenge in a game he considered himself an expert in, a game that for him seldom lasted more than twenty minutes.

He looked at this girl, four years younger than he and almost as tall, a girl with bitten fingernails and long red hair, a girl who seemed not at all impressed by him, a girl who he knew would win the tournament the following day.

With a shrug she accepted his challenge for another match. Now that she knew his approach, could judge the way he set up his defense, the game would last less than an hour.

He believed he knew her strategy. He would beat her, quickly and cleanly, and then ask her out to dinner, perhaps, to soften the blow.

They met at the library. When the library closed, they marked their positions and took the chessboard to the country club where his parents held a membership.

Again, he lost.

He was sure it was only a matter of time before he was going to beat her.

Capturing Nick's queen one evening, four weeks later, Megan looked up and knew she wanted to marry him. It surprised her, confused her. He hadn't even tried to kiss her.

25

—Marriage? Kissing? Come on, Megan. Is that all you can think of? This is taking too long. I didn't plan you this way. You aren't nearly as strong as I wanted you to be. I don't want you to drift submissively into some marriage and turn into one of those meek, bitter, and frustrated women who let themselves be victimized by their husbands. Most of the novels and stories we read in our seminar on contemporary women's fiction are about women like that, women who are dissatisfied and leave their old life only to walk into a new life that seems just as bleak. It doesn't make any sense to me, because the women in the seminar are not like that. There are fourteen of us, all women, including the professor, ranging in age from twenty-two to forty-two, single, divorced, married without children, married with children, women with independent minds and strong opinions, women who are imaginative and who trust their own decisions.

—But the fiction we discuss tells us that to be a woman is to be a victim, that all men are villains. Why? It doesn't have to be that way. There are good relationships between women and men, between men and their children. Aren't there? I won't let you be victimized by your husband, your children, your house, Megan, and I won't let you keep a card file of rooms to be cleaned and silver to be polished. You won't have to leave one baby lying on the sidewalk while carrying the other child and four bags of groceries to a third-floor apartment. I'll give you a backpack to carry the baby, or I'll make your children old enough to walk. They'll be wanted and spaced at least two years apart. I'll provide you with a baby-sitter, Megan, a kitchen on the first floor, a car, with enough imagination to improvise. You'll be bright, assertive. . . . Say something assertive, Megan.

—
—Anything.
—
—Just one thing, Megan.
—
—Please?
—I hate to pick blueberries.
—What does that have to do with . . .
—Forget I said it. Just forget—
—No. Really. I'm glad you said something. I just don't
know what to do with it. What does it mean? Can you tell
me?
—
—Megan?

26

Although she tried to ignore her feelings, they didn't go
away.

She began to wait for Nick's first move, not in chess, but
in displaying something that would match her own feelings. Twice she considered letting him win. The first move
would have to come from him. Megan, at twenty, felt that
the male had to make the first move—except in chess, of
course, where her strength lay in the opening.

Growing resentful of her self-imposed submissiveness,
she not only defended her position on the board, but tore
aggressively into his flanks, pushed her way past his pawns,
seized his knights, and took possession of his bishops.

Once, she almost let him win. She went through with
her plan during the opening, sacrificing four pawns, both
knights, and one castle. She felt like a fraud. It wasn't fair
to him. In the end game she castled, exchanged a pawn in
the eighth rank for a second queen, and fought like a
demon to make up for her early losses. The game ended in
a draw.

Perhaps he would lose interest as soon as he won. The challenge would be gone. He still hadn't tried to kiss her, much less attempted to go after what Aunt Judy said all men were after.

While maintaining her defense on the chessboard, Megan lowered her own defense. The first time he kissed her, although he still hadn't beaten her, they went to the Howard Johnson's Motor Lodge.

The earth did not move.

She heard no bells.

After he was asleep, she got up and sat in the orange chair by the window. Indians don't cry. It would be dumb to start now. Just because she had expected something different. Real dumb. She pulled her knees up in front of herself and clasped her arms around them. Her feet were cold.

27

Attitude makes a great difference.

A disciple of Norman Mailer, let's call him Henry Nelson, certainly would have handled the preceding chapter differently.

"Why the understatement?" he would ask. "You're finally getting to something of importance. Nick takes bold revenge for his losses on the chessboard and exerts his dominance."

"You're misinterpreting, Mr. Nelson. He is not—"

"Listen to me, child. You want to get this published, don't you? Then forget about this whole equality shit. Nobody buys it. Believe me. I've been writing books a hell of a lot longer than you. Just look at your vocabulary: there's a whole range of words you're shirking. Let me tell you how to write that scene."

"Thank you, but I'd rather—"

"No need to thank me. This is how you should do it:

She thrashed beneath his powerful virility. Savoring her struggle, he masterfully forced her thighs apart with his right knee. Consumed by inflaming lust, he felt the pulsating power of his penis, a loaded gun . . ."

"Listen, Mr. Nelson. You're in the wrong book. I don't want—"

"Wait, there's more:

He dominated her, bruising her breasts with his strong mouth as he prepared to grind into her. This was no game of chess; this was life, the battle of life, and he came as the conqueror. With a powerful thrust he mastered her, pronging her shuddering cunt while she lay subdued, submitting to his . . ."

"No."

"What's the matter? Too descriptive for you?"

"Too offensive. It's my story, and I don't want you to intrude. The characters I'm creating are not like that. Dominance and submission are destructive in a relationship."

"What else is there? Wake up, kid. Face up to reality."

"There's trust. Understanding. Respect for one another. Love."

"Bullshit. You're a dreamer. Deep down all women want to be dominated. They're just afraid to admit it."

"That's just a role you'd like to force on women. Haven't you heard, Mr. Nelson? Most men are beginning to reject it too; many have already."

"Fool. You probably also believe that there can be friendship between men and women."

"Of course."

"Hopeless. Absolutely hopeless," Mr. Nelson would mutter.

28

I might take Chapter 27 out. Editing it, I blush as much as when I first typed it. What if my sons read it someday? Or my mother-in-law? Or my very first teacher? Or my friends? Or the people in this town? Or the gas-station attendant?

Would I think of Chapter 27 every time somebody said: "By the way, I read your novel."

Would I want to wear dark glasses and become a recluse? What if it were translated into German and all my relatives overseas read it? Could I ever go back for a visit? Would the post office discontinue my mail? The oil company cease to deliver? Would I have to burn this manuscript to keep my children from freezing to death?

My husband? He hasn't bought any dark glasses for me. Still, I might take Chapter 27 out. Maybe next week. Maybe . . .

29

After Houdini, Megan would have liked to have a child as soon as possible, but Nick kept postponing the decision for a number of unchanging and not very imaginative reasons, which he insisted were valid:

1. I'm not ready; I'm too young to be a father.
2. I don't want our conversations to boil down to strained spinach and the price of baby shoes.
3. We won't have time for each other anymore.
4. Any combination of the above reasons.

With the children in the neighborhood he was reserved, almost cautious. They lived in a West Hartford development with several dead-end streets, ideal for bringing up children, according to the realtor who had sold them the white Cape with three bedrooms. The previous owner had left a huge sandbox under the dogwood tree.

Megan kept her part-time job at the university library, working mornings from nine to twelve. Twice a week she had a Shakespeare class in the afternoon. At the rate of one course a semester, she figured it would take her at least five years to finish her B.A. But she didn't mind; there was no rush. She felt content spending her free afternoons decorating the house, reading, or meeting some of the new neighbors.

Most of the couples on the street had been married less than eight years, had one to three children, a dog and/or a cat, and one to two cars. Most of the children were preschoolers. Sometimes, when Megan picked up a child and held it, Nick would smile dutifully at the child, perhaps even nod, but under no circumstances would he hold it or play with it. She never saw him fake an emotion, something she respected in their private life but felt compelled to overcompensate for when faced with a new baby in the neighborhood and Nick's unenthusiastic: "Very nice." Later, she would be annoyed with herself.

When the Beckers next door had their second child through natural childbirth, and Wayne Becker couldn't stop talking about how great it had been to see his son born, how great it had been to be with his wife during labor, how great it had been to know that he was actively taking part in the birth of his child, how great it had been to know that he was making things easier for Jill by helping her with the breathing and relaxation, Nick whispered to Megan, how great it would be if Wayne never said great again and would hit upon another subject.

But the following week he picked up two paperbacks on natural childbirth, and the next time Megan brought up parenthood, she was spared the familiar objections one through four.

After she stopped taking her pills, it took her five months to get pregnant. Every month, when she discovered the familiar red stains, she felt depressed. She began chewing her fingernails again, a habit she had outgrown when she moved out of Aunt Judy's duplex. Her first missed period filled her with such hope that she began shopping for white booties and maternity clothes. After two weeks she made an appointment with Jill's obstetrician, Dr. Wilkins, who, according to Jill, was just great because of his small hands.

30

I have this whole stack of potential characters, some of whom I haven't brought into the plot yet. For each of them there's at least one white three-by-five index card covered with penciled notes to which I add and refer frequently. I know a writer who is haunted by a character in one of his novels whose change of eye color not only escaped him but also his editor. A nightmare. I make sure to check the eyes of my characters repeatedly.

Then there are the index cards with groups: family, neighbors, friends, etc. And the cards with dates. Dates are very important. Wouldn't it be terrible if I started the novel with Megan walking on the beach in 1976 and then let her remember that walk in 1975? What if I got her wedding date wrong or told you that the children were three instead of two years apart? Wouldn't you doubt everything else I said?

Some of my cards have key phrases, maybe a bad habit or pet grievance. I could have introduced these characters to you gradually, illuminated them through flashbacks or fantasies, or even invited them all to a party at the Stones' house. After all, they are in this manuscript because they touch upon the lives of our protagonists. Instead, I shall let you look at them through my index cards. Let me just open the plastic recipe file where I keep them. Here. They get shuffled a lot and aren't in any particular order. Don't worry, I won't write:

judy donovan/1920/aunt/div.feb.62/gray-short/brown-ey/
vibrators/lotion/square-fa/"Ifyouaskme"/

Instead it will go like this:

JUDY DONOVAN

Megan's aunt. She was born in 1920. "If you ask me . . ." is one of her pet sentence openings. I might still cut it. It's only on her card to remind me that I should begin several of her sentences with it. Eventually you'd recognize her way of speaking without my having to resort to my thesaurus's eighty-four verbs to replace the not very original: to say. Instead of saying: Aunt Judy said, I could say: Aunt Judy gave utterance to, Aunt Judy shot her mouth off, Aunt Judy talked a blue streak, Aunt Judy had her say, Aunt Judy put into words, Aunt Judy was eloquent, Aunt Judy shot the breeze, Aunt Judy held forth, Aunt Judy held back, Aunt Judy uttered, pronounced, chattered, asserted, speechified, orated, stumped, flourished, spouted, ranted, expatiated, allocated, harangued, ejaculated, mouthed, preached, sermonized, invoked, etc. etc. etc.

Aunt Judy never does anything in moderation, whether her interests are of domestic or political nature. Always she adheres strictly to what, at that time, she considers to be RIGHT, and she tries to make others follow her concept of RIGHT. Her attitude is one of rigidity, although her priorities change occasionally. In other words, she climbs on different bandwagons and tries to hold the reins. Although most organizations initially appreciate her energetic involvement, they soon tire of her manner, which tolerates no difference of opinion. There's a peculiar discrepancy between Aunt Judy's actions and words. If she just did things without talking about them or trying to make others conform to her view, she wouldn't be half as intimidating. Actually, she's quite decent, but she wrecks that impression as soon as she opens her mouth.

When this novel starts, Aunt Judy is fifty-six, wears her gray hair short, and has, according to her index card, brown eyes and a square face. She still lives in her side of the duplex and rents the other half to the elderly couple with the cats, which are not the same (the cats, that is, not the couple).

From her dining-room table she runs two mail-order services, one for vibrators (PPP: Pulsating Pleasure Pals), the other for a pink lotion in white plastic bottles, guaranteed to fade freckles, brown patches, and age spots. Aunt Judy firmly believes in the merit of both products.

VINCENT DONOVAN

That's strange. Usually their cards don't touch. Anyhow, he's two years younger than his ex-wife. Since he's a minor character, you already know as much about him as necessary for this novel. As far as I can see, he won't reappear, other than perhaps in conversations or deodorant-commercial flashbacks.

Since I haven't given you a physical description of him, you may use the blank space below to describe him as you imagine him. Make a little sketch, if you feel like it. It won't make the slightest difference.

EDWARDS FAMILY

Mrs. Edwards - VW, Uncle V., Easter dinner, Salada
Mr. Edwards - teacher, back of VW, frogs
Maureen - Megan's best friend, cinnamon, leaves
Oliver & Butch - twins, knee socks

DONALD HENEGAN

Nick's neighbor and tennis partner. They've been winning the men's doubles for three years in a row at the club. Don is a dentist who considers himself extremely handsome and charming, an asset to any party. At first glance you barely notice that he is overweight. He carries his two hundred twenty plus pounds well hidden under sporty blazers, and his weight does not keep him from skiing and sailing. When he wears his Frye boots, he is just about six feet tall; the rest of the time he's almost five eleven. His passion in life is an antique car which he only takes out on Sunday afternoons for family rides. He keeps it in a rented garage close to his office, ever since one of his daughters scratched the right front fender with her scooter. Every other evening he works on it, polishing, waxing, whatever.

Donald likes to have his dinner served to him when he gets home, which can be anywhere between seven and nine, depending on the polishing. He likes to have his dinner served to him after the children have eaten and are in bed. He likes to have his dinner served to him in the den on the card table so he can watch TV.

Donald likes to have his dinner served to him.

MINOR CHARACTERS

Dr. Hamilton - delivers Megan's brother, booties, hands
Dr. Wilkins - "You're coming along nicely," stuffed fox, small hands

Mrs. Chadwick - cleaning woman, red sneakers, sex edu-
cation
Appleface - nurse, mini - prep, bitch
Norm Vallencourt - first crush
Daniel F or M - fat, green eyes, lousy spelling, missionary
Houdini - the baby that didn't happen

SARA HENEGAN

Megan's best friend, aside from Nick. Sara has five
children, four of them girls. Easily influenced by whoever
pressured her last, she has a difficult time saying no to
organizations, children, friends, especially Donald. She's
the one who goes around collecting for the Heart, Kidney,
and United Fund, who bakes pink and green cupcakes on
Valentine's Day and St. Patrick's Day for nursery school,
who takes care of the family pets: two turtles, one
half-blind hamster, a canary, three cats, one goldfish, and a
partridge in a pear tree.

She always seems to be in the process of running, trying
to live up to everybody's expectations. Motivated by
Megan's trips to the university, Sara enrolled in a Chaucer
seminar once, but dropped after two classes because it
interfered with Don's dinner. She has devised a method of
keeping food warm between six P.M. when she eats with
the children and the time she dines with her husband. Her
children do not like to eat alone. Donald does not like to
eat alone. Sara is twenty-seven pounds heavier than when
she got married.

No. This is too much: the weight, the five children, the
pets, the husband. Cut the goldfish and one of the turtles.
I'm having problems with Sara. She's turning into a victim.
This is my seventh revision of her. I've changed the color
of her eyes, the color of her hair, the color of her Formica
counter. Still, she remains a victim, even with the present

combination of blue eyes and shoulder-length black hair. My husband saw a bumper sticker a few weeks ago:

INSANITY IS HEREDITARY.
YOU GET IT FROM YOUR KIDS.

He thought it was funny.

I wondered.

Yet I would rather have five children than one Donald. Perhaps I should give Sara only two children, eight and six years old, two well-behaved daughters who make their own beds. But then why would she bake cupcakes for nursery school? Either way, I can't win. What if I sent her to law school and she divorced Donald as part of her course work during the first semester? Would you give her an A? Would you give her an A *and* a lover, an intelligent man strong enough to be gentle? Would you kill Donald with a heart attack? A dagger? Kindness? Or would you have him suffer a fatal accident in his polished antique car? You think I'm being heartless? I'm only letting you in on the possibilities. There are deliberate choices to be made. Perhaps you'd feel as I do if you knew what Donald told Megan while he was leaning against the Beckers' frost-free twenty-four-cubic-foot side-by-side Whirlpool refrigerator-freezer. "She only thinks I control her," Donald stated when Megan remarked that it would have been nice if Sara could have finished at least one semester and received credit for it. —*She only thinks I control her.* —Megan shivers whenever she remembers.

31

Some of the other characters could be introduced to you in a COUPLES section: Jill and Wayne Becker; Nick's sister Pam and her husband, David Turner; Nick's parents,

Beverly and Robert Stone. But I think I'd better get back to the story before this card section gets too long and you lose interest. Besides, there are some characters I might decide to leave out. When I first started this novel, I had several potential characters, but suddenly they don't fit in anymore. Take Michelle Grant, for example, a very good listener who finds friends easily because she assumes their identity. Men see themselves when they look into her eyes. While at first they are flattered, they eventually get bored looking into a mirror and listening to a soft voice reciting their opinions. Michelle doesn't have any close women friends for the same reason. Maybe I'll have to write a short story for her to exist in.

Then there is Dr. Wilkins's wife, Norma. You haven't met her yet. She's the one in green under glass. It might have been interesting to explore the thoughts and emotions of a woman married to an obstetrician who is treasured by his patients because of his small hands and his positive attitude. Neither shall I include Megan's history professor, who wrote *Brilliant!* under her essay on the influence of women in fourteenth-century politics, nor limit myself to the characters introduced to you. What about a dermatologist who does not make a pass at Megan?

Relax.

Just imagine you have a glass of wine in your right hand, your choice of year and vineyard. Mouton-Rothschild 1929? I'm in a generous mood. Imagine I'm taking you around, meeting my characters, whispering a few things to you I couldn't possibly say in front of them. You understand, a party after all. Here, let me refill your glass and remember to stay away from the heavy man with the blue blazer and the Frye boots, leaning against the refrigerator.

32

DR. WORDEN'S FEMALE PILLS
FOR ALL FEMALE DISEASES: A
great blood purifier and nerve
tonic. Cures all diseases arising
from poor and wasted condition
of the blood, pale and sallow
complexion, depression of spir-
its, lack of ambition, palpitation
of the heart, coldness of hands
and feet, pain in the back, nervous headache, dizziness, loss of
memory, feebleness of will, ringing in the ears, early decay. ALL
FORMS OF FEMALE WEAKNESS,
hysteria, hunchback, decayed
bones. Women can be beautiful.
All weakness and disease removed by taking Dr. Worden's . . .

"Mrs. Stone?" A tall nurse came to the door of the
waiting room. "You may come in now." Her white uniform
hung on her loosely, as though she'd recently lost thirty or
forty pounds.

Megan closed the paperback with the advertisement of
the wonder pills, a reproduction of a 1903 Sears, Roebuck
catalog, and returned it to the low, imitation-wood-grain
table. She followed the nurse into a large office, paneled
with blond wood. Most of one wall was covered with large,
rectangular frames showing enlargements of four children
—three boys and one girl—blond smiling children, smiling in childhood, early puberty, and frequently in between. *Trust me, my patients, I'm a father. Those four children
trust me. See their smiles?*

The nurse drew a white curtain around the examination table and handed Megan a light blue johnny. "The doctor will be with you in a few minutes. You can open the curtain when you're ready."

"Should I leave anything on?"

"No. He'll want to do a pelvic exam."

Struggling with the Velcro fasteners in back of the johnny, Megan wondered if Dr. Wilkins would be able to tell without the tests. She hoped she wouldn't have to wait. As she opened the curtain, she noticed a psychedelically painted filing cabinet; perched on top of it was a fox, its bushy tail climbing the window frame like a trained vine. Eternalized by a taxidermist with a flair for the dramatic, it hovered above a glassy-eyed, light gray rabbit, as if preparing to shred it to bits. One red-brown paw was draped across the rabbit's neck, its rich coloring like blood against the pale fur, as if only the rabbit were dead.

Megan looked away from the limp shape. The rabbit never had a chance.

Arranged in a stair pattern on the wall across from the window hung four hunting prints, framed in identical wide strips of brown wood. Next to the black base of the desk lamp hovered two white ceramic rabbits. School projects? He must have a thing about rabbits, pale rabbits. TO DADDY FROM SHAWN was printed in large, irregular letters on the bottom of a faded child's painting, tacked above the desk.

See this. I hang on to things. And I'm young at heart. You saw that filing cabinet. My oldest son painted it. I value children. Come closer. Take a look at all the photos under the glass on my desk. It'll pass the time while you're waiting. Photos of my children. Yes, that's my wife, Norma, over there, in the green. And the family pets. See the family pets? No, we never had a rabbit. Why do you ask? The pencil holder? My youngest son made it from an empty orange juice can and covered it with material and rick-rack. Touching, isn't it? I

*mean that I actually use it. Not too many professional men do.
It must clearly show that I'm a family man. My wife gave me
that wooden clock in the shape of a squirrel. Original, don't you
think so? And since you asked about rabbits, that picture over
there, the white rabbit sitting in a patch of snow, see it? It's one
of my all-time favorites. I guess I do have a certain fondness for
rabbits, after all. No, I never wondered why there isn't any
snow on the branches of the pines in the picture.*

Jill had said that Dr. Wilkins had small hands.

Jill had said that Dr. Wilkins had a very positive attitude,
that even if she felt depressed during her pregnancy
because of pains in her legs, dizziness, headaches, she
always left his office feeling good about herself, so much
more positive than when she came in, as if he had given
her a magic cure.

Megan pictured him as a slight man with blond hair and
quick movements. Instead he looked like a retired prize-
fighter who had gained weight and lost most of his dark
hair.

His hands were abnormally small.

The speculum felt cold.

He did not ask: *What does your husband do?* a predictable
question Megan had grown to dread when meeting people
for the first time. When she first got married, it never
bothered her, but lately she had begun to wonder if all
married women had to put up with that question. Did any
of them ever reply: *What difference does it make?*

"What do you do?" he inquired and listened attentively
when Megan told him about her studies and her job at the
library.

"Are you hoping for a boy or a girl?" he asked and
listened just as attentively when Megan told him that the
sex of the child wasn't important as long as it was healthy,
and that, although it would be nice to have one of each,
she wouldn't mind at all if she had two boys or two girls,
that she thought it would be nice to have two children

while she was in her twenties and, perhaps, two more after the first two were in school.

Nodding occasionally without interrupting, he made her feel as though she were his only patient, that there was nothing he'd rather do than spend an extra ten or fifteen minutes talking with her. Even though Megan suspected that he would exhibit the same effective combination of patience and enthusiasm toward the next patient, she felt comfortable with him.

"I'll call you as soon as I get the results from the lab," he told her before she left. "I hope the news will be good."

Driving home, she wondered if he found that statement equally effective for patients hoping not to be pregnant.

33

—Can't you be a little more original, Megan? This spiel about two children now and two later, the sex of the child not being important as long as it's healthy. Everybody says that. Not that it's wrong or anything. It's just so . . . so unoriginal. If I were an obstetrician, I'd scream each time a patient gave me that line. I had such plans for you, Megan. Why are you dragging like that? Can't you be positive? Assertive? Strong? Do I have to go back and rewrite you?

—If you do, Ursula, take out the beach part.

—What's wrong with walking on the beach?

—I'd rather be polishing silver. Just because you want solitude doesn't mean you have to send me across ten miles of sand until my feet bleed.

—I didn't know you felt that way.

—Do your own walking the next time you get a craving for solitude.

34

Although her breasts grew uncomfortably large and she felt nauseated most evenings, Megan eagerly went through those experiences, fascinated by the changes in her body. Sometimes she was afraid Dr. Wilkins had made a mistake, that she wasn't pregnant, that it was just another Houdini. But then all she had to do was touch her swollen breasts or remember the queasiness of the night before. She welcomed her discomforts as proof that within her a child was growing. Soon summer would be over. And then fall. Christmas. And then only three more months until the baby would be born.

She spent hours imagining her child, what he would look like, how he would react to her. She thought of him as a boy, a boy with blond hair and blue eyes like Nick's. Through him she would learn what Nick was like as a child, would find out about the years before she knew him. Perhaps the child would have her features. It was easy to picture him at two or three years of age, even up to five, since most of the children in the neighborhood were preschoolers. Although she tried, she couldn't picture him at ten or twelve.

There was a secret excitement to being pregnant, as if she had invented it. Surprised by the strength of her feelings for the child she carried, she turned into herself, her perceptions greatly changing as they were filtered through her womb. She went for long walks by herself, listening to her body, aware of its changes and needs.

Although she didn't show, she began wearing maternity clothes in her second month, not anticipating that six months later she'd be thoroughly sick of cone-shaped dresses and tent tops. For the first time in her life there was no need to hold in her stomach; with a sense of wonder and pride she watched its expansion.

In her third month she began decorating the nursery. She painted walls, sewed curtains in a pale green trimmed with white, went through every carpet store within a radius of twenty miles to find a matching green carpet, and finally settled on a thick white shag. She made green-and-white window shades, appliquéd a green lampshade with white replicas of the Three Bears. She, who hated to darn Nick's socks, who put off mending or sewing on buttons for as long as she could, found great pleasure in sewing for the baby. Aware of her contentment, she embroidered tiny kimonos and shirts and began working on a crib-size quilt.

35

A dream.

Playing on the dirt pile in back of the house with Michael. Tufts of grass and weeds. Digging tunnels. Tunnels that become garages for the cars:

> one red firetruck
> one blue car with doors that open
> one blue car with a wheel missing

Tunnels big enough to stick her arm in. Stick her arm in all the way up to her shoulder. Bigger. Tunnels she scoops out with an old soup ladle. Tunnels she crawls into. *Michael.* NO. Knowing she's dreaming. NO. And still going on, crawling, crawling. NO. Until the tunnel ends. Dark. *Michael.* Screeching. Too tight to turn. Screeching soundlessly. The taste of dirt. And falling. Falling. Earth on her shoulder. Her face. Her tongue. Trying to push her eyes open. *Michael—*

"Megan?"

Trying to push her eyes open.

"Megan?" Nick's hand on her shoulder, shaking her.

"What?" She tried to sit up, oddly frightened and out of breath. "What is it?"

"Are you all right?" He turned on the reading light. "You were having a nightmare. You were calling for Michael."

The tunnel. Dirt. On her tongue. On her eyelids. On—

"Are you all right?" He was bending over her, his blond hair falling across his forehead, his eyes squinting. "Here. Lie down."

"It's just a dream." She let him pull her close. "I used to have it all the time. After the funeral. I haven't thought of it in years."

"You want to talk about it?"

She shook her head.

"Can you go back to sleep?"

"I guess so."

"You want me to get you anything?"

"Like what?"

He thought for a moment and then grinned. "A pickle? Pregnant women are supposed to crave pickles."

"No, thanks."

He pulled his arm out from under her and turned off the lamp.

"Nick? Thanks."

"That's okay."

The fluorescent dial of the alarm clock radio was the only light left in the bedroom.

"Nick?"

"What?"

"Nothing."

If she watched the minute hand, she could see it move very slowly. There was a second hand, but it wasn't fluorescent. Although she couldn't see it in the dark, she knew it was moving.

"Nick?"

He was breathing evenly.

The baby would be all right. It had to be.

36

The first time she felt her child's movements, a light fluttering as though it were a small bird held within her hands, she called Nick at his office, and they went to Ferranti's that evening to celebrate with veal Parmesan, Ruffino Chianti, and spumoni. Nick's initial mild interest in the baby increased when the movements became strong enough to be felt by him. Although his involvement with the pregnancy was not as continuous as Megan's, it became intense. At night he liked to fall asleep with one hand on her abdomen. Sometimes, in the morning, he would hold conversations with the fetus, asking it to kick once for yes and twice for no.

"Would you like your mother to get up and make breakfast for us?" he would ask, or: "Are you the only one in there?"

Christmas morning she found three stockings hanging above the fireplace in the living room. The one in the middle, a small red one, was filled with nuts, oranges, two rattles, a teething ring, a pacifier, and a cloth picture book with a yellow duck on the cover.

37

Writing adds a rather strange perspective to my life. Something within me records experience as it happens. During a conversation I often see the other person's sentence on paper, modified to suit one of my characters.

I feel a fork slip from my hand as I empty the

dishwasher. Fascinated, I watch it fall, prongs down. It hits my right sandal and clatters to the floor. While observing this, I'm also aware that I'm seeing and recording it, imagining the words on the page.

But there is more than that; there are the possibilities of what could have happened:

The fork could have stuck in my flesh.

There could have been blood.

Lightly swaying, the fork could have remained stuck in my foot.

Why did the ambulance driver have a glass eye?

Who left the bomb in the emergency room?

Where was the father of the triplets, born in the parking lot?

Why didn't . . .

It could go on endlessly, each fantasy a catalyst for yet another one. And as I'm aware of that which happened and of that which could have happened, those visions are already becoming a memory. But they are kept separate.

Somehow.

I know the difference.

Still, at times I wonder how narrow the line between them is, how delicate the balance.

38

(I dedicate this chapter to Captain Kangaroo for sixty minutes of only infrequent interruptions by my youngest son.)

Together they attended childbirth classes every Tuesday evening in the living room of an old Victorian house, where they sat in a large circle on the wooden floor with five other pregnant couples, each of them armed with two pillows for the exercises. Megan noticed that the other women were all under five foot six, while only two of the men were her height.

The instructor, Donna Bell, a dark-haired divorcée in her early thirties, spoke of the joy in seeing one's child born, of actively participating, of experiencing the togetherness of husband and wife, of feeling in control of labor through various methods of panting and relaxation. It was so important to give the baby the best possible start by not being drugged during labor and delivery. Several times she pointed out that this was not natural, but prepared childbirth.

To Megan all this sounded wonderful. After only three classes she could barely wait to go to the hospital. How she longed to control her labor, to actively push her child through her vagina. She'd be calm like the woman in the film of an actual delivery Donna had shown. The camera had frequently focused on the woman's features, concentrated in labor. Labor, according to Donna, meant hard work. A smile of euphoric dimensions spread across the mother's face as her child was born and handed to her. There was no indication that she might have been experiencing pain at any stage. She never flinched. She never even bit her lip.

Not once during the eight-week course was the word *pain* mentioned.

39

BAG OF TRICKS:
1. cornstarch - powder
2. paper bag - prevent hyperventilation
3. lollipops - Schrafft's lemon/not too sweet
4. Chap Stick
5. Wash 'n Dri's
6. washcloth
7. tennis ball - backache
8. food for husband
9. stopwatch - time contractions
10. books, cards, etc.

By the first weekend in February, Megan's suitcase was packed, including most of the items from the photocopied list Donna had given each of them. The lollipops were to keep her mouth from getting dry during labor, while at the same time providing energy. According to Donna, it was very important that they weren't too sweet. Schrafft's lemon lollipops, Donna said, were ideal. But nobody sold Schrafft's lemon lollipops in Canton, Avon, Farmington, or West Hartford. Megan experimented sucking three other brands, became hooked, and gained eight pounds in one month. Finally, Nick found some in Hartford and brought home one dozen long-stemmed, yellow Schrafft's lemon lollipops.

More and more she felt altogether too noticeable. The combination of weight and height made people in stores turn and look at her. Being pregnant wasn't as wonderful as in the beginning. She felt awkward and uncomfortable. Impatiently, she waited for labor to begin. Maybe the baby would be born a week or two early.

40

Oh, you sweet expectations, only to be challenged, crushed, or modified by what is commonly referred to as reality.

Nobody ever mentioned it would hurt.

Nobody.

Afterwards, it would be hard for her to believe she had gone into labor expecting it to be a totally joyful experience, to be smiling euphorically like the woman in the film, instead of cursing Dr. Wilkins, using words that would make her feel guilty for the duration of the predicted postpartum blues which she would not experience.

Instead of being a week or two early, as she had hoped,

she was five days overdue, five long days, and when her labor began, it was just as Donna said it would be: the contractions were weak and short. It gave her confidence to realize how easily she could control them. They felt almost like menstrual cramps, only lighter, and she longed to exercise her command on something more substantial. When they began in the late evening of the fifth overdue day, they were half an hour apart. She stayed up, reading Faulkner's *Light in August,* eagerly waiting for the intervals to decrease.

Nick went to sleep upon her urging that he would need his strength the next day. He agreed.

By two A.M. the contractions were still thirty minutes apart, not even strong enough to keep her awake. At this rate it would take weeks before she'd have the baby. Years. the *Guinness Book of World Records* would cite her labor as the longest in history. She would continue to expand. After a few months she'd barely notice the mild contractions every half hour. They'd finally have to excavate the child, and he'd be fully toilet trained, maybe even ready for college.

When the alarm went off at seven, she woke up. Her contractions were no closer than twenty minutes.

"You might as well go to work," she told Nick. "This is going to take forever."

"Are you mad at me because I slept?"

"No."

"You should have woken me up."

"They're probably not even real contractions. Jill had false labor with her first baby. Remember? Wayne told us."

"At least let me call Dr. Wilkins and ask him," Nick said. She shrugged.

But Dr. Wilkins seemed to think that her labor was for real when Nick told him that her contractions were twenty minutes apart, that they had started at thirty. Dr. Wilkins suggested they come to the hospital.

Driving slowly, Nick held her hand. There was barely any traffic. The date was March 27, 1971. Spring was beginning to exhibit itself. The air was zooming with metaphors of renewal and birth: a perfect day to have a child.

41

How close to Megan you have grown in the last months, Nick. How you enjoyed those practice sessions at home, faithfully supervising her exercises every evening on the green carpet. How she huffed and panted and simulated pushing, timed by you with your new dark blue 1/5-second shock-resistant trackmaster stopwatch with sixty-minute color-coded time-out capability and color-coded push buttons for start, stop, and return to zero. Kneeling by her side, you announced: "Beginning of contraction," and then, at intervals: "Fifteen, thirty, forty-five seconds, relax, relax, sixty seconds, end of contraction, take a deep breath, very good, relax."

You practiced the effleurage with her, massaging your fingertips across her tight abdomen. And remember the relaxation exercises, Nick, your favorite part of the ritual. You would announce: "Right leg," and she would contract her right leg, lifting it slightly off the floor while you lifted the other leg to make sure it was totally limp and relaxed, shaking it just a little to see it wasn't tense and then doing the same with her arms. "Relax your right leg," you'd say, and then go through the entire sequence: "Right arm; left leg; left arm," testing her relaxation in the other limbs, sometimes moving her head from side to side to make certain her neck wasn't tense.

How proud you felt when she managed tricky combinations such as: "Left leg; right arm," or: "Right leg; right arm," or: "Left arm; right arm," or: "Right leg; left arm."

You made sure to always show your approval. And how she, lying on the carpet with two pillows stuffed beneath her knees, followed your voice totally, never questioning your variety of orders. Not once were you repetitious. You felt good knowing that because of these sessions, labor would be easier for her: during childbirth she would relax automatically to the sound of your voice while her womb contracted.

The existence of fathers' waiting rooms in hospitals struck you as absurd. How could any man *not* want to see his child born?

42

They left their car in the parking lot across the street from the hospital.

"How are you feeling?" Nick asked, calm, considerate, and, oh, so much in control of the situation.

"Fine," Megan smiled, a sort of brave smile, a smile, oh, so much in control of the situation.

"Just think," he said. "Today our child will be born."

She squeezed his hand.

While he signed her in, she was taken to the maternity floor via wheelchair; it lent tremendous authenticity to her weak contractions. How she longed for the challenge she had prepared for so eagerly.

She was welcomed by a short, round-bodied nurse in her forties, a red-cheeked woman with blond curls and a motherly smile packed with efficiency. As she listened to the nurse's instructions, Megan felt the start of a light contraction, a contraction she could have handled without the panting, without the fingertip massage; however, she lifted her right hand.

"Just a minute, please," she said, panting and effleuraging until the contraction stopped.

"Thank you," she said, with that brave little smile to the apple-cheeked nurse, who appeared relatively unimpressed, as though she'd seen it all.

She only stated: "Your first."

"Yes." Megan beamed.

Appleface nodded as if she'd known it all along.

Megan managed to get through the enema with less difficulty than she had expected when she first saw the size of it. Clad in a limp hospital gown, she lay down on the starched bed, waiting for Nick and/or her next contraction, happily anticipating whoever or whatever would arrive first. Instead, the nurse, who had remained unimpressed with Megan's considerable show of control, arrived with the equipment necessary to turn Megan's pubic area into something resembling the skin of a recently plucked chicken.

It came to a clash of wills.

"Pull up your johnny, please," said Appleface, saturating a large cotton wad with something strong-smelling from a plastic bottle.

"I've talked to Dr. Wilkins about having a mini-prep," Megan stated bravely, covering her curly hair of a darker color with her right hand. In her seventh month she had discussed the prep with Dr. Wilkins, since she remembered how uncomfortable it had been when her pubic hair grew back after her appendectomy the year before she met Nick. She still—

"A mini-prep?" My husband is looking over my shoulder. "You had that with the children, didn't you?"

"Yes, and the first time I had to fight for it."

"Isn't that rather personal?"

"Why? It's her mini-prep, not mine."

"Then why bring it in?"

"Because I want Megan to start fighting for what she wants. Besides . . ."

"What?"

"I'm still angry at myself for letting a whole class of student nurses watch me being prepped for my kidney surgery."

"But that was ten years ago."

"So? You know what bothers me most about it? That nobody asked my permission. I still remember how embarrassed I was. Embarrassed and at the same time scared of the surgery. I was convinced I would die."

"Why didn't you ask them to leave?"

"I didn't know I could."

"Still, it's rather personal."

"Just because I'm giving Megan one of my experiences doesn't mean I'm Megan. Lots of women have mini-preps."

"What's for dinner?" my husband asks.

What a transition. "What time is it?"

"Five-thirty."

"You want to order pizza?"

"I guess so," he says without enthusiasm. "What do you want on it?"

"I don't care. I'll cut up a salad to go with it."

I think of Tillie Olsen's book *Silences*. According to her, the women writers of the last century whose achievements endured for us in one way or another nearly all never married or married in their late thirties. She only names five who married and had children as young women. All had servants. How reassuring it would be to know there was a cook downstairs, slicing vegetables and roasting meat, maybe even a nanny to see after the needs of my children. How nourishing is pizza? Tomorrow I'll make a real meal, simmer fresh vegetables to perfection (whatever that is), maybe even bake some bread and . . . I'd better write a shopping list.

43

"We don't do mini-preps," Appleface said without a motherly smile.

"But Dr. Wilkins agreed to it," Megan said stubbornly, not daring to take her hand away for the next effleurage, although she felt the beginning of a contraction. Her body tensed, rising toward a tight center. It hurt. Just a little. Donna must have been right when she explained how important it was to do the breathing and massage right from the beginning, in order to stay on top of a contraction.

Appleface closed the plastic bottle as though trying to wring its neck, dropped the cotton wad into the green metal wastebasket below the sink, and stormed out of the room. Ten minutes later she marched back in, her round features screwed into a tight fist.

"Spread your legs, Mrs. Stone," she commanded, her voice below freezing.

"Did you check with Dr. Wilkins?" Megan asked, fighting the evaporation of the wonderful happiness earlier associated with this day, the day she was going to give birth.

"I don't have all day, Mrs. Stone."

"Did he say it was all right?" Megan insisted in a small voice.

The red of the cheeks spread across the face and stained the plump neck. "Yes, Mrs. Stone, you will get your way. Now, if you please would spread your legs."

Another cotton wad was subjected to saturation from the strangled bottle. Megan stiffened as she felt it wet and icy against her vulva. The strokes of the razor were firm and quick, too quick to be safe, it seemed to her. Weakened by her earlier resistance, she didn't dare to object. The thought that the nurse was trying to hurt her came just before she felt the sharp, stinging pain.

"You cut me," she said, trying to raise herself on her elbows to see if she was bleeding. "You just cut me," she repeated, helpless with anger.

"If you stopped squirming, Mrs. Stone, this wouldn't happen." There was a smug satisfaction to the fat voice. "You're making this extremely difficult for me."

Biting her lower lip, Megan lay back and submitted to the hostile hands. Nick would be coming soon. She'd tell him.

But Appleface didn't let him in for half an hour, and then he had to leave again, because Dr. Wilkins came and examined her, stating that she had begun to dilate and that she was coming along nicely.

44

—Hey, I'm proud of you, Megan. The way you stood up to Appleface.

—But I got hurt. Are you pleased about that too?

—Of course not. How can you even think of that?

—Because you're pushing me. You've given birth twice, and—

—Pushing you?

—Yes. This is my first time, remember? I don't know all those things. I don't care if I get a full prep or a mini-prep. Just because it was important to you once doesn't mean it has to be important to me. I don't want to fight the battles you never resolved for yourself. I'm not a rebel.

—Yes, you are.

—No. I'd much rather have a peaceful labor and delivery.

—Peaceful? There you go again with your expectations.

—You make mistakes too. Why don't you just leave me here in the hospital with Nick? Get away from that desk. Spend some time with your children. Cook a decent meal. Clean the house. Anything. Just stop making me do and say things that are out of character. How can I possibly develop if you constantly intrude on my space, nudging me into directions I don't want to take?

—But it's important to fight for what you want, Megan.

—What if I don't want it?

45

Six hours later Megan was still coming along nicely. This is what happened during those six hours:

Nick ate his sandwich.

Megan sucked five Schrafft's lemon lollipops.

Megan threw up the equivalent of five Schrafft's lemon lollipops.

Nick massaged Megan's abdomen with cornstarch.

Megan and Nick played gin.

Megan told Nick that he was more interested in playing cards than in helping her through labor.

Megan told Nick she loved him.

Megan told Nick she didn't think it would hurt like this.

Dr. Wilkins said he was going to break Megan's water.

Dr. Wilkins inserted a long instrument into Megan's vagina.

Megan asked him when he was going to break the water.

Dr. Wilkins told her he had just done so.

Dr. Wilkins left after telling Megan she was coming along nicely.

Nick followed Dr. Wilkins.

Nick came back and told Megan he had talked to Dr. Wilkins about Appleface.

Nick pulled the washcloth from the bag of tricks.

Nick moistened the washcloth and laid it across Megan's forehead.

Megan took the washcloth from her forehead and sucked on it frantically.

Nick tried to tell Megan a joke.

Megan said Donna was a fraud.

Megan told Nick she knew he didn't love her.

Nick reminded her that Donna had said women in labor tended to act irrationally during the transition phase.

Megan pulled the tennis ball from under the small of her back and threw it at Nick.

Megan said she was sorry.

Nick timed her contraction and told her to relax.

Megan thanked Nick for being so wonderful.

Nick put Chap Stick on Megan's lips.

Dr. Wilkins came and told Megan she was coming along nicely.

Megan told Dr. Wilkins to go to hell.

Nick said that this was a good sign because she must be in transition.

Megan threw up bile that tasted of Chap Stick.

Nick said he was proud of her.

Megan sent Nick to the coffee shop to keep up his strength.

Nick came back after ten minutes smelling of apple pie.

Megan made him promise to take care of the baby if she died.

Nick said she was not going to die.

Nick held Megan's head as she threw up.

Nick told Megan he knew she could do it.

Megan sucked on her washcloth.

Nick told Megan he was proud of her.

Megan listened to a woman screaming in the next room.

Megan remembered a square hand holding two white booties.

Nick told Megan the woman was alone.

Nick timed Megan's contraction with his shock-resistant trackmaster stopwatch.

Megan told Nick she had always known the stopwatch was more important to him than she.

Megan said she couldn't go through with it.

Megan said she knew she was going to die.

Nick asked her to lie on her side and massaged her back.

Megan told Nick she could never manage all this without him.

Nick told Megan he loved her.

Megan felt sorry for the woman in the next room.

Megan told Nick he was conceited thinking he deserved the credit for her not screaming like the other woman.

Nick pointed out that he hadn't said anything like that.

Nick told Megan she was very brave.

Megan began to hate the stopwatch in Nick's right hand.

Nick told her he knew how the contractions were hurting.

Megen used obscene language in telling him he could never know how the contractions were hurting.

Nick talked about transition symptoms.

Megan said Donna was a fraud.

Nick told Megan she was doing wonderfully.

Nick said he was hungry.

Megan told him to go to hell.

Megan said she was breaking apart.

Megan told Nick she had never felt so trapped.

Nick said they were going to see this through together.

Megan thought that he had the option to leave.

Nick kissed Megan's hands.

Dr. Wilkins came and told her she was coming along nicely.

Megan told him she knew he was trying to kill her.

Megan felt guilty and tried to apologize.

Dr. Wilkins said something about transition symptoms.

46

—As a character in this novel I object.

—Object? To what, Nick?

—You were going to write a positive book. No victims

or villains, remember? You already have forty-five chapters, and so far my character is flat and condescending. Just take a look at the end of Chapter 26:

> The earth did not move.
> She heard no bells.
> After he was asleep, etc.

You make it sound as if I just made love to her and then rolled off. Somewhat crude, don't you think so? It wasn't like that at all.

—Then what was it like?

—There should have been three or four pages of dialogue between *no bells* and *After he was alseep.* Do you have any idea how restricted I feel by your choices and omissions? In Chapter 24 you even distort my thoughts:

> He believed he knew her strategy. He would beat her, quickly and cleanly, and then ask her out to dinner, perhaps, to soften the blow.

Why should I accept a perceptionally incorrect statement like that? Of course I wanted to beat her in chess, just as I try to win when I play against men. It has something to do with challenge, all right? And I thought of asking her to have dinner with me because I wanted to know her better. She was very reserved when we first met, afraid to let anyone get close. That's why I didn't try to kiss her for quite a while; she seemed to carry this barrier of glass around herself. Megan and I were friends before we were lovers. I—

—Do you know how pompous that sounds, Nick?

—Why? I do consider her my best friend. We trust each other. There's no letting down. I admire her intelligence, and I think she's beautiful, even though she doesn't believe it. She has an incredibly poor self-image.

—That's certainly not one of your problems!

—What's wrong with liking myself? Megan and I've talked about it. She grew up believing that to love yourself is a sin. Love your neighbor and let him strike the other cheek. But she's beginning to outgrow that attitude and trying to accept herself.

—Listen, your wife is in labor, and you're wasting time trying to explain her to me.

—There's plenty of time. Dr. Wilkins just took another look at her and told her she's coming along nicely.

—That does sound like Dr. Wilkins.

—Besides, you don't know Megan nearly as well as I do.

—What do you mean? I made her up.

—But I live with her, remember? I care about her.

—You do? Then why did you let her walk by herself to the lighthouse?

—Because once she decides to do something, she gets very upset if anybody tries to talk her out of it. When we were first married, I used to try, but it just wasn't worth the aggravation. Besides, it doesn't happen all that often. And about those roles you mentioned earlier—

—Shouldn't you be timing Megan's contractions?

—Don't worry. I can do two things at the same time. *Relax, Megan. Thirty seconds. Fifteen seconds. You're doing beautifully.* Where was I? Oh yes, roles. I believe Megan was to some extent looking for a role when we got married. She overidentified, perhaps because she hadn't let herself love anybody since her parents died. She was afraid of losing me, worried I might get killed on the way to work. At times she clung too much. And she was always looking for approval. I don't want to tell her what to do or who to be.

—What about the breakfast thing?

—I only kid her about it two or three times a year. I have to admit that I could easily be reconciled to the idea of a breakfast-making wife, but I was offended by your version of the second Mrs. Stone. Really, she sounds as though you pulled her right out of a soap commercial. *Relax, Megan. Relax. Here, let me rinse your washcloth. Is that better?* And that brain recipe. Before you ransack your cookbook for another one of those and commit plagiarism, let me point out that I was referring to Megan's intelligence.

—But you did make that statement about being a leg man.

—I might have. After several drinks. You wouldn't want me too perfect, would you? A complex character should be neither black nor white; you have to touch upon the shades of gray. Right? Many shades. How about a light pearl-gray for me? I told you I like myself.

—But do you have to prove it constantly? Now what about the dialogue, those three or four pages between *no bells* and *After he was asleep?*

—All right. I didn't ask her if she had come. I knew she hadn't. And we didn't talk about her family. That, too, came later. Actually, we talked about chess. She told me about the nun who had taught her the game when she was ten. Her name was Sister Maria. I met her after we were married. Her mother had been the Czechoslovakian chess champion for three consecutive years in the early twenties. The family emigrated in the thirties. *Relax, Megan. Forty-five seconds. Thirty seconds. Fifteen seconds. End of contraction. You're doing fine.* Sister Maria won quite a few tournaments in New York and Hoboken, New Jersey, where they lived before she entered the convent. Megan told me that one of Sister Maria's grandfathers had been a Grand Master, one of the five leading players in 1914 during the Great International Championship in Leningrad. It was still called St. Petersburg when Czar Nicholas II gave him the title of Grand Master. I tell you, finding out about that impressive background made me feel a lot better about having lost consistently.

—That's all very interesting, but I'd rather concentrate on your wife's labor.

—All right. But I want you to know that there are things I've done today besides eating my sandwich and going to the coffee shop for a piece of apple pie, which, by the way, gave me tremendous stomach cramps.

—I didn't know that.

—There are lots of things you don't know about me. Look at Megan. She's dozing off again. She's tired from staying up most of the night, and she keeps falling asleep between contractions. There. They are much closer together now. If I lay my palms on her abdomen, like this, see, I can feel the tightening just before the next contraction begins. It's the strangest feeling. It just draws up, hard as rock. *Wake up, Megan. Beginning of contraction. Fifty seconds. Forty. Thirty. You're doing fine. Keep breathing. Twenty. Ten. Beautiful.* Did you see that? I did the pant-and-blow breathing we learned in class, and all she had to do was imitate.

—All she had to do? Maybe you should have the next kid, Nick.

—Funny, real funny. But seriously, if you don't take more care with the development of my character, I'll walk out of this novel and you're going to be stuck with one of those single-mother plots.

—What's wrong with a single-mother plot? Sounds like a good option. But maybe I should first give you a chance to redeem yourself. What if I wrote the chapter of your son's birth from your point of view?

—Are you sure it's going to be a boy?

—Positive. I decided that very early. Take a look at his index card.

—Do you have one of those for me?

—Sure. It took me some time to make up my mind about what you look like. But here it is. You have blond hair, blue eyes, dark blue, your left ear sticks out just a little, and you're about six foot two. Too thin to look athletic, you are, however, a strong tennis player, a demon at the net.

—A demon at the net. I like that.

—I thought you would. You also ski, too fast, always looking just a little out of control. Since I certainly exhausted your interest in chess, I thought I'd let you read a lot, maybe *The Wall Street Journal* as well as contemporary fiction and poetry.

—What's that on the back of my card?

—You have an M.B.A. from Harvard. You see, I've provided you with an excellent education. You're vice-president of Stone, Inc., a company founded by your father. Stone, Inc., manufactures wheels for roller skates. No keys. Although you're not unhappy with your work, you become impatient at times. It's just too easy. For a man who—

—Hold it. *Relax, Megan. Sixty seconds. Forty-five. You're coming along nicely. Thirty. Fifteen. It won't be much longer now.* For a man who what?

—For a man who enjoys challenge, there isn't enough of it in a position that has been waiting for you since you were born. You dread spending the next thirty years of your life dedicated to roller skates.

—Sounds depressing. Can't you come up with something better? I always wanted to be a spy.

—I can't stand spy stories. At least most of them. And I don't see you as a spy type. I can picture you breaking in a new pair of ski boots after coming home from the office. You're still wearing your suit pants, but have taken off your jacket, shirt, and tie. Stalking through the living room in your T-shirt and ski boots, you carry your attaché case to the chair by the fireplace. Well, do you like yourself better now?

—I'm not overwhelmed, but I guess I could perform within that frame.

—What am I going to do with you?

—You could always transfer me to a different century. Put my head under a guillotine or throw me to the lions.

—I might do that to Henry Nelson. But I need you in this manuscript, Nick, although I don't much like to admit it. Are you ready to do your version of the birth chapter?

47

—Megan was wheeled into the delivery room at 11:45 P.M.

Timothy Michael was born at 12:20 A.M.

Standing behind the delivery table, I pushed both her shoulders forward as Dr. Wilkins guided the small, wrinkled shape from her body.

"Quick now," he said, lifting it dramatically. "What is it, boy or girl?"

I saw the genitals, just as I saw that he had two arms, two legs, a rather large head, and I heard my voice, the same instant Megan said: "A boy."

"We have a boy," she repeated.

Later, in her room, we would laugh and say that Wilkins had missed his calling to the stage, that he probably put on this little performance all the time. But at the moment when we both said: "A boy," I felt a bond between us as strong as the umbilical cord still connecting Megan to our child.

His screams were loud and thin.

He was handed to Megan, covered with a moist film of cheese-colored stuff and a few small blood streaks.

He blinked. I saw that his eyes were blue.

His nose was covered with tiny white blisters.

He was perfect.

"Look at his wrists," Megan said.

They were scratched: his fingernails were long.

I bent over the two of them as Megan freed one of her breasts and brought his face against her nipple. He didn't nurse. From the books we had read during pregnancy, we knew he wouldn't.

"Congratulations. He's a fine-looking boy," Dr. Wilkins said, waiting for Megan's placenta. He winked at me. "Haven't lost a father yet."

"Congratulations," said the night nurse, waiting with a small rubber-ball contraption to suck mucus from our son's mouth and nose.

Timothy flinched and threw his arms wide open, as though startled by the abrupt change from darkness to light.

"I'm so proud of you," I said.

"He's perfect," I said.

"He has your hair," I said and touched the fine reddish down.

She held him, his cheek against her nipple, as Dr. Wilkins cut the cord. She held him while Dr. Wilkins stitched her perineum, which had torn during the last pushes. Earlier, when she had refused an episiotomy, he had warned her she might tear. She took my hand and laid my index finger against the baby's palm. With surprising strength he grabbed it, his hand closing around it.

She said she barely felt the stitches.

Reluctantly I freed myself from my son's fingers as Megan handed him over to the nurse. We watched her cleanse him of the last traces of his existence in the womb.

48

She did not get the postpartum blues, although she had read about them and expected those predicted feelings of irritation, confusion, fear, sadness, and insufficiency.

Instead she felt high.

Incredibly high.

She had a private room with twenty-four-hour rooming-in. Interrupted only by doctors, nurses, and Nick's frequent visits, she took care of her child in the white room.

She cleansed him, examining each toe and finger, every inch of his body.

She tried to nurse him. At first they were both clumsy about it.

She nursed him, flinching at the greedy pull against her nipples, which became sore in spite of the toughening exercises. During the last three months of her pregnancy, she had tweaked each nipple twenty times before going to bed. Standing in front of the bathroom mirror, she had pulled and twisted faithfully, according to Donna's instructions, wondering about latent masochistic tendencies only during the first few weeks.

She barely slept. She was too excited, too high. At night she listened to her child's breathing. When he cried, she nursed him and kept him in her bed until he fell asleep again. During the day she spent hours watching him, whispering to him.

49

The second day the florist delivered a potted tulip plant from Aunt Judy and two dozen white roses from Dagmar. Nick visited four or five times daily. Since he had a cold, the nurses made him wear a surgical face mask before they let him into the room.

He brought flowers.

He brought a Raggedy Andy, taller than the baby.

He brought his parents, who seemed awed to find the child in Megan's room, who were used to looking at newborns through the window of a nursery, who told her she didn't even look sick.

"I'm not sick," Megan said.

"You must be glad it's a boy," Nick's mother said. "With your being tall and all that."

Nick's father began to cough and said quickly that they'd better be going.

They left two large savings bonds made out to Megan Stone and/or Timothy Stone and a black velvet box with a heavy gold charm bracelet and two charms: a boy's profile with Timothy's initials and birth date, and a heart without anything engraved on it.

Beverly Stone patted Megan's hands. Then she patted Megan's cheeks.

"Thank you," Megan said.

They walked from the room, apparently somewhat puzzled and uncomfortable.

"My mother was all geared to bringing comfort to a sick person. You're just too healthy." Nick grinned. "Oh, I almost forgot. Your aunt stopped by this morning with all kinds of frozen casseroles. She said she'd visit you after you get home. She wanted to know if there was anything you needed."

"Not really. I'll call her later to thank her."

"I'm surprised she hasn't visited yet."

"She can't stand hospitals."

"Why?" He was playing with his son's toes.

"I don't really know. She says she can't breathe in hospitals. When I had my appendix out, she called twice a day and sent all kinds of stuff. But she didn't visit."

Nick examined Timmy's heels.

"Remember the woman who was in labor in the room next to mine?" she asked.

He nodded.

"She didn't have her baby until the next morning. They put her out completely. She's across the hall now.

Yesterday I could hear the nurse trying to wake her up to tell her she'd had a boy."

"Aren't you glad you didn't have anesthesia?"

"Now I am. But while I was in labor, I wished they'd knocked me out in the parking lot."

"At least we know we have the right one," Nick said.

"Were you worried they might get mixed up?"

"Not really." He shrugged, looking a little embarrassed. "But at least now I'd recognize him anywhere."

She nursed Timmy while Nick watched. Afterwards he held his son. Before he left he changed Timmy's diapers, laid him gently on his stomach in the glass bassinet, and wheeled it next to Megan's bed so she could watch him.

"I'll be back early tomorrow," he said.

Lying on her side, she watched her son, his knees tucked under his belly, his face turned toward her, his eyes closed. His eyelashes were incredibly long. On her night table were Dagmar's roses. She suddenly wished her grandmother were with her.

50

Dagmar—where does she come from?

Until today I thought she'd come entirely from my imagination, but now I'm not that sure anymore. Driving home from the university where I teach, I found myself wondering what my grandmother would have been like, had she lived. I haven't thought of her in years. When she died in 1949, I was only three. One of her legs was amputated during the war by a pediatrician. Afterwards she suffered from complications. There were no surgeons available; they were taking care of the *real* war casualties: men; they didn't have time for an old German woman with varicose veins.

I don't remember my grandmother. My mother told me

that I liked to ride on my grandmother's wooden leg, that I held on to it and let her drag me around. My mother tried to stop me many times. I don't remember. Yet I felt guilty when she told me.

I'd like to think that it gave my grandmother pleasure to be with me, that she enjoyed rather than endured me. She was the third wife of my grandfather, a Dutchman who had come to Germany as a young man. His first two wives died in childbirth. The first left him a daughter; the second, a son and a daughter.

Driving home, I wondered what it had been like for my grandmother to be pregnant with her only child, my mother. Did she lie awake at night, thinking of the other wives who had died giving birth? What if I wrote a poem about her? The third wife of the Dutchman. The other children? What about them? The children of the dead mothers. While driving, I started scribbling down notes. Finally I pulled to the side. Maybe my grandmother took the children to the Rhine River. I used to go there as a child and watch the river, the barges. It was only half an hour's walk from the house where I grew up, the house where my grandmother used to live. The Dutchman built it. She survived him; there was no fourth wife.

The photos I have of her show her from the waist up. Never her legs. What if I wrote the poem about the family grave where the two other wives were buried, where she and the Dutchman are buried now? On All Saints' Day my parents used to take my sister and me there to put flowers and wreaths on the wide grave.

What would she be like, had she lived? I would have liked her, I believe. She'd be strong. Nobody would tell her what to do. Nobody tells Dagmar what to do. Dagmar doesn't feel obligated to explain her reasons for doing something. Is she an extension of what I imagine my grandmother would be like, had she lived?

51

The year before Timmy was born, Dagmar had moved from her Manhattan brownstone to Golden Acres, an elegant nursing home five miles out of Boston.

"Why Boston?" Aunt Judy had asked. "You don't know anybody there."

"That's right," Dagmar had nodded.

Her relationship with her daughter was ambiguous, at best. For years she had resisted Judy's attempts to take over her life. Although she found it amusing to watch Judy's attempts to reverse the mother/child roles, the struggle, at times, was draining.

Even Megan had tried to convince her grandmother to move to a home or apartment in Connecticut where she could visit her more than two or three times a year. But Dagmar was firm about staying in the Boston area. She had a large room with a high ceiling at Golden Acres, to which she had brought some of her favorite things: a carved wooden chest, her Victorian rolltop desk, a large blue oriental rug, her stereo, and her husband Rudi's collection of books about Indians. Although she had sold or given away his other things after he died, she had held on to the books. She kept them on two shelves between the arched windows of her light room. Sixty-two of the books were written by Karl May, a German writer whose imagination roamed America, although he never actually left Germany. In 1912 Karl May died at the age of seventy, still fighting ugly rumors that some of his books had been written in prison. Bound in leather, the books were printed in ornate German script. Rudi's favorites had been the Winnetou books: Winnetou I, Winnetou II, and Winnetou III. In Winnetou III, the chief of the Apaches, Winnetou, dies. Until Rudi died, he used to reread Winnetou III every three years. It was the only book that ever brought him close to tears.

"They'll be yours someday," Dagmar had told Megan.

52

Picture this: a woman bending over her sleeping infant, bending down and waiting for him to wake. Her red hair is long, almost to her waist. Whenever she nurses her son, she pulls it back so he won't tangle his fists in it.

You recognize her?

Her days center around her child. It is as though she lives a fluid dream as she takes care of this small being that began in her center. The outside world does not count. Patiently she waits for him to wake so she can smile at him, bathe him, play with him. Poems and fairy tales she reads to him. When he falls asleep at her breast, she holds him, watching him breathe, his chest miraculously lifting and falling. She is needed, wonderfully needed and totally accepted. His needs are immediate; only she can totally satisfy them. Her child is surviving and growing from the nourishment he sucks from her breasts. In two weeks he will eat his first jar of baby food, strained bananas, but right now, she is his one source of life. Imagine the extreme satisfaction, the rush of love when she feels his fierce tug at her nipple. This is what she was born to do, she believes; she has never felt this content.

53

Yes. This is better than the forty-two pages I wrote describing in detail Megan's early months as a mother. It needed to be tightened. Had I remained in the background and merely shown it to you, you would have asked:

So what? By the time I subtly weaved in Megan's first signs of dissatisfaction, you'd have been far ahead, telling me impatiently that you knew this couldn't last, that nothing is permanent, that the outside world would penetrate before too long. You are a cynic.

Does it have to be all that predictable? When I turned on the light an hour ago to write this in bed, I thought I was onto something I didn't want to forget during the night. I didn't think I would get into this. But what do you want me to do? Deny her those feelings of satisfaction, of acceptance? They are valid, believe me, just as valid as her early dissatisfaction, those first indications of evaporating euphoria. A gradual process. She doesn't notice it. Only afterwards will she look back and wonder why she missed the first signs. When does she stop waiting for her child to wake up, hoping he'll sleep a little longer so she can finish something she wants to do? When does she begin reading while nursing him, looking at the letters on the page instead of into his eyes? She knows she still loves him, loves him more each day. Perhaps the wonder is wearing off; she is getting used to being somebody's mother.

The immediate fulfillment of her child's needs no longer satisfies her so completely. At times she'd rather sleep through the night than nurse him. And although Nick takes turns and brings Timmy to her every other night so that she may linger in half slumber while letting her child empty her breasts, she only rarely recovers the early joy.

She gives all her attention to her son's needs, and if she feels a slight resentment at this, she promptly reacts with guilt, that rampant growth Aunt Judy cultivated in her. With two children, there'll be even more opportunity for guilt.

—Have you noticed this smooth transition, Megan? Four years in one sentence. Nicole has been born, is two years old; Timmy is four. All those opportunities to feel guilty. Just consider having to decide between the priority of your children's and Nick's needs. And what about the awareness of dissatisfaction? The natural reaction is guilt. If you—

—Why are you leaving those years out? The transition might be smooth, but it's too fast. It doesn't work for me. I don't have enough time to get used to my children. Why are you rushing me?

—I'm not rushing you. I—

—You should bring out how different the children are. Even as a baby Nicole was much sturdier than Timmy. Tougher. She still is. She'll probably always go after what she wants, while Timmy will worry about the feelings of others. At times he is too sensitive. They even look different. Timmy has blue eyes and reddish-brown hair. Every year it darkens a little. By the time he's in high school, it'll probably be brown.

—The novel won't go that far.

—How far is it going to go?

—I don't know. But not that far. What about Nicole?

—Her hair is white-blond and very thin and curly. It often frizzes, surrounding her face like a halo. It gives her a very angelic look—totally misleading. Her eyes are brown now. A strange contrast. They started changing color the day after she was born, and by the time she was ten days old, they were brown.

—I'm glad you pointed out the children's differences, Megan; still, I don't want to deal with those years in detail. It could become too repetitious. And I honestly believe you wouldn't want me to. Just look at yourself. Sometimes you can't even wait to get through the day, to start all new the next morning. You don't know why. There's not enough of a change in your life to make you look forward to the next day. Why is that, I wonder? You have an understanding husband, two healthy children, a beautiful house with a garden, your own car. Why isn't that enough?

54

Instead of working on the novel, I've been revising the poem about my grandmother. After many revisions it's ready to be sent out. I've called it *The Third Wife of the Dutchman*. How good it feels to actually finish something and to see it all on one page. This novel will take forever, I sometimes fear, and it helps to get the illusion of actually having finished something.

> The third wife of the Dutchman
> takes the children of the dead mothers
> to the river.
> She gathers camomile that soothes bellyaches,
> camomile to rinse her hair.
> On Sunday she sings hymns
> on the women's side of the church
> from a black prayer book.
>
> In spring the third wife of the Dutchman
> tends the tulips on the wide grave.
> There will be room for her,
> for the Dutchman and his children.
> He is a shrewd merchant.
>
> The third wife of the Dutchman
> is not afraid to be strong.
> At night she lies with him
> and smells the tobacco
> on his Kaiser Wilhelm mustache.
> She listens to the movements of her girl child
> and wills herself to live
> long beyond the birth.
>
> On All Saints' Day
> the Dutchman takes his children
> to the grave of their dead mothers.

They carry circles of white flowers;
a cross of holly.

In the evening
the third wife of the Dutchman
sings lullabies
to the blond children
to keep the dark away.
On Saturday
she sweeps the sidewalk
in front of her house.

55

"What did you do today?" Nick asked brightly, closing
the kitchen door behind him, dropping his attaché case on
a chair, and advancing for his predictable coming-home
kiss.

Megan resisted the impulse of replying: *Nothing much.*
There must have been something she had done. She
couldn't possibly feel this tired and dragging from doing
nothing. But what had she achieved today? There wasn't
anything to show, no accomplishments to point to and say:
Look at what I did today.

Even if she were a dedicated cook (which she wasn't)
and had some three-hour delicacy baking slowly and
succulently to perfection, she would know that soon it
would be consumed. It wouldn't last. What was the sense
in telling Nick that she had fed the children breakfast and
lunch, not to mention morning and afternoon snacks of
sliced apples and carrot sticks; that she had cleaned up
after them each time; that she had washed, folded, and put
away two loads of laundry which soon would be dirty
again; that she had bought two half gallons of milk, a
pound and a half of haddock, four strawberry yogurts, two

loaves of whole-wheat bread, and a few other items she'd run out of; that she had meant to clean the bathrooms but had not gotten around to it; that she'd written checks to pay the phone and electric bills.

There was nothing lasting to her accomplishments.

No evidence of change.

The furniture she had dusted would require the same mechanical task again; everything: making beds, vacuuming, washing windows, faces, dishes . . .

"Just the usual," she replied.

"That's nice," Nick said and went into the living room.

How she wished there was something she could show him and say: Look at the change. What if she became involved in decorating projects like Janet Dial down the street, who was always changing things with scraps of material and trim she bought on sale, who had sewn matching covers with rickrack for her toaster, blender, coffee maker, youngest daughter, and electric can opener last week. Janet had five different sets of curtains with color-coordinated comforters and tissue boxes for each bedroom. Janet also moved her furniture into different groupings during the first week of summer, fall, winter, and spring. Did her husband comment on the change when he came home? Show his approval? What would happen when nothing else needed to be redecorated? Would she paint the house again? Wallpaper the ceilings? Perhaps she kept a schedule to make sure it never came to that, always saving something that needed to be changed.

The children. They changed. But how could Megan take credit for their growth? Although she delighted in their development, she knew it did not reflect her accomplishments. Sure, they learned things from her, molded their words after hers, tried to imitate her. But their physical development was something that would have happened without her and would continue.

Last year she had tried canning, motivated by the rows

of jars with fruits and vegetables on Sara's shelves. How tempting it sounded to preserve something, to make it last, to have something to show for *beyond* the immediate preparation and consumption of food. She bought five dozen jars, examined their tops for cracks, soaped and rinsed them. Fruits and vegetables she washed, cut, cored, pared, chopped, sliced, or stirred. She cooked, steamed, measured, and poured them into the clear jars. With the satisfying feeling of having completed something worthwhile, she sealed the hot-bellied jars and handprinted blue-rimmed labels with contents and dates. It didn't matter that her fingers were cracked and stained. She imagined the garden she would have. She would grow all her vegetables, maybe even order fruit trees from the nursery.

The green beans spoiled.

The blueberry jam grew fuzzy patches of mold.

The tomatoes tasted all right but looked disgusting.

56

This is written while I'm waiting for my dentist appointment. Behind the words on this page, I hear the sound of the drill. Don't try to tell me that apprehensions such as this don't influence writing. To give you a completely unbiased, uninvolved *slice of life,* I would have to write in a vacuum, subjected to screened, identical stimuli. A lobotomy might have the same effect.

"How do you like the tomatoes?" Megan asked, following Nick from the kitchen where she had just given him a sample of the stewed tomatoes she was cooking for dinner.

He took off his tie. "I don't know."

"What do you mean? You just tasted some. You must have some opinion."

He shrugged.

"Well?"

"Are they supposed to look like that?"

"Like what?"

"Like that. Why is it so important?"

"Because I canned them, and because we have nineteen more jars in the basement." She tried to keep her voice level.

"Why did you do that?" He sat down with his *Wall Street Journal.*

"Because I thought you'd like them."

"I like them. I'm wild about them. All right?" He turned the pages to the stock-market section.

"You don't really care, do you?" Her hair was falling forward. Impatiently, she pushed it back with both hands.

"You're squeaking."

"Dammit, stop reading. I'm talking to you."

He raised his eyebrows and lowered the paper.

She stood in front of his chair. If only she could shake him out of his composure. She crossed her arms in front of her chest and then dropped them to her sides. "Aren't you going to answer?"

"I didn't think an answer was required."

She took a deep breath.

"What was the question?" he asked.

"Just forget it. Don't pretend you care what I do. I spent two weeks peeling those fucking—"

"Where are the kids?"

"In the den. Why?"

"Your language."

"My language was enriched by you, if you remember correctly. Don't act like a damn saint. And stop staring at my hands. I know exactly what you're doing. You always stare at my hands when we have an argument and you want to confuse me. I'm going to move them if I feel like it. See?" She waved them back and forth in front of his face. "Get a good look. See how chapped they still are from canning and—"

"I didn't ask you to go through all that trouble."

"Excuse me for letting myself be interrupted by you." She hoped he noticed the sarcasm.

"I didn't know you were still talking."

"Well, I was."

"Maybe you should say 'Ping' or something like that when you're finished."

"You're a real bastard, you know that, Nick Stone? A real bastard. You could have—"

He turned a page.

"I haven't pinged yet," Megan shouted, hating the sound of her voice, hating Nick for getting her this upset.

"I can read and listen at the same time," he said calmly.

"It's rude."

With exaggerated patience he folded the paper and laid it on the table in front of him, taking great care in lining it up with the edge of the table.

"Why couldn't you be honest enough to tell me you hate canned tomatoes instead of letting me go through all the work. I even told you before I bought the jars and the canner. I told you . . ." She turned away abruptly and stared out of the window. She was not going to let the bastard make her cry. She was not going to let him. The blue spruce in front of the window became blurred. Damn.

"Listen, I'm sorry you're getting this upset," he said.

"I'm sorry you chose to interpret my words incorrectly," she mimicked the tone of his voice, turning around quickly. " 'I'm sorry you're making such a fool of yourself.' Isn't that what you mean? Stop apologizing for my reactions. I know exactly what you're doing. It doesn't count." She sniffled. "There, you should really be proud. You got me so upset I'm crying."

"It's good for you to cry."

"Good for me? What right do you have to tell me it's good for me to cry? I hate to cry." She tried to ignore the sound of her voice but remained aware of its "mean chipmunk" sound, as Nick had referred to it in the past. For a moment she couldn't remember how the argument had started.

"Why don't you just buy canned tomatoes from now on?" he asked. "It would be easier on you and probably a lot less expensive."

"You want me to get a job to pay for the damn jars?"

"You know there's no need for you to get a job. You're pulling this entire thing out of proportion." He got up and tried to draw her close.

She shook off his arm.

"Come on, let's be friends again. I'm sorry you misunderstood what I said."

"I didn't misunderstand," she said, trying to speak as slowly and calmly as he.

"Friends?" He put on his little-boy smile, which, at certain times, held irresistible charms. This wasn't one of those times.

"Certainly," she said.

He quickly kissed her left cheek, sat down, and looked at the open page with the column of figures. "Congoleum is up half a point."

"You're incredible," she shouted and ran up the stairs.

57

Clutching his green Oscar puppet, Timmy was sitting on the top stair. His cheeks were wet.

"What's the matter?" She sat down right next to him and put one arm around him. "Why are you crying?"

He looked at his knees. "Daddy and you. The yelling."

"It must have upset you."

He nodded and wiped the back of his right hand across his nose.

"It's all right." She took his hand and helped him up. "Where is Nicole?"

"In my room. Playing with Legos."

"I thought you two were still in the den."

"You didn't hear us. You were fighting too much."

She looked quickly into Tim's room, where Nicole was sitting on the floor, playing. "Let's go into my bedroom and talk," she said to Tim.

He sat down next to her on the green bedspread.

"Remember how you and Nicole fight?" she asked.

Timmy looked up.

"Sometimes you get so angry at her that you cry."

"When she breaks things I make."

"And sometimes Nicole cries and you both start yelling at each other."

"She's always breaking my stuff."

"I know. But just think. After you fight, you settle things between you, or your father and I help you to settle things. And then you play again. You see, grown-ups have fights too. Arguments. We get angry, just like you. But it doesn't mean we don't love each other. We always settle things afterwards. Sometimes it takes a little while. And you know what?" She laughed and pulled him close. "We make a lot less noise than you two monsters."

He giggled.

"A whole lot less noise than you and Nicole. You should hear yourself sometimes, screaming and yelling, until I feel like sitting on the top stair and crying. But you always make up, right?"

"Did you and Daddy make up?" He squirmed.

She moved her arm. "Not yet."

"Can I go play?"

"How about a kiss and a hug?"

"Okay." He quickly squeezed her neck with his wiry arms and dabbed his mouth against hers.

He darted from her room, the green puppet forgotten

on the bedspread. Slipping her right hand into its soft material, she made a few unenthusiastic movements with her thumb, Oscar's left hand. Nick had made her behave in a manner she detested. It was always that way. The calmer he remained, the more upset she became until at times she forgot what their arguments were about. He stayed so damn uninvolved. And the less he said, the louder she shouted, until she felt like a fishwife. She had planned the evening to be special, had even fed the children early so Nick and she could have a quiet dinner.

They would have sat down at the small table close to the fireplace. She had defrosted veal cordon bleu and a package of those baked, stuffed Penobscot potatoes Nick liked. The cauliflower in cheese sauce was simmering in its plastic pouch next to the back burner with the stewed tomatoes on low. In the refrigerator waited a salad with Bacos, black olives ("Trying to get me sexy?" Nick would ask), croutons, blue cheese, and radishes. Nick would have lit the candle and put on her Hurricane Smith record.

NICK: These tomatoes are excellent.

MEGAN *smiles modestly and touches her wineglass against his.*

HURRICANE SMITH:
". . . Who was it that caught you falling
and put you back on your feet . . ."

NICK: You must have worked very hard. These potatoes are very good, better than my mother's.

MEGAN: I bought your favorite brand, all prestuffed.

NICK: After dinner let's look at all the jars you filled.

MEGAN *smiles.*

HURRICANE SMITH:
". . . and who was it that tripped you anyway
in order that the two of us could meet . . ."

MEGAN: Why is it that in our actual conversations I seem to do most of the talking, while in my fantasies you are the verbal one, Nick, you communicate so beautifully, while I only need to smile graciously and say a few occasional words.

URSULA: I'm getting out of this chapter. This is over my head.

58

—You and your fantasies, Megan. Don't you see that reality can't match your expectations? Why are you always planning ahead? Can't you let—

—Do you know what he told his sister Pam? He told her Nicole's birth was easy. I'm sure it was easy for him. He only watched. He didn't feel a thing. If I ever have another child—

—But that's not what I'm talking about. All I wanted to know was—

—If I ever have another child, I won't let him into the delivery room. I'll let them knock me out in the parking lot, and he can sit in the fathers' waiting room with the rest of them.

—But he only meant that you were brave. He was proud of you for having both children without medication. That's all. He didn't mean there was nothing to it. Maybe "easy" wasn't the right expression for what he wanted to tell his sister.

—You're taking his side again.

—What do you mean, his side?

—You even let *him* do Timmy's birth chapter. I'm the one who gave birth. Why didn't you listen ˙me instead?

—I tried, Megan, but I couldn't hear your voice.

—Because you're too busy listening to the voices of men.

—That's not true.

—Just look at your intruders: Henry Nelson, Nick, your husband, your sons.

—What do you want me to do? Invent daughters who interrupt?

—You don't understand.

59

It has been some chapters since you met Nick's mother, departing from the maternity ward with pats and clucks. Before you forget her, let me tell you a little about Nick's side of the family. Beverly Stone (I might still change her name to Mildred or Eleanor) is very satisfied with her life. She knows the right people, invites them to her house, and is invited to theirs. Beverly believes in God, Mother's Day, her manicurist, the New York Stock Exchange, a change of sheets every day, Waterford crystal, her horoscope, and the importance of class distinction. While never forgetting her housekeeper's and twice-a-week gardener's birthdays, she maintains a friendly but distinctive distance. She likes music and exercises her baby grand quite pleasantly. She also likes expensive things she can feel against her skin. Silk. Pearls. Mink. At five foot two, Beverly has always felt that Megan's height is barbarous, that Megan laughs too loud, eats too much, makes her presence too noticeable. Beverly means well and really plans to help her daughter-in-law with Tim and Nicole once they are a few years older and not quite so noisy. In the meantime she shows her support by the periodic statement: "How I admire you young mothers. I don't know how you do it."

Her occasionally tactless remarks are frequently covered up by her husband, Robert, with a series of quickly fired, disjointed questions or with a nervous cough. He believes his manners are continental. Although he discusses a great number of subjects with seeming ease, he manages to never say much of depth. He is devoted to his children, loyal to his wife, and incorrect in the assumption that the toupee he wears is his secret.

His daughter, Pam, has an opinion on everything and makes sure everybody is aware of it. She loves a good argument with others, except with her husband, David. Her life centers around keeping him happy and avoiding anything that could cause a disagreement between them. While she advocates independence for her children, Pam tries to anticipate what might possibly irritate her husband, so she can protect him. Interested in politics, she serves on three different town committees and on the board of the League of Women Voters. She has a B.A. in art history from Smith College, as well as a red T-shirt with the inscription:

A CENTURY OF WOMEN ON TOP
SMITH COLLEGE CENTENNIAL
1875–1975

She only wears it to bed. The shirt, that is, not the degree.

David Turner seems blissfully unaware of being protected. He is a stockbroker and likes to listen to himself talk. An amateur cook, he is always trying to exchange recipes with the "girls." The word "woman" makes him uncomfortable; it's so much easier to lump females of any age into the unthreatening label "girl." His standing repertoire of little jokes is referred to by Nick as early-puberty jokes. Although David is only thirty-five, his hair is already gray but still quite thick. Once a year he tries to grow a mustache, but always shaves it off after a few weeks: it never fills out. David is the one who wore beads in the late sixties and still wears Indian shirts to parties. He also is the one who insisted Megan give him the fabulous recipe for the beef in mushroom sauce she served at a dinner party for twenty, making her admit in front of everybody that it had come from the back of a Campbell's soup can.

Pam and David did not misunderstand Nick when he told them after Nicole's birth that it had been easy. When they noticed Megan's expression, they assured her that Nick surely had meant it as a compliment to her and to her endurance. Beverly Stone said she preferred to have her children the way they used to be had, with the husband waiting somewhere else, that she could not understand why Nick wanted to see all that blood. She did not say she suspected he was talked into it by his wife.

60

"Good morning," he said cheerfully, coming down the stairs.

"Good morning," she replied without looking up from the book she was reading.

"When did you get up?"

She shrugged.

"The children still asleep?"

She nodded.

"Still mad about those tomatoes?"

She turned a page.

"You weren't very affectionate during the night."

"I don't remember."

"You kept pushing my hand away."

"I was asleep. I don't remember."

"I tried. Really."

"Any witnesses?"

"You're stealing my line. What are you reading?"

She tilted the cover of her book.

"*The Woman Warrior*? Sounds as if I'm going to be in trouble. What is it about?"

"A woman warrior."

"I would never have guessed."

She didn't say anything.

"Hey, I thought it wasn't polite to read when someone's talking to you."

She closed the book.

"You're going to lose your place."

"Don't let it worry you." Her voice was barely above a whisper. If she could keep it there, she'd be fine. When they were first married, she used to react with silence when she was hurt by something Nick had said or done. It had taken him years to convince her that it was better to voice her hurt or anger instead of swallowing it silently. She had learned to express her feelings, but now she sometimes wished she'd never left the safe dignity of silence.

"Maybe you're mad at me because you're getting your period," he suggested hopefully.

She traced the capital *W* of *Warrior* on the book cover.

"Still angry at me?" The little-boy smile again.

"I'm not angry."

"Disgusted?"

She shook her head. A strand of hair tickled the side of her neck. Sometimes she got so tired of it that she wanted to cut it. But it had taken so long to grow to her waist.

"Disappointed?"

She felt very calm.

"Annoyed?"

As long as she didn't answer, she wouldn't shout or cry.

"Furious?"

How he enjoyed his stupid little game. Either sad or upset would be next. They'd had the same conversation so many times that it had become totally predictable.

"Disgusted?"

"You're repeating yourself."

He grinned. "But I got you to answer."

"I'm glad you're having so much fun."

"Listen, I think it's very nice that you went through all that trouble with those tomatoes."

Nice. She stared at his hands. But they weren't moving. He didn't even seem to notice her waste of strategy.

"And I will eat those tomatoes," he said. "All of them."

She heard the upstairs toilet flush. Timmy must be up.

"I really will. Ping." He sat down next to her on the sofa.

"Then why did you pick on me last night?"

"Oh, I don't know." He put his arm around her shoulders and she stiffened. "Things at the office, I guess. They just don't change. It's so damn smooth."

"I thought you talked to your father."

"I have. Twice in the last six months. He listens to what I say, tells me how he appreciates my thoughts and that he'll give me more responsibility. But everything stays the same. He can't let go."

"I might cut my hair," she said.

"I didn't have to study finance and business administration to do what I'm doing. I could have started right out of high school."

"You think it would look better short?" she asked.

"For six years he had to send me away. Six years. Only the best schools would do. And I cooperated."

"He asks your advice, though. Only last Sunday—"

"He always asks. It doesn't mean a damn thing. He does whatever he was going to do anyhow. He doesn't want my opinion; he wants my approval. It's a gesture. No more. And I feel totally useless."

She'd always thought he liked his work. "But don't you at least get a feeling of accomplishment?"

"From what?"

"Maybe from a financial statement if it looks good. I don't know. The total sales for a month?"

"No, I don't have enough influence to feel good about it."

"At least you get paid well. That must give you some satisfaction."

"I feel like a fraud accepting forty thousand a year for a job I'm not allowed to do. He doesn't need me in there."

"Then why do you stay?"

He frowned.

"What if you left? Just for a couple of years. You could work for another company, couldn't you?"

"He'd throw a peppermint stroke. Listen, I've been programmed to take over that company since I was born. I haven't . . ."

She could see a crib in the shape of a roller skate, a gigantic roller skate. Inside of it sat a skinny blond baby with a ruffled bonnet, chewing on a wheel instead of a teething ring. Next to the crib stood a younger version of Nick's father, wearing a toupee and reading to his son from a profit-and-loss statement.

". . . sitter and go out?" Nick asked.

She blinked. "What?"

"Let's talk about it tonight. You want to get a sitter and go out?"

"I could check if Mrs. Olsen is free."

"Why don't you pick a restaurant and make reservations. I'll call you later." He kissed her quickly on the mouth.

61

I've been in a fit of writing. It's going too fast. I write at gas stations, in the parking lots of supermarkets, on my Exercycle, and while I'm driving. Nothing must get lost. Most of the communications come from Nick, although I try to listen to Megan's voice. Today, when I was driving to the university, Nick got into the car with me. He just wouldn't stop talking. Leaning over the pad on the passenger seat, I put down jagged words that would be difficult to decipher later.

—Not so fast, Nick.

After finding myself twice in the wrong lane, I finally pulled to the side of the road, scribbling furiously.

"Anything wrong?"

I hadn't even noticed the police car. "No. Not really."

"You can't stop here. It's for emergencies only. Let me see your registration and license."

Poetic license? "Well, this is sort of an emergency," I replied, handing him my car registration and driver's license.

"Why? Are you feeling sick?" he asked, looking at me over the rim of his glasses.

"I'm . . . not being myself, officer. I thought it would be better to wait a few minutes until I . . . felt more like myself again, you know."

"Dizzy, huh?" He didn't seem to expect an answer. "Are you sure you can drive?" He looked just like the Southern sheriff from a car commercial I'd seen last week.

"I'm already feeling much better," I said, relieved that apparently he wasn't going to give me a ticket. "Much better, thank you."

He nodded and handed my papers back. "Where're you from?"

"Gilford."

"I mean that accent."

"Germany."

He nodded as if he'd guessed right. Once, a little boy asked me the same question in his own way: *How come you talk funny?*

"Just take it easy."

The cruiser followed me until I got to the turnpike.

"See what you did?" I asked Nick without turning my face toward him or moving my lips. I wouldn't want anybody to think I'm conversing with what might appear to them an empty seat.

—So? It's your own fault. Besides, it could be a lot worse. You could have made me an ax murderer. Or a pervert. Or a Holy Roller who'd follow you around, trying to convert you. Instead I happen to be a likable character, intelligent, diplomatic, relatively handsome . . . Hey, what's the matter? Why aren't you answering me? Watch out, you just missed our exit.

62

Have you ever had a crush on someone? Megan suffered from one for almost a year until the frightening attraction of Dr. Bogan began to wear off. He was the children's pediatrician. After Timmy was born, she developed the strangest crush on him; strange, because she could not rationally explain to herself why she felt drawn to him. In his late forties, he was old enough to be her father. His skin was smooth and hairlessly pink; his hair and eyebrows yellow-white; his eyes a watered-down blue. One shade paler and he would have looked like an albino. About half a foot shorter than she, he was of slight build, with an ass so skinny that he wore concave trousers.

When Timmy was one month old, she suddenly became aware of how much she was looking forward to his checkups, how much care she took in choosing what to wear to them, how she could actually feel her heart beating wildly whenever she looked down into Dr. Bogan's eyes.

It didn't make sense. He looked repulsive.

She tried to ignore her feelings.

But when Tim's appointments changed from weekly to biweekly, and then to once a month, she imagined for weeks what Dr. Bogan would say, how he would look at her, what she would answer, what she would be wearing. Whenever she caught herself in one of her fantasies, she felt guilty, angry at herself; but within minutes she'd be back in one of her imaginary dialogues with him. She knew just how it would eventually happen. He would come into the examining room. His eyes would light up.

DR. BOGAN: Megan, my dear, how are you today?

MEGAN: Fine.

DR. BOGAN (*examining Timmy*): What a perfect child. You're doing a wonderful job taking care of him.

MEGAN *smiles modestly/mysteriously*.

DR. BOGAN: May I be honest with you? I've fallen deeply in love with you and want . . . [*No. He wouldn't come right out with it. He'd be more subtle, leading up to it.*] Megan, dear— [*No. Not "dear." Maybe "darling."*] Megan, darling. [*That's better.*] I've been meaning to talk with you about something— [*But that could lead to a talk about the weather or Timmy's digestion.*] Megan, darling, I've tried to hide my feelings for you, but they are stronger than I. I want us to be together for the rest of our lives. I can't imagine living without you . . .

Her fantasies always ended at this point. What would she reply? What would she do? Would she be strong enough to say no to him? She felt as guilty about her fantasies as though they had actually occurred. What was happening to her? Once she caught herself putting the names Megan and Bogan next to each other in her mind. It frightened her. Was she hoping something would happen to Nick so she could be free? Or was she merely frightened because Megan Bogan sounded dreadful? Megan Began Mogan Bogan? Dreadful. How come her heart didn't beat anymore when Nick walked into the room? What if her love for him had just disappeared? She hadn't even felt it go away.

She felt like a traitor.

She'd have to be honest with Nick.

He had a right to know.

A right to know what?

Nothing had happened.

Maybe if she changed pediatricians, it would go away. But Dr. Bogan, Bob Bogan, was so good with Timmy. He had taken care of him since birth. He was familiar with him. Most of all, he approved of her as a mother. He knew the answers to all the questions she wrote down on lists and took to his office because she could never remember her questions when she looked down into his pale, pink-rimmed eyes. Reading her list to him, she tried to keep her voice from trembling, and to keep the memories of her fantasies separate from the memories of what had actually happened during the office visits. She was petrified that someday they might blend with one another, blend with her many imaginary dialogues; she wouldn't be able to distinguish between what he had said and what she had fantasized. With each visit it became more difficult; the quantity of her memories increased, while the quality of her fantasies remained at the same level, a safe level: they always included Timmy in them, were fully dressed, and shared as a setting the first examination room on the left.

If only she could talk to somebody about it.

She waited for the right time, the right person to confide in.

63

This is my Waiting for the Mail chapter. Do you know how much time I waste six days a week waiting for the mail? How many futile trips to the mailbox I take? The mailman may come anytime between 11:00 and 1:00. Since I can't see the mailbox from the house, I usually walk down our long driveway at 10:55, in case he's early. He never is; yet, there might come a day when he'd be early. I'd be ready: a mail junkie, waiting for her fix.

The next trips are at twenty-minute intervals: at 11:15, 11:35, 11:55, 12:15, 12:35, 12:55—until the mail gets there. Manila envelopes with my address in my handwriting are rejections of a story or a group of poems. A magazine's printed return address on a skinny letter-size envelope might mean an acceptance. Or an invitation to subscribe. Recently a magazine used my return envelope to send me an acceptance letter. So I'm kept in suspense until actually tearing open the envelopes.

I get a lot of exercise walking up and down our driveway between 10:55 and 12:55, but not enough to make up for the eating. Waiting makes me hungry. Between trips I nibble. I'm positive I could lose ten pounds if the mail were delivered punctually and predictably at 10:55 every day. And I'm trying very hard not to suspect the mailman of maliciously keeping the acceptance letters in his car for an extra day or week.

One of my friends, a writer, has solved her Waiting for the Mail problem by renting a box at the post office. Her husband picks up the mail on his way home from work. How can she stand waiting until 5:30? She tells me it works for her, although there were certain withdrawal symptoms in the beginning. It would drive me insane. I'd be parked outside the post office every morning by 7:55 with a Thermos of black coffee, pencils, paper, and a spyglass aimed at my P.O. Box in case something were added during the day.

Sundays? Holidays? I wait for the next mail day, of course.

64

Megan couldn't very well ask Nick's sister what to do about her irrational feelings for Dr. Bogan. Pam's first loyalty would be to Nick. Besides, she was too efficient, too rational, and might have trouble understanding what Megan felt guilty about, especially since Megan herself had trouble understanding why she felt so miserably guilty.

Sara would listen. She'd understand. But Sara had enough problems of her own: Sara had Donald.

How much easier it would be to write a book about Sara and Donald. I'd have a villain and a victim: the plot would present itself with more than enough conflicts for a medium-sized novel. All I'd have to do would be choose from the obvious solutions:

a. Sara leaves Donald
b. Sara kills Donald
c. Sara's lover kills Donald
d. Sara dies slowly from a rare blood disease and Donald changes
e. Donald is hit by a paving truck and changes drastically
f. Sara has a sex-change operation without telling Donald
g. Donald has a sex-change operation without realizing it

Megan did not talk to Sara about Dr. Bogan. And she didn't even consider approaching Aunt Judy. Although her aunt had tried not to show it, she had been hurt by Uncle Vincent's affair with Mrs. Edwards. She never mentioned his name after he left, but one afternoon, coming home from school, Megan found her in the bedroom, looking through some old snapshots. Her eyes were red, and when she saw Megan, she quickly shuffled the pictures together and said something about sorting through old junk that needed to be thrown out. One faded photo fell down: a young woman and a man in bathing suits, sitting on a rock by a lake, smiling at each other. When Megan bent to pick it up, she recognized her aunt and uncle; she'd never seen them look at each other like that. Aunt Judy's hand trembled when Megan handed her the photo.

She thought of talking to Jill, but Jill wouldn't understand why she would develop peculiar feelings for a man on whose head she could rest her chin. Jill had a very strange attitude toward love anyhow. One evening, driving home together from the movies, they had started talking about their marriages, and Jill had freely admitted that she didn't love her husband.

"You must have loved him once." Megan had felt shocked. "You married him."

"I wanted to get away from my parents."

"But the two of you seem so close. You get along so well."

"Wayne says he loves me. But I've never said that to him."

"Maybe you're just calling it something different. I think you love him. You're always doing things for him, cooking his favorite foods, keeping your house nice. You seem so content with him."

"I am content. I like to cook. I like taking care of my house. And I do like Wayne. But it's not the same as love. I love my kids. Believe me, I know the difference."

"How about when you were growing up? Didn't you ever think that someday you'd meet someone and—"

"Dream of a prince, you mean?" Jill had laughed. "No."

Jill was a very practical woman who made dental appointments six months in advance and then actually kept them. Very organized, she sewed on buttons as soon as they came off and never forgot to water her plants or turn off her stove. Sometimes Megan envied the ease with which Jill seemed to do all those chores she detested. Jill had the habit of looking up into the face of the person she was talking with. To those who didn't know her, it gave a falsely submissive impression. When Jill wanted something, she usually got it. Her approach was direct and effective: there were no wasted moves. When she wanted an addition to their house, she convinced Wayne that it would be a good idea to expand his TV and radio store to include CB's. It increased his net by forty-three percent and paid for another bedroom, a den, and a second bath.

Wayne Becker was a slim man with brown hair and blue eyes. He walked very erect. One of the most considerate men in the neighborhood, he was constantly trying to help others, lending out tools, his wheelbarrow, his lawnmower. Always enthusiastic about one thing or another, he tried to incite others with his enthusiasm.

Even if he had to walk across the room, he'd light his wife's cigarette. Megan often noticed how his eyes followed Jill wherever she moved. Idly, she wondered if he brought the same reverence to their lovemaking.

She could just imagine Jill's reaction if she told her she felt guilty about the fantasies involving her son's pediatrician.

"Bogan?" Jill would ask, tilting her face, her long blond braid hanging down her back. "Skinny little Bogan? Has he made a pass at you? Have you gone to bed with him? Are you planning to leave Nick? No? Then what right do you have to feel guilty?"

Perhaps there had been some wisdom, after all, to the weekly confessions of her childhood. How comforting it would be now to enter a dark cubicle and, without eye contact, confess and be absolved. Absolution, would she always be waiting for it?

65

—Quiet, Nick. You're going to wake my husband.

He follows me everywhere, intruding into my thoughts, my house, my dreams, even my bed. I have no privacy.

—Stop messing up the blanket, Nick.

He doesn't even look guilty about waking me up.

—About this sex education thing . . .

—I don't feel like talking.

—Megan is upset. She feels you limited her character by making her so naive. I've never heard of anyone who believed herself pregnant because she thought of somebody. Why don't you leave that part out?

—Tell her to talk to me about it. I'm always trying to listen to her, but she won't communicate.

—At least change her age. Make her ten or eleven. What really bothers us—

—Us?

—Megan and me and the rest of us. We discuss things. Do you think we just accept those bits of dialogue you imagine and put on paper? You don't have more than twenty, maybe thirty percent of our conversations.

—You discuss the novel you're in?

—Of course we do. You talk about your life with others, don't you?

—But that's different.

—No, it isn't. What really bothers us about Megan's imagined pregnancy is that you were only guessing. Maybe in Germany thirteen-year-olds are that naive. But not here.

—Author's prerogative, Nick. Just think, I could have given you arthritis or lockjaw. I chose not to, so don't tempt me.

—I know all about author's prerogative. What about author's responsibility?

—It has to do with truth. But my truth might be different from yours.

—Are you telling me that truth is subjective?

—Consider our conversation. You probably think you're doing me a favor by giving me your opinion. I think you're rude to wake me. I'd rather sleep. We're both looking at the same incident, but from different perspectives.

—Then what about the color of this blanket? We both see that it's blue.

—But that's a fact, Nick. You don't have to invest any belief in it.

—Well, I have another question. How do you account for Megan's naiveté, considering her aunt was selling vibrators right from her dining room?

—Not while Megan was living there. She started the mail-order business the summer after you two were married.

—You never mentioned that.

—Consider it mentioned and let me go back to sleep.

—That doesn't solve anything.

—All right, then. Maybe I'll take the vibrators out. Satisfied? Aunt Judy could be working for one of the insurance companies in Hartford. There certainly are enough of them. Make her an office manager, a claims investigator, anything you want. Just let me go back to sleep.

—Haven't you ever heard that a writer can't follow a manuscript around, explaining and making changes? But that's what you're doing. Don't think they won't catch up with you.

—Nick, I'm tired. Go and nag someone else.

—I don't nag.

—You mean men don't nag?

—I didn't say that.

—Go away.

—But I'm in *this* book. One more thing. I don't like that name: Megan. It reminds me of flowered housedresses.

—I'm sorry, but you're stuck with it. I have sixty-four chapters so far, and I'm not going to retype them just because you don't happen to like your wife's name. You think you can choose that in real life? Besides, I like the name.

—Real life? How can you say my life isn't real? Can you prove your life is more real than mine?

"Leave me alone."

—Another thing: my sister doesn't have children. You wrote: *For her children she advocates independence.* But they're waiting to adopt. They've had their name on the list for two years, ever since they found out that David is sterile. They do have two dogs, however, English sheepdogs: Purdy and Isabel.

"I didn't know that."

—Stop yawning. There are many things you don't know about us.

"Wait, you're wrong. I'm the one who is making this up. I invented you, Nick."

—That's what you think.

My husband opens his eyes. "What is it?"

"Nothing."

"Having a bad dream?"

"I'm sorry. I didn't mean to wake you."

His voice thick with sleep, he mumbles something.

For some reason I feel almost unfaithful.

—Nick. Nick? Get out of my bed.

No answer.

—Nick?

My husband's breathing is loud and regular. Tomorrow morning he'll probably tell me I talked in my sleep again. What if Nick is in my study, editing the manuscript. What if he's changing everything around, crossing out names? What if . . .

Quietly, I slip out of bed. Try to find my slippers in the dark. Bump my toe against a dresser. The door to my study is closed. I open it. The desk lamp is on.

I shiver.

—Nick?

What if I woke up in the morning and couldn't remember typing this chapter?

66

Each time I'm wrenched away from Megan's story, it becomes harder to return, no matter if the interruptions are caused by my doubts, by the beings who inhabit my mind, or by those who inhabit my house. The loudest voice, the most urgent need, usually wins, becomes the most real, obstructing everything else.

Where was I? Absolution. I was trying to listen to Megan, to her wish for absolution. How comforting it would be for her to enter the dark cubicle of her childhood and, without eye contact, confess to a nameless priest and be absolved.

Confessions are so much easier in the dark.

"Are you sleeping?" she whispered.

"Not anymore," Nick said. "Why?"

"Nothing. I was just thinking."

"About what?"

"It isn't important."

67

Timmy was ten months old when Megan, who had gained ten pounds worrying and eating while waiting for the right time to confess her crush, tried again.

"Do you ever feel attracted to other women?"

"Not really," Nick said, turning over on his stomach and dropping his right arm across her. "Why?"

"I don't know. Just . . . I mean, what would you think if I ever felt attracted to another man?"

"What do you mean by attracted? Go to bed with him?"

"No." She sat up; the blanket slid to her waist. "I mean thinking about somebody. Not sleep with him."

"I'd say you're human." He fumbled with the blanket. "You can't help the way you feel."

First in fragments, then in hints she began to tell him, afraid he'd say he would leave her. Nick listened to her fully clothed fantasies and imaginary dialogues. She felt as if, after months of sleeping outdoors under a pile of leaves, she had finally been permitted her first bath.

"You aren't upset?" she asked when she finished.

"Of course not. I just wish you had told me earlier. I thought you'd been acting sort of weird."

"I was not . . . It doesn't really matter. But don't you ever feel that way about someone else?"

"I look. I mean, I'm not blind. But I haven't really wanted to have sex with another woman."

"Would you, though? If you wanted to?"

"I don't know."

"What do you mean?"

"Not if it would risk our marriage. I can't predict something like that, but if you need an answer right now, it'll have to be that I don't intend to."

"Actually, it's kind of unfair that . . ." she started.

"What?"

"You had sex before we met. I'll never have a basis for comparison."

"Go and compare if you have to."

"You can't mean that." She tried to see his expression in the dark. He couldn't possibly be serious. She couldn't even tolerate the thought of him with another woman. Consciously, she pulled her imagination from the beginnings of a love scene, in technicolor, between Nick and a blonde with beautiful legs.

"I think I mean it." He sounded infuriatingly calm.

"It wouldn't bother you?"

"Hey, it's getting late. I have to get up in the morning."
She was wide awake. "I can't believe that."

"What? That I have to get up in the morning?"

"That you can honestly say it wouldn't bother you."

"Listen," he said, his voice just a bit impatient. "I love you and I don't want to tell you what to do or what not to do."

She could easily think of several ideal answers he could have given instead.

68

Once properly confessed, her crush dissolved as gradually as the ten pounds she had gained feeling guilty about that crush. The first time she was able to talk to Dr. Bogan without her heart beating irrationally, she felt as though she held a secret power over him.

—I think it was more anger than a feeling of power.

—Why anger, Megan?

—Because he was able to make me feel that way. It was absurd. He was so repulsive with that pink skin.

—But he didn't do it on purpose. He probably didn't even know.

—I hope he didn't notice. I don't think he did. Still . . .

—What?

—Nothing.

—Don't stop now, Megan. Please. How do you feel about him now?

—He's a good doctor. I can trust his judgment when something is wrong with the children. At least I know I won't ever have another crush on him.

—How can you be so sure?

—Because I figured out why it happened.

—And that'll make you immune?

—Yes. I think it happened because he approved of me. He used to tell me I was a wonderfully competent mother. That's what he said: "wonderfully competent." He held all the answers. During Timmy's first year, I was so unsure; I worried about accidents and about doing the wrong things. What if he suddenly stopped breathing? I used to check on him whenever I woke up at night.

—What about Nick? Did he worry?

—Nick? He never worried. You should know that by now. He just expects things to turn out the right way. It's infuriating. Couldn't you have made him a little less secure? He used to tell me that babies are tough. He bounced Timmy on his shoulders, rolled around with him on the floor. Stuff like that. I don't think it ever occurred to him that we could lose him.

—Babies *are* tough, Megan.

—I know. But it took me a while to realize that. I was much more relaxed with Nicole when she was an infant. But with Timmy I became very dependent on Dr. Bogan because he could have handled any emergency, even a tracheotomy.

—And you would have liked to move in with him so he'd be right there if anything happened? Megan Bogan sounds dreadful.

—Of course it does. It's what you wanted, isn't it? Why else would you have picked that name from the phone book?

—How did you know?

—You think I should cut my hair?

—We weren't talking about . . . Okay. Why would you want to cut your hair?

—I'm not sure I want to cut it. I like the way it looks long, but it takes forever to dry and gets tangled and . . . You're probably not interested in my hair.

—I'm interested. Really.

—Then why did you have to make it red?

—Why not? Red. Blond. Brown. I had to pick something.

—Do you like red hair? Is that why you gave it to me?

—No particular reason. I just . . .

—Don't you think there has to be a reason for your choices?

69

"Could you do me a favor?" Sara asked.

"Sure," Megan said, wiping the last traces of oatmeal from Nicole's cheeks. "What is it?"

"Are you doing your grocery shopping today?"

"Yes. You want me to pick something up for you?"

"No. But I was wondering if I could come along and do my shopping at the same time."

"Sure. That'll be fine."

"I have to lose some weight," Sara said. "I just have to. And I read last night that the first step is to change your buying habits. The article suggested shopping with a friend, to check out each other's buys. All you would have to do is make sure I don't buy any junk food, to convince me not to buy half a gallon of butter-crunch ice cream."

"Should I ask: Why don't you buy some broccoli instead?" Megan lifted Nicole from the high chair.

"I guess so. But you have to be firm about it. Especially if I start to argue. And I'll do the same for you. I won't let you buy any junk food."

"But Nick likes potato chips, and I have ice cream and graham crackers on my list." Her hair felt heavy against the back of her neck, and she lifted it, briefly, and then let it fall down again.

"Why don't you buy fresh fruit instead?"

"I'll buy fresh fruit in addition to potato chips and ice cream."

"Well, maybe I could help you pick the best buy, you know, check the unit pricing to make sure you're buying the most economical brand and size."

"No. That would get too complicated." Megan pictured their shopping carts, side by side, blocking the aisle. She disliked shopping enough as it was, and usually timed it for when Timmy was in nursery school. To attempt shopping with both children was a mistake. A disaster. They were always asking her to buy things she didn't need, and Timmy usually managed to get lost at least once. It was much easier to push the cart with only Nicole around the store, to fill it up as quickly as possible. She could just see herself in the cookie aisle, arguing vehemently with Sara against the purchase of a bag of Keebler's Chocolate Chip Cookies.

"We can take my car," Sara said.

What if their bags got mixed up? She'd end up with half of Sara's groceries unpacked on her kitchen counter before she'd realize that she hadn't bought sardines and brown sugar. And how did those Oreos get in there?

"I really appreciate this," Sara said.

Was it too late to tell Sara she'd rather not do her that particular favor? That she already felt angry at herself for letting Sara push her into something she didn't want to do? But what if Sara really needed her help? After all, this was the closest she had ever come to admitting she couldn't control her eating habits.

70

Sara's eating habits. What about them? It could be a funny chapter, funny and sad. I once saw a play in which the main character was an overeater who called herself a junkie foodaholic kleptomaniac. Or was it junkoholiac? Something like that. Of course she changed at the end of the play and became gorgeously skinny. I'm wondering if Sara could change like that. It would be such a nice ending. Endings are hell to write. I still have a long way to go till the ending.

This chapter isn't going anywhere. To face an almost empty page is scary. Especially if it remains almost empty after an hour. The only thing worse is a *totally* empty page. Fortunately that only happens two or three times a week. Maybe I'll think of something if I sharpen my pencils again and make another cup of coffee. I want something to happen, to change.

The weather has been the same all week.

The dog. Maybe if I watch the dog closely, I can see him grow.

He is growing a pound a day.

Three quarters of an ounce every hour.

A fascinating change.

I sit at my desk and watch the dog change.

When we got him from the Humane Society last month, the index card attached to the door of his kennel read: 13½ weeks. He wasn't very large. Probably he'd be a nice, medium-sized dog once he was fully grown. Perhaps I should have been suspicious when he kept stumbling over paws the size of tennis balls. We took him home, bought him a collar, two dishes, a leash, a rawhide chewy toy. He was more interested in chewing the living-room rug and eating his way through a Sheetrock wall. Our younger son wanted to call him Princess Lea, Darth Vader, or Obi-Ben-Kanobi. Our older son voted for Benjamin Franklin. Ben seemed a good enough compromise.

The vet took one look at Ben and told us he was no more than five weeks old. Suddenly, he looked enormous to me. For five weeks he was enormous. The vet told us he'd be huge. Part collie, part shepherd, he is a gentle yet

alert dog with a coat the color of burned butterscotch
pudding. I've weaned him from Sheetrock and carpets by
giving him an old leather shoe. If I watch him closely, I can
see him grow.

71

Have you ever met a foodaholic? Someone who hides
Twinkies in the hamper? Brownies behind the socks?
Tootsie Rolls and Oreos under the sewing machine? Three
Musketeers and Baby Ruths in the tackle box?

Since her wedding Sara has gained 1,263 pounds. She
has lost 1,236 pounds in weekly up and down shuttles.
Mondays are her best days to start new diets. Sara is the
only woman in the neighborhood who always insists on
serving something with coffee. Once a week she bakes, for
family and company, she says. She is always trying to send
leftover desserts home with her friends, as though petrified to be left alone with any combination of starch and
carbohydrates.

Until Megan found eight Marathon bars and three
Charleston Chews under the driver's seat of Sara's Volvo,
she assumed that her friend's weight gain was merely
unfortunate. She couldn't remember ever having *seen* Sara
eat cake or sweets of any kind. But that afternoon, when
her own car didn't start and she borrowed the Henegans'
Volvo to take Nicole to Dr. Bogan because of an earache,
she began to wonder about Sara's eating habits. Nicole's
panda fell down and slid under the seat. When she bent to
retrieve it, she found eleven candy bars and six empty
wrappers.

She began to wonder if her friend was one of those
people who only indulge when they are alone, who sneak
out of bed in the middle of the night, no, not to meet a
secret lover or bookie, not even to reach for a hidden

bottle of Scotch or Chianti, but to seek out camouflaged reserves of potato chips and black jelly beans, chocolate turtles and Hostess fruit pies.

She began to see things she hadn't noticed before. Once she forgot her keys at Sara's and returned, only to discover two fewer donuts on the table than five minutes earlier, a delicate film of powdered sugar adorning the left corner of Sara's mouth. And another time she could have sworn there was a trace of caramel on Sara's breath.

72

His knees pulled up to his chin, he is sitting in my shopping cart. I feel conspicuous wheeling a grown man down the cereal aisle. He is heavy.

—Get out of my shopping cart, Nick. I didn't ask you to come along.

—But I'm just trying to help you with your research for the next chapter.

—I don't want your help. I need to think, to imagine what it feels like for Megan to shop with Sara, to stop and discuss each purchase, to—

—Better move along. You're blocking the way.

—If you don't leave, I'll—

—What?

—I'll fill this cart with frozen spinach until you have frostbite.

—Don't make a scene. It would have been so much easier to have Megan tell Sara that she'd rather shop alone, that her idea is stupid, a complete waste of time.

—I know you wouldn't have any trouble doing that. But Megan lets herself be talked into things she doesn't want to do. She'll have to learn to say no.

—Learn to? Are you trying to do this gradual development shit? To be subtle? You?

—Leave me alone or I just won't write that shopping chapter.

—That probably would be better anyhow. You don't have any idea how those domestic scenes bore me.

—Get out.

—Stop acting weird. People are staring at you.

—

—Pretending to cough? Not very original. They noticed your lips were moving. And you should have seen your face when you were hissing at me.

—

—Ignoring me? Now if I were in your situation, I'd read the labels of canned goods. Some people read with their lips moving.

—

—Hey. Stop it. You didn't really mean that about the frozen spinach. Don't. Careful. That's a very sensitive area.

73

Megan stood in front of the bathroom mirror, her red hair parted in the middle, hanging straight to a hand's width above her waist. Lifting both hands slowly, she separated her hair into two thick strands, closed her fingers around them, and brought the halves forward, bending them at the level of her breasts to see what it would look like shorter.

For over a year she had been thinking about cutting it, wondering what it would be like without the soft familiar pressure on the back of her neck. Each time she asked him, Nick had said she should do what she thought was right, that he didn't want to influence her decision even *if* he liked long hair. A very unsatisfactory answer from a man who asked her every morning what he should wear, which suit went with which shirt, and whether she thought he should wear the tie with the blue stripe or the solid red.

Perhaps she should ask him once more.

Perhaps she should wait until he came home from the office. After all, she hadn't told him this morning that this was the day she was going to cut her hair. She hadn't told him because she hadn't started thinking about it until after Jill had picked Timmy up for nursery school; not until after she had cleaned the kitchen, made the beds, and put Nicole down for a nap; not until after she had gone to the bathroom, washed her hands, and seen herself in the mirror.

How she hated the limbo state of sluggishness that came with prolonged indecision and made her move as though she were walking under gray water. Anything was better than that, even the wrong answer, anything but the slow drowning in her doubts. Nick said she rushed into decisions; she believed he took too long making them. What a different feeling afterwards, an almost giddy lightness, even if her choice was not the best.

Perhaps she should call Nick at the office to make sure he wouldn't mind. But then again he would tell her it was her hair.

What if she called Jill and asked her to come over? Jill loved to give advice. But she was out shopping; she always shopped on the days she drove the children to nursery school.

With her right hand she took the narrow scissors from the drawer next to the sink, while firmly holding the left half of her hair. She began to—

—Wait, Megan. Think it out *before* cutting it. You have beautiful hair.

—I have thought about it and thought about it and I can't stand thinking about it anymore.

—But—

—If I wait any longer, I might change my mind again,

and I'll have to cut through my own doubts and through
what I imagine Nick's objections will be.
    —He won't object. He'll—
    —Don't interfere.

74

She began to cut, thinking *no,* cutting, feeling the hard
metal of the blunt scissors against her fingers, *no,* cutting,
no no, forcing, swallowing, forcing the scissors through
until it was too late to reverse her decision incision.
    Without blinking she looked at herself in the mirror.
Half of her hair barely covered her left breast anymore.
She unclenched her left hand and released the severed red
strands. They dropped into the sink, a few hairs flattening
against the wet porcelain. The other side still hung down
to her waist. Turning her face from side to side, she
wondered which half looked better. When she became
aware of what she was doing and its futility, she began to
cut the other half slowly.
    The feeling of urgency was gone.
    She thought of the way she had often felt in her room at
Aunt Judy's house, when she tried to look out of the
window and only saw her own reflection, imagined her
reflection raising one fist to shoulder level and pushing it
forward, catapulting it through the glass. She remembered
the effort of holding on to herself, of keeping herself
separate from her image in the window. But behind the
delicious torture of the idea had always been the certainty
that she wouldn't do it. After all, there was no reason for
it. She had resisted, until today, when the woman in the
mirror forced the scissors through her hair, when she gave
in, perhaps because she was not as sure as she had been
back then of their separation.
    The sides were uneven.
    She began to make corrections, here and there, thinking

it would take a little time getting used to it at this length, imagining she could still feel it against her back, something within her crying over the loss. Before she could reason with herself, before she could come to a deliberate decision, she cut one thick strand on her left side to shoulder level. There. It was done. Now she would have to even it out.

She wondered how Nick would like it, although he had said, among other maddeningly wise things, that he wished she were free of the need for his approval.

75

The approval of Aunt Judy had been terribly important to her as a child. To be an adult, she had believed, meant to be wise and firm and, above all, sure of oneself. After she was married, she sometimes wondered if others felt as she did, if their concept of being an adult had also been wrong in that it did not bring the maturity and answers they expected.

Once she had asked Nick about it: "Do you ever feel disappointed by what it's like to be grown-up?"

"Not really. Why?"

"I don't know. I used to think that once I was an adult, I'd feel more secure. But even being a parent is different from what I thought it would be. You know, sometimes I catch myself saying things to our children that sound just like Aunt Judy, things I never thought I'd say to them."

"Like what?"

"Well, Timmy said to Nicole yesterday: 'Let's make a rule you can't play with my Batman car.' Aunt Judy was always making new rules. I suddenly realized that I say things like: 'Let's make a rule not to wear muddy boots in the living room.' "

"That doesn't sound very unreasonable to me."

"I should be able to handle things on a one-time basis.

You know what worries me? That there are more things I know I don't want to do in bringing up our children than things I know will be right for them."

"Just wing it."

"I do know that I want them to feel good about themselves, to love themselves. I grew up believing that it was selfish to love yourself. And I do want them to feel good about showing affection. I never saw my aunt and uncle hug or kiss."

"We're certainly demonstrative enough in front of them. Thanks to me you've learned to show your affection."

"You're taking full credit for that, of course."

"Of course."

"You're the most conceited . . ."

"You know what your problem is?"

"Yes. Your conceit."

"Seriously. You always picture things ahead of time in all details. You expect too much. You should just let things happen. They do anyhow."

"But sometimes it's nice to look forward to something like a vacation, almost better than actually being there."

"Because you have control over it when you picture it?" he asked.

"I don't think it has anything to do with control. Imagining things I dread magnifies them, like going to the dentist or visiting Aunt Judy. I think about it ahead of time. I worry. When it actually happens, it has grown out of proportion."

"Why don't you just stop doing it, then?"

"You think it's that easy? Knowing your weakness doesn't automatically correct it. I know it happens in books. A character suddenly realizes what causes her to do a certain thing. She has this terrific insight, preferably in some analyst's office or while walking along a deserted beach, and all her problems are solved. I just don't believe that kind of shit."

Nick laughed.

"Don't you sometimes wish that things were more certain?" Megan asked. "That we could look at ourselves, at our lives, and say: 'Yes, this is the way it is' or 'This is my reason for doing something'?"

76

But what if you weren't sure of your reasons?

What if the process of decision making was at the mercy of an impatient hand holding scissors?

Her hair looked awful.

She tried to even it out, always ending up with it just a little shorter and not much more even. When she could see her right earlobe but not the left, she stopped, afraid to go any further, and stared at herself in the mirror. Her faced looked changed, rounder somehow. Her neck seemed longer, her shoulders more noticeable.

Would she be confused the next morning when she looked into the mirror? Would she remember immediately that she had cut her hair the day before? Had others ever cut their hair while asleep and stepped in front of the mirror in the morning, trying to piece together what had happened during the night? What if there had been other changes? What if a woman woke up one morning and found herself metamorphosed? What if she had gained weight and her face showed lines that hadn't been there before? What if her hair were chopped off unevenly? What if she discovered she'd been in a mental ward for years, that she had lost her sane self years ago, the self she remembered as though it had belonged to her only yesterday, the self that she was separated from by a night of years, the self . . . *Stop it!*

She blinked.

It didn't look all that bad. She'd get a professional haircut. As a matter of fact, she'd call right now and make an appointment. By the time Nick got home, she'd look fine, with one of those shaped cuts that practically took care of themselves, that could be washed and dried in a matter of minutes. Nick would like it. He would admit he hadn't thought she'd look so good with short hair, that he actually preferred it, that she should have done it years ago.

She called the four local salons. The earliest appointment she could get was in three days.

Perhaps she should call Nick's mother and ask her to stay with the children while she quickly drove into Hartford. She should be able to get an appointment somewhere there. But it would take at least two hours to bring her house into any kind of shape suitable for leaving Nick's mother alone with. She'd have to dust, clean the bathrooms, vacuum, wash the kitchen floor, empty the dishwasher, clean the top of the refrigerator, rearrange her shelves . . . Make that four hours. Her mother-in-law's house was always immaculate, intimidatingly immaculate. Even when her housekeeper was laid up for weeks with a broken leg, the house remained intimidatingly immaculate, which led Megan to believe that its intimidating immaculateness was not merely due to the existence of a highly paid housekeeper, but that her mother-in-law herself was intimidatingly immaculate.

Enough word games. Megan's hair—

"Yes, I'll be finished with this chapter in a minute. Just pour some juice for yourself and your brother. The red juice? I don't remember buying— No. That's wine. Wait—"

77

My youngest son wants to show me a picture he drew of his room, not as it is, but as he would like it to be.

"I want my bed next to the window," he tells me. "That's my dresser. See? Over there's my beanbag." He points to a sheet of paper filled with irregular shapes. "The circle next to the closet is the lamp."

"We can't move the ceiling light."

"Can I use your eraser?" He erases the circle and makes another one in the middle of the page. "Like this?"

I nod.

"You like it?"

"I do. What's this over here?" I'm looking at an obscure rectangular shape with a square on top of it.

"My toy chest."

"Of course. And that's your fish tank on top of it."

"It's a book. My dinosaur book. Oh no." He suddenly looks upset.

"What's the matter?"

"I forgot the fish tank. I better draw it real fast or the fish are going to die."

78

"Oh my God," Jill said when she dropped Timmy off by the kitchen door.

Megan instinctively reached up and touched the sides of her hair. Her neck felt cold. "It looks that bad?" She tried to grin.

"I'm just surprised," Jill said quickly. "Turn around. Let me see. "It's just that you look so . . ."

"Awful?"

"Changed. Yes. That's it. You look different. Are you going to leave it like that?"

"What's for lunch?" Timmy asked.

"I've been trying to get an appointment to get it fixed. The earliest one I can get is Friday. But if I drive into Hartford . . ."

"David gots a new truck," Timmy said.

"Has," Megan said. "David has a new truck."

"How about my sister-in-law's cousin?" Jill asked.
"Remember her from my last picnic? Elaine. She's the one
who had the baby last summer after all the miscarriages.
She used to be a hairdresser. I could ask her."
"I don't know. I hardly know her."
"David gots a new truck."
"I'll call her if you want me to," Jill said.
"Let me first check if I can get a sitter. If I bring the
children along and keep turning my head watching them, I
won't have any hair left."
"They can stay with me."
"What's for lunch?" Timmy asked.
"Nicole is still napping," Megan said.
"I'll get her. Don't worry. I'll take them both home with
me and give them lunch. You like egg salad, Timmy, don't
you? Here, let me call Elaine."
Megan remembered the cousin of Jill's sister-in-law as a
heavy young woman with black teased hair and smudged
eyeliner. Maybe it would be better to wait until Friday
when she could get a real appointment. She hoped Elaine
would not answer the phone. Perhaps she was out shopping or, if not out, taking a shower and unable to hear the
phone ringing. She could be sitting under a hairdryer with
a head full of rollers or in a chair, tied up and gagged after
the burglars got away.
"Elaine? Hi, it's me, Jill. Thanks, fine. Yes, next Sunday,
Wayne too. Listen, I was wondering if you could do me a
favor. Remember Megan, my neighbor? You met her at my
last picnic. Yes, that's the one. Only it isn't long anymore.
She started cutting it and . . ."
Megan hoped Elaine would say no. Maybe her baby had
a check-up. Maybe she had to go to her dentist, analyst,
mother-in-law's. Maybe the baby didn't like company.
Maybe she had a highly contagious disease and wasn't
permitted to cut anybody's hair. Maybe a diaper-service
truck had just missed a turn and crashed through the
living-room window. At least a moped . . .

"Great, thanks a lot." Jill hung up the phone. "She said to come right over. You know where the house is?"

"No. I'm terrible about directions."

"It's easy to find. You remember the house where—"

"I don't want to impose on her. You know, I can really wait until Friday. I don't mind wearing a bandana kerchief for a couple of days. Besides, I still have to change Nicole's diaper."

"I'll take care of her. You better get going. You remember the house where Ellen Brown used to live? On Ridgewood?"

Megan nodded. She used to play tennis with Ellen until the Browns moved to Fort Worth.

"It's the brick ranch with white shutters two houses from there, just across the street. You can't miss it. It has a real unusual mailbox. It's covered with all kinds of different color-streaks." Jill quickly glanced at Timmy, who was taping a drawing he had made in nursery school to the door of the refrigerator. She whispered: "Actually, it's 'fuck the mailman' in thirteen different languages and then camouflaged with paint streaks. Wayne and Robby, Elaine's husband, did it after the baby's christening party. They were both smashed."

Why couldn't she just say "No, thank you, but I don't want my hair cut by someone who used to be a hairdresser"? It should be so easy to tell Jill she didn't want to go.

"Jill?"

"Yes?"

"I'll find it."

79

Backing out of the garage, she remembered the dinner she had not wanted to send back two months ago. They had gone out to dinner on Valentine's Day to the new restaurant that had opened in two plush dining cars from an old train. She had ordered curried lamb on a bed of rice.

The train was drafty. She felt sorry for the waiter, an elderly man who walked quickly with a stoop. His eyes were watery; while taking their order he coughed twice.

"You want my jacket?" Nick asked her.

"But then you'd be cold."

"I'm warm enough. Here, take it for a while at least."

He got up and laid the jacket around her shoulders: it kept the draft away. It must be awful to work in such a cold place.

The food took forever to come. When the waiter finally walked through the swinging door several feet behind Nick, a clear drop of liquid fell like a tear from his nose into the curried lamb. He seemed to be unaware of it, because he was watching where he was going, a pathetic old man, smiling apologetically while saying he hoped they hadn't minded waiting so long. What in heaven's name was she going to do?

"Is there anything else I can get for you?" the pathetic thin old man asked, bowing humbly.

Numbly, she shook her head.

"No, thank you," said Nick and began to eat.

Her stomach felt like a fist.

"Enjoy your dinner," the waiter said and left.

"Why aren't you eating?" Nick asked.

If only she were one hundred percent certain where *it* had landed. Maybe she could eat around *it*. God. She felt ill at her thought. But what if Nick made him take the food back? What if the sick old man lost his job because of her?

"My stomach is sort of queasy. I don't think I can eat."

He frowned and stopped chewing his filet mignon.

"Nick? Will you promise not to do something?"

"Not to do what?"

Haltingly, she told him.

"I think we should send it back," he said. "That is, if you

are sure you saw a drop from his nose fall into your food."

Never again would she eat lamb.

"I think I saw it." She looked away from the moist meat. Suddenly she understood vegetarians. "But I can't really prove it. And what if they fired him? I don't want to send it back. I couldn't eat anyhow after this. They'd probably insist on fixing another dinner, and who knows what would happen to that in the kitchen. Maybe the chef has cholera or hepatitis."

"Thanks a lot." He put his fork down.

"I didn't mean that. I'm sorry."

"It's all right."

80

She passed Ridgewood without taking a right. There was no way Jill could make her go to Elaine's. One homemade haircut a day was more than enough. She would not let herself be maneuvered into something she didn't want to do.

The following right was a dead end with a cul-de-sac where she turned her car. She could always tell Jill she had a flat tire on the way, or that she was stopped by a gang of Hell's Angels in the center of town, dragged into Nimmelberger's Delicatessen, and gang-banged in front of the imported-crackers section.

Maybe she should just drive by the house to see what the mailbox looked like. If a repair truck from the phone company was parked in the driveway, she would take it as a sign to go in. She felt like a conspirator when she passed the streaked mailbox that was stuffed six times weekly by an unsuspecting insultee.

There was no repair truck in the driveway. She felt tolerant enough to concede that any kind of repair truck would have counted.

There wasn't even a red tricycle.

The second left off Ridgewood was Elman Circle, which was only a semicircle and brought her right back onto Ridgewood, spilling her twenty feet from Elaine's driveway.

81

I read the chapter in which Elaine completes Megan's haircut to my writing students and tell them that, increasingly, I'm becoming worried about Elaine turning into a stereotype, that already I've revised Elaine's chapter eleven times and still am dissatisfied with her character.

"Why don't you give her some issues of *Vogue* instead of *Family Circle* and *Woman's Day?*" Sandy suggests.

"I like her just the way she is," Dominic tells me. "She reminds me of my sister. She even looks like my sister."

I tell them that I sent the haircutting excerpt to *Ms.* magazine, and that they rejected it because "The kitchen chaos at Elaine's was overkill or even seemed snobbish about class distinction."

"But there are kitchens like that," Gloria insists. "Wouldn't it be even more snobbish not to admit it?"

Cynthia tells me: "I've been thinking about cutting my hair. But I don't think I'll do it now."

I take the section home and revise it once more, pulling poor Elaine out of the black hole of stereotype. I up her IQ, change her reading habits, weight, hairstyle, kitchen, interests, even her daughter's name. When I proofread my new version, I can't picture Elaine anymore. Where before she was somewhat overwhelming but vivid, she now is a mere shadow. I take my revision to my students.

"I don't think Elaine's new image and her gossip of your earlier draft go together," Noelle points out.

"I like her better this way," Henry says. "She's not as predictable as the first Elaine."

"Why don't you let her join a few feminist groups?" Denise asks.

"I like it when Elaine wonders how long it's been since she cut anybody's hair," Bruce says.

Daryl shakes his head. "The new Elaine isn't funny anymore. And that blue ribbon in her hair makes her look like a little kid."

"Couldn't you combine the two versions somehow?" Andrea wonders.

"Are you trying to write a version that *Ms.* will accept?" Dick asks.

"No." I assure them that, ultimately, I can only write for myself, not a specific audience; although it means a lot to be accepted now and then. I tell them how helpful it is to listen to different opinions, especially if I'm uncertain about a character or an incident. This helps me to lead into a little lecture about criticism, how they, too, have to be selective about the criticism they accept from others about their writing; that it is good to listen to everything and then to reject what they can't work with.

I point out to them that, obviously, I cannot accept all their suggestions, but that it helps me to get their reactions. I thank them for letting me bounce Elaine off them.

82

I dedicate this chapter to my students for being so responsive.

Eleventh Revision	*Twelfth Revision*
Megan rang the bell by the front door and was still listening to the chimes chiming "Strangers in the Night"	Megan rang the bell by the front door and was still listening to the chimes chiming the "Ode to Joy" from Bee-

when Elaine opened the door.

"Oh my God," Elaine said.

"How are you, Elaine?" Megan asked, wondering if *ohmygod* was the traditional Becker clan greeting.

"Don't worry," Elaine said.

Ohmygoddontworry, Megan thought. She would greet Nick like that tonight. *Ohmygoddontworry.* There wouldn't be much left for him to say about her hair. She might even chant it: *Ohmygoddontworrynick* . . .

She dutifully admired Elaine's baby, a fat-cheeked girl of eight months with a tremendous amount of very black hair. She briefly wondered if Elaine teased the baby's hair. "What's her name?" she asked.

"Tracy Louise."

Standing on rather unsteady legs, the baby bobbed back and forth in the playpen. Megan held out her right hand, and the baby reached for it with sticky hands, promptly losing her

thoven's Ninth Symphony when Elaine opened the door. She looked different without makeup.

"How are you?" Elaine asked.

"How are you?" Megan asked.

Elaine looked thinner than Megan remembered her. Her hair was pulled back and tied with a blue ribbon.

cut

She admired Elaine's baby, a round-cheeked girl of eight months with a tremendous amount of black curls. "What's her name?"

"Melissa."
ditto

balance. Megan helped her back up.

"She has beautiful hair." She rubbed her hands together, trying to get rid of the stickiness.

Elaine smiled. "You want to sit right here?" With a generous gesture she moved two egg-stained plates, a crusted cereal dish, three empty juice glasses, and an almost empty coffee cup to the opposite side of the table. "I have to clean up in here anyhow, so we can do it right here."

Tracy Louise began to wail.

"Listen, if you're too busy to cut my hair, I'd understand," Megan began hopefully. "I wouldn't mind if . . . "

"I have plenty of time." Elaine loosened her daughter's chubby hands from the padded top of the playpen. "She's just learning to stand up. But she doesn't know yet how to sit down by herself."

"I remember that stage," Megan said, remembering that stage and wishing she were somewhere else. "It took my daughter almost two weeks until she trusted herself enough to just drop down."

"Here, let me put this

"She has beautiful hair. My daughter's hair hardly grew until she was almost a year old. It still isn't nearly as full as Melissa's."

Elaine smiled. "You want to sit right here?" With quick movements she pushed aside several books, pencils, a legal pad, and an empty coffee cup. "I help with the publicity for the League of Women Voters. I'm doing some research on women in management."

Melissa began to wail.
ditto

ditto

ditto

"Here, let me put this

around your shoulders." Elaine took a dishtowel from a hook next to the sink. "Tracylou, here, Mommy give you cookie? Goodygoo. Tracylou."

around your shoulders." Elaine took a large clean dishtowel from a drawer next to the sink. "Here, Melissa."

She handed her daugher a long thick teething cookie. The small fist closed around half of it, while the other half disappeared in the baby's mouth. The round cheeks inflated and deflated as the sucking sounds began.

ditto

There was still enough time to walk out. She could say she had a dentist appointment or that she had promised to sing in the church choir (what church? what choir?), that this was the day she was supposed to start ballet lessons, cake decorating lessons, waterskiing lessons . . .

ditto

"How do you want it cut?" Elaine, whose hair was teased into magnificent proportions, inquired. Her eyes were as smudgy as the rim of her coffee cup.

"How do you want it cut?" Elaine asked.

"What do you think?" Megan asked, missing her long hair so much that she almost felt like crying. But just almost.

ditto

"Well, I could layer it, you know, the way Maxine Foster wears it. You know her?"

ditto

Megan shook her head.
"She was at Jill's picnic."
"I don't remember."
"Her husband is the one who had the affair with the wife of the veterinarian who sued him for alienation of affection. They used to take their Dalmatian there. Remember?"
Megan shook her head.
"What happened to him?"
"He lost his case."
"No, I mean the Dalmatian."

ditto
ditto
ditto
ditto

ditto

ditto
ditto

Elaine frowned. "Gee, I don't know. They separated. Jack Foster moved to Boston. Maxine is a hostess at the Blu Gnu."

Elaine laughed. "I don't know. Maybe they had a custody fight over the dog when they separated. Jack Foster moved to Boston. Maxine is an administrative assistant at UConn."

Tracy Louise threw the teething cookie out of the playpen.

Melissa threw the teething cookie out of the playpen.

Elaine retrieved it. "So you don't want it layered," she stated.

ditto

"I wish I knew," Megan said.

ditto

"How about all the same length or with bangs? I think you'd look cute with bangs."

ditto

"Do you have any pictures of hairstyles?"

ditto

Elaine pursed her lips and began looking thoughtful. "I got some *Family Circle* and *Woman's Day* in the living

"I have some *Ms.* and *Redbook* in the living room. Sometimes the ads have nice haircuts. Let me get them. I just

room. Sometimes the ads have nice haircuts."

Megan leafed through several issues quickly, finally settling on the haircut of a blonde advertising tampons. While Elaine, softly humming to herself, began cutting her hair, Megan closed her eyes, idly wondering about truth in advertising. Although the ad said Soandso Tampons gave the blond model the freedom to swim, dance, and hang-glide, there was no proof whatsoever that the model was wearing a tampon in the photograph, that she had ever used Soandso Tampons—or any other brand, for that matter—or that she had her period when the picture was taken.

Tracy Louise began making sounds of distress.

"Just a minute, sweetiepie," Elaine said, taking what seemed like a tremendous amount of hair from Megan's—

bought the new *Vogue* too."

ditto

Melissa began making sounds of distress.

"Just a minute, sweetheart," Elaine said, taking what seemed like a tremendous amount of hair from Me-gan's—

83

—Wait.

—Why, Megan?

—Those two columns. Why are you doing that?

—Because the first Elaine was a stereotype.

—Then why don't you write the chapter with the revised version of Elaine?

—I don't think that's enough. I can't visualize her.

—You could add more details.

—I know.

—But somehow I don't think it would be enough. Besides, I do want to get across how just a few changes —hair, interests, reading material—change a character.

—But which Elaine do you like better?

—That's not important, Megan.

—Why not?

—You're pressuring me.

—Why isn't it important? It should be.

—All right, then. What if I don't want to choose between the two Elaines?

—But you're always after me to make choices.

—That's different.

—Is it?

—Do you think it was so easy typing two columns? It was driving me insane. I constantly missed the margin and had to do pages over again. I'd much rather continue the haircutting scene without the columns. Anyhow, Elaine is almost finished with your hair, and—

—How does it look?

—Can't you wait? I'll get to that. In time. Both versions of Elaine are beginning to blend into one. I don't really need those columns anymore. The only difference remains the baby's name. Should I use Tracy Louise or Melissa? What do you think, Megan?

—Make your own decisions.

—I will. I'll just combine the names. TLM. Tracy Louise Melissa.

—You can't have both.

—And why not?

84

TLM's sounds of distress became very distressing. Her open mouth was surrounded by wet particles of teething cookie. With a sigh Elaine laid the scissors on the table and loosened her daughter's hands. Softly, TLM plopped down and immediately scrambled up again, pulling herself up by the fine mesh of the playpen.

"You went through this for two weeks with your daughter?" Elaine shook her head. "One more day of this, and I'll be ready to be taken away." She gave the baby another cookie, which was quickly absorbed in the small fist and rushed to the open mouth with frightening familiarity.

"It's just a stage," Megan said.

"Keep convincing me, please. How old are your children?"

"Four and almost two," Megan replied, feeling the scissors move in a straight line above her eyebrows.

"You going to have any more?"

"I'm not sure." Not even Nick's parents had asked her that. When she first got married, she had thought she'd like four children. But that was when she still felt that sudden rush of warmth whenever she looked at a baby. Lately, she hadn't felt that anymore. "I'm not sure," she repeated.

"This is fun," Elaine said. "I've really missed cutting hair. It must be about fourteen or fifteen months since I've cut anybody's hair." She critically tilted her head and fluffed Megan's bangs with her left hand. "You look cute with bangs." She began to trim them.

Megan winced as a small avalanche of red strands catapulted past her eyes. She wished there was a mirror.

"I'd like another one real soon. Maybe two years apart like your children," Elaine said. "You think it's a good age difference?"

"They get along well. At least most of the time," Megan said, wondering if it would be insulting to give a tip to the cousin of her neighbor's sister-in-law. How much was the correct tip anyhow? She hadn't been to a hairdresser for almost eight years, not since her wedding, when Aunt Judy insisted that she have her hair done properly.

Swaying lightly, TLM was standing in her playpen.

"Don't you just love them at this age?" Elaine asked.

Megan nodded.

"Hold still. Careful. I'm almost finished. I just love the color of your hair. I always wanted to have hair like that."

"Really?" Megan felt a glow of interest. She had never met a volunteer for red hair before.

"There. Let me see. Yes. That's it." Elaine smiled. "Let me get a mirror for you."

TLM's mouth quivered.

Elaine returned, extending an oval, chrome-plated mirror.

Looking at her reflection, Megan first noticed her eyes, wide, as if dreading what they might see. Her hair fitted closely, slanting back from her face. Like a helmet, she thought, a smooth copper helmet. Her cheeks, usually partly covered by her long hair, were suddenly visible, adding areas to her face she wasn't used to.

"It suits you," Elaine said and lifted TLM from the playpen.

Megan turned her head to the side. No bulk of hair trailed her movement. She became aware of the back of her neck; it had a gentle curve to it. Stretching her neck, she noticed the tightening of skin over the unfamiliar shape of the bones between her ears and her chin.

"You'll be surprised how fast it'll grow," Elaine said, almost too eagerly.

Megan shook her head. It felt light. Nothing superfluous was left, nothing but the most essential was covering her head.

"I think I like it," she said and, hearing her voice, she

suddenly knew that it wouldn't matter all that much if
Nick or Jill or her mother-in-law liked it. "It feels right,"
she said.

85

Some of the intrusions are nice.

My husband brings me black coffee in my favorite blue-
and-white mug. If only I weren't so suspicious. Has he
come into my study to be with me, or has he brought the
coffee because he knows I'm including some of the
intrusions in my manuscript? Does he want to keep up a
good image? Already I'm feeling guilty about my thoughts.
However, I still ask him. You see, I have this honesty
hang-up. After all, who is forcing me to include my nasty
suspicions in this chapter when I could have pretended
well-balanced serenity?

My husband calmly tells me that, of course, he came to
be with me. He sits down on the hide-a-bed, and I stop
writing.

He tells me he ordered lumber for the deck, that he's
planning to start building it this weekend. He did a lot of
the work on this house. Secluded, it sits on ten acres. We
designed it together; I brought most of the ideas, he drew
them to scale in a workable compromise: no cathedral
ceiling, but a wooden ceiling in the living room; no arched
windows, but an arched front door; no wraparound deck,
but a deck by my study and our bedroom. A house of
compromises, yet it turned out well and is almost completed.

He asks me how my day was, and I show him the chain
our youngest son made this afternoon from all my paper
clips. There is nothing quite as distracting as having a
four-year-old standing by your right elbow while you type,
emptying your top desk drawer gradually and depriving

you of paper clips. When you finally realize that he's gotten into your folders in the lower drawer and is taking paper clips off your poems, rejection slips, and stories, it's too late. It will take hours to restore order.

I tell my husband that sometimes I wonder what it would be like to have one entire day to myself, to write without interruptions. I tell him that sometimes I fantasize living alone for a week or two, renting a cabin by a lake, at the shore, or on top of a mountain. In the mornings I'd get up early and write until eleven, maybe twelve. There would be no demands on my time, no meals to make for anybody. I'd only eat food that didn't need to be prepared: bread, cheese, fruit. After lunch I'd go for a walk, a swim, lie in a meadow, pick wild flowers. I'd wash my hair in the lake and let it dry in the sun. There'd be a canoe. In the afternoons I'd—

What if it rains? my husband asks me.

In my fantasies it never rains.

My husband reminds me of the long weekend, five months ago, when he took the children to see his parents in New Jersey.

He reminds me that I had four full days to write.

He reminds me that I told him, upon his return, that I couldn't concentrate in the silence, that the absence of interruptions drove me out of the house and made me seek out crowds in shopping malls and movie theaters.

He reminds me that I told him of the loud conversations I staged with invisible policemen and their equally invisible but ferocious attack dogs every time I came back to the empty house, just in case someone was hiding under a bed or in a closet.

He reminds me that his memory is much better than mine.

86

This chapter begins with a dream.

You wish I hadn't told you?

You wish I had let you find out, all on your own, that it is a dream at the same moment when Megan wakes up and realizes it's only a dream? Let me explain. You see, I need your assistance to pull this off. You're responsible for overseeing the lighting and the operation of the camera used for recording this dream. You are the cinematographer. We'll start with a moving shot. Ready? You suggest high-key lighting? I don't have any objections. After all, you come to me highly recommended.

—Cut the shit.

—Nick, this is between the reader and me. Get out of the script. You aren't even in this dream. You're off-page until Chapter 87.

Please, don't let this character annoy you. He is just one of those spectators who force their way onto a set. An intruder. Maybe we should give him three dollars and use him as an extra, put a tree suit on him and place him next to the garage of his parents' fourteen-room brick colonial. You recognize the statues on the front lawn? Yes, you're right. We did get it from Rent-A-Colonial, Inc., on North Elm Street. No, they didn't charge extra for the bricks.

High-angle shot. Megan's car is coming down the driveway. Any kind of car will do. I haven't specified make or color. Take your own if you want to.

Megan opens the door of her car. You pan to her mother-in-law's powder-blue Lincoln in front of the garage. Megan walks to the front door and rings the bell. No answer. Close-up of her right hand ringing again. Nice effect.

She walks back to her car. Close-up of her face. Reaction shot. She's thinking, wondering why her mother-in-law's car is there. She walks to the garage, long shot, bends to lift the garage door. You think they would have an automatic opener? I hadn't thought of that. We could always assume it's broken. Anyhow, Megan bends to lift the door.

Low-key lighting. Subjective angle. Megan's eyes get used to the dimness. Master shot to show the entire inside of the garage. Zoom lens to cover several areas without moving the camera. First the heaps of dirty laundry. Three heaps. Waist high. Diameter: five to six feet. Cement floor. The ironing board; gray cover. Good. You got the hands? From an extreme close-up of Beverly Stone's veined hands to a medium shot. Tattered bathrobe; limp terry cloth with stains. Close-up of her face wearing neither teeth nor makeup. Her hair untinted and uncombed. Frazzled. Extreme close-up of the pinched-looking skinfolds around her lips. No dentures.

Reaction shot: Megan. Stunned. Her nostrils quiver, implying old-musty smell in the garage. Long shot: Megan. Crisp blouse. Smooth blue skirt. Simple, but effective. Good contrast to her mother-in-law.

Reaction shot: Beverly. Horror. She has been found out. Covering her mouth with one hand, she frantically motions with the other for Megan to go to the front door.

Wipe transition. Megan standing by the front door, looking back over her shoulder.

Cut.

No. That's all. This is where the dream ends. You were magnificent. Thank you. We better get out of the way. She's waking up.

87

Waking up was a shock for her, the same as every morning. It was as though she knew moments before actually waking that she only had a short time of sleep left.

Closing her eyes tightly, Megan tried to hang on to the vague fragments of the dream that had left her with a strange feeling of satisfaction. If only she could piece the scattered parts into one meaningful—

"Daddy. I'm up." Nicole was giggling as she slipped into Nick's side of the bed.

In the bathroom the thin stream of Timmy's urine hit the surface of the water in a powerful morning trickle. He flushed before he was finished. He always flushed before he was finished because he liked to watch it go down in a whirlpool while aiming for its center.

Megan pulled the blanket up to her ears. Against the pillow her head felt tight. No mass of hair to get tugged under her shoulders or back whenever she turned. She kept her eyes tightly shut. In movies she had seen women waking in various poses, all equally graceful as they opened their eyes with anticipation and greeted the morning with a smile on their lips. For her, waking was always like being wrenched from something infinitely more important. Even the children knew her morning mood and usually snuggled in on their father's side of the bed.

The long body next to her stirred and moved closer, pushing her right to the edge. She heard the sound of damp kisses. The mattress bounced. Damn. She didn't even have peace in her own bed. It was easy for Nick to let the children in, to play house with them. He'd be gone in less than an hour, while she was left to play house with them for the rest of the day. On mornings like this, separate beds were at the top of her list, even separate bedrooms.

The blanket was pulled from her shoulders.

Without opening her eyes, she jerked it back. She wanted to remember everything the way she had seen it in her dream: the laundry heaps, the bathrobe, the no-teeth. Even the smell she remembered. Keeping her breathing steady, she tried not to let her annoyance surface: it would mean waking up fully. Nick was hopeless. Dozens of times she had asked him *not* to let the children into bed until she was awake. Didn't he understand that she hated to be woken up before the alarm went off? Once she was awake, it was different; then she liked to feel their small warm shapes close to her. Nick refused to understand. Just because he was a light sleeper who didn't have to cross long bridges between sleep and awareness, he had no sympathy for her need to cross those bridges safely.

She heard the regular clicking sound of Nicole sucking the middle finger of her left hand.

"That must taste good." Nick made his usual morning statement.

Once, just once she wished he'd say something different.

As usual, Nicole giggled and the clicking stopped. "I go get Bunty," she said.

The blanket was moved down to Megan's shoulders as her daughter used an unreasonable number of movements to climb out of bed. Impatiently, she pulled it back.

"You awake?" Nick turned and fitted his body against her curved back. His left hand closed around her breast.

Why did she have to marry a morning person? "Please, I want to sleep," she said in a small voice, shifting free from his hand.

"It's almost time to get up."

"Then let me stay here until *almost.*" She buried half of her face into the pillow.

"Good morning, Bunty." Nick greeted Nicole's panda with a cheerful voice.

Bunty was a name Nicole had created. Her first word, it had seemed a possible combination of "blanket" and "bear." Other children said "Mommy" first; for Nicole it was "bunty" and then "Daddy."

A separate bedroom.

It was a tempting thought. To wake up on her own when she was ready, not because of the children's noise or

Nick's alarm clock. To just lie there, remembering her dreams, imagining their continuation while slowly adjusting to the day. To have the blanket move only when she moved, nobody pulling it from her. Nobody.

But what about evenings?

What about nights?

What about feeling the warmth of Nick's body next to hers?

What about long talks in the dark and making love?

What about a compromise? She could always fall asleep next to Nick in the big bed. During the night she could get up and go to her own room, slip under the covers of her own bed so that in the mornings she would wake up alone. But the bed would be cold. Even an electric blanket took time to warm up. Besides, she'd have to leave the warm bed to get to her own room. If she used an alarm clock, everybody would wake up. The kids would want to play at three or four A.M., and Nick would hint about a six-course breakfast.

So much for tempting thoughts. She felt she was being watched. Cautiously, she opened one eye. Tim was sitting on the rug next to her bed, observing her seriously. She felt a sudden rush of longing to hold his small, wiry body. He loved it when she read to him, and he was always thinking, often surprising her with the depth of his questions. Above all, he knew she didn't like to talk until she was completely awake.

Wordlessly, she lifted the blanket, and he settled against her with a smile. His feet were cold. Pulling him closer, she kissed the top of his fine reddish-brown hair. It still smelled from Johnson's Baby Shampoo. She had washed it the night before.

Nick's mother—did she really own a bathrobe like the one in the dream? The details still were so vivid. The tower of perfection had crumbled. The elegant dresser, the gourmet cook, the president of half a dozen charitable organizations was only human after all, disgustingly human. Human wasn't even the right word. How much easier it would be to face her from now on, to look at the carefully made-up face, the manicured hands, and the expensive clothes. Even if it was only a dream. She felt her lips move into a smile against Timmy's hair, as she was overcome by a giddy feeling of superiority over the woman who inevitably made her feel like a klutz, five inches taller and twenty pounds heavier than she actually was. From now on—

"What should I wear today?" Nick asked.

88

—You know, this could go on forever, scene after scene, without anything really happening.

—Things are happening, Megan.

—Where?

—Well . . . In your mind.

—That's not enough.

—Why not?

—I'm not satisfied. I want something to change.

—Like what?

—I don't know.

—Maybe if you were more impulsive, you'd—

—Impulsive? How impulsive can I possibly be with two small children to take care of? With all the responsibilities you've given me? To even treat myself to the illusion of being impulsive, I'd have to make all kinds of plans: arrange for baby-sitters, meals . . .

—You want me to tell you something that happened to me, Megan? It's about my typewriter.

—Do you have to?

—Once upon a time I had an electric typewriter.

—I don't want to know about it.

—I'm going to tell you anyhow. Have you ever been attacked by a purring wildcat, a lion, say, or a tiger?

—What does that have to do with your typewriter?

—Be patient, please, Megan. It'll help you to understand this chapter. Once upon a time, six months ago, I bought a used electric typewriter from an office supply store. I took it home, barely able to wait until I could write on it. After all, I had wanted one for years. I rushed my youngest son through *Sesame Street* and lunch (he loves yogurt with crushed pineapple and honey), planted him into bed for his nap with two Richard Scarry books, and rushed to my study to plug the typewriter in. And then I flicked the ON button. The typewriter began to hum. I put in a double sheet of unblemished paper, poised my fingers in the correct position, and waited for inspiration to strike. I tried a few exercises: zxcvbnm.,/ᶜ;lkjhgfdsaqwertyuiop _ß-0987654321!"#$%-&'()*"_POIUYTREWQASDFGH JKL:@?.,MNBVCXZ. It felt great not having to lean on the keys. I barely touched them and they obeyed. The typewriter purred. I turned it off. Silence dropped around my elbows as I waited for that one spark to get me going, to generate other sparks. Finally I thought of something, but the instant I was going to impress it upon the above unblemished paper, my fingers hit the rigid keys, shocking the idea clear out of my system. I turned it on. It began to hum. It sat there, humming, waiting for me. It growled: *Write, write,* as though it would devour me unless I came up with an idea.

—Aren't you exaggerating?

—Not really. I did feel pushed by it, nagged. I feared I'd never be able to write again. Once upon a time I had an electric typewriter. Once upon a time I had an electric typewriter for three hours. I dedicate this chapter—

—Not to me, I hope.

—Don't worry. I dedicate it to the man at the office supply store who did not make any wisecracks when I took my electric typewriter back three hours later and told him it was driving me insane, and who returned my check since he hadn't deposited it yet. I love my little portable manual. I've been fiercely devoted to it since the day I tried to replace it with an aggressive typewriter twice its size. If only it didn't have this little thing missing on the left side of the roll, you know, the one you push in with your left forefinger to adjust the height of the paper. Only a sharp little nail is sticking out. My youngest son tells me he doesn't remember what he did with the little part after he played with it, and that he is sorry it hurts my finger where the little part is missing.

—That's not exactly what I had in mind when I wanted something to happen.

—All right, you want something to happen to you? Let's just jump then to July 25, 1977, the day before your thirtieth birthday. We'll get to Nick's overdue reaction to your haircut in a later chapter. Should I forget to tie up this and all the other loose ends floating around this manuscript, please, remind me just before we get to the end, so I don't have to write a sequel called *More Intrusions* or *Further Intrusions* or *The Intruders Strike Again* . . .

89

It felt weird to be almost thirty, and there was nothing quite as almost thirty as one day before. Megan felt as though something monumental should happen to signify the passing into her thirties, an injection of wisdom, a change of hair color or perspective, an orgy, or a new pair of tennis sneakers. Nick had asked her several times what she'd like for her birthday. She wished she knew. How about having her conscience kidnapped and thrown into the Atlantic with a block of cement tied around its middle? Years later, when it would be found, there would be no identifiable details left to link it to her. And even if they traced it back to her, she would deny it: *Officer, I never saw this conscience in my life.* And whatever made her think of an orgy? She didn't even know anyone who had ever been in an orgy, unless, of course, she knew someone who had been in orgies but kept it secret, except to the other participants. How did one arrange an orgy anyhow? The Yellow Pages? Tennis sneakers would be safer.

She hoped Nick hadn't arranged a surprise party. They were not his style; but perhaps he thought she wanted one on her thirtieth birthday. All in all it was depressing to be almost thirty. There were no apparent changes.

90

"Open it," Nick said, handing her a small, soft package.

She set down her wineglass and untied the red string.

"Careful," he said.

Inside the paper was a small plastic bag with two thin, yellow, cigarette-shaped, irregular things.

She frowned. "Are these . . . ?"

He grinned. "If you don't try it before you're thirty, you never will."

She felt like a child about to do something forbidden. For over two years she had wanted to try it without ever actively attempting to get hold of grass. But there had been a mild curiosity in her mind, prodding her now and then into wondering what it would feel like. Nick had told her she wasn't missing anything, that he had smoked occasionally at school and that there wasn't much to it.

"Wherever did you get it?"

"Trying to make me reveal my sources?"

She laughed. "Keep your secret then."

"I've had it for over a week. Al Pernidge got it for me. I was saving it for tonight. Happy last day of not being thirty yet."

Timmy took forever to fall asleep. Four times he came

out of his room to get a drink of water, to go to the bathroom, to tell them about a bad dream he thought he would have if he fell asleep. When Nick promised to leave the light on in his closet and the door half open, he finally settled down.

After Nick lit the first one, she took a cautious draw. Nothing happened.

"Should I inhale it?"

"If you want to get high." He reached for it and put it between his lips.

She had read about perceptions becoming heightened, impressions being filtered through deepened awareness. But her living room still looked the same. The rug would get up and walk away on its own if she didn't vacuum it soon. The drapes . . .

"Are you sure this isn't something Al grows in his backyard?" she asked.

"Don't force it." He handed it back to her. "Just relax."

The phone rang.

"I'll get it." He walked into the kitchen, the back of his light blue shirt hanging over his pants.

Holding the soft thing between her lips, Megan took a deep draw. Both eyes closed, she tried to make herself available to the influence of the experience she had wondered about.

It was definitely disillusioning.

What if Nick had bought some tobacco and rolled it himself? He knew she couldn't tell the difference. She had never seen grass, although she had read about its sweet smell. But she had smelled pipe tobacco a lot sweeter than this. What if Nick was trying to protect her? She felt herself getting angry. He had no right to do that to her. Reaching for her wineglass, she was careful not to let the yellow thing slip from between her right forefinger and thumb. It had become very short. She leaned forward and took the other one from the plastic bag. When she tried to

light it from the soft, crimped stub, it didn't take. She drew
on it once more and dropped it into the ashtray.

From the kitchen came Nick's voice: "Yes, I've ordered
dinner for two hundred and sixty. One setup for each
table. No. The retirement watches will be delivered
tomorrow. I have . . ."

She cringed. He was talking to his father about the
annual Stone, Inc. employee party. It would be held in
another week in the same building as last year. How she
dreaded another evening in the rented hall with recessed
fluorescent lights, speckled with dark shapes of dead
moths and flies.

91

Last summer, when they got there, the hall had been
packed with dressed-up people. By the door they were
presented with plastic leis by the girls from the steno pool.
Hawaii was the motif for the annual social event. Why
Hawaii? she had asked Nick. He had shrugged: Why not?
The year before it had been Paris, the decorations travel
posters with the Eiffel Tower, balloons, crepe streamers,
and red tablecloths.

As she squeezed her way to her table set for eighteen,
she noticed that the decorations had barely changed with
the theme: balloons, crepe streamers, red tablecloths, and,
hanging from the ceiling, white plastic bird cages filled
with artificial fern. The lei scratched her neck. Was she the
only one who felt uncomfortable? She studied the faces
around her; most of them looked eager, a few drunk or
bored.

Standing in the buffet line, she talked to the wife of the
shop superintendent, Cynthia Engelhart, who was wearing
a large black dress with one single rose printed between
her knees and cleavage. She felt like running away when

Jack Hill, the accountant, always one of the first to make it through the line, came up to her with a Styrofoam plate overlapped by gravy-covered meat and gave her advice on what to get. Only five foot four in spite of his platform shoes, he smiled up at her, making her feel huge, and advised her not to load her plate with potato salad and macaroni salad, but to wait until she got to the end of the long table where they kept all the good stuff, the roast beef and the ham and the turkey and the lasagna and the scalloped potatoes and the cheeses and the desserts.

For a while she was afraid he'd stay by her side to supervise her choices, but she convinced him to sit down and eat before his food got cold. The next day he would tell Nick at the office that he'd taken care the wife was getting a good meal.

After dinner she danced with her father-in-law to the tunes of a band of four little old men singing:

> I left my heart
> i-hin West Hartford . . .

While smiling through the presentation of retirement watches and the awards for the two most efficient employees, she fantasized walking out, leaving her coat and all those faces behind and climbing to the top of a mountain, any mountain, where she would see no one for days.

But she had stayed.

92

She struck a match and lit the second yellow cigarette. So much for smoking grass. She might as well finish it, no matter how disappointing it was. At least she hadn't missed anything by not smoking in the past. No feelings of euphoria. No heightened perceptions. Just Nick's voice droning on about that party. It was only nine-fifteen, too early to go to bed, too late to call a sitter and go to the movies.

Finally, Nick was hanging up the phone.

"Sorry I took so long. That was my father. He wanted to know if—" He stopped and looked at the butt in the ashtray, then at the second one in her hand.

"Admit it," she said. "You bought some regular tobacco or some other kitchen weed and wrapped it in weird yellow paper, right?"

"No." He seemed annoyed. "I told you where I got it."

"This isn't doing anything," she interrupted him. There was a sudden tingling behind her skin, behind her forehead. She took a deep draw. "Hey," she said slowly. "Now I feel something. It isn't much but . . . Is it supposed to tingle like that?" The wheels inside her knees started racing, setting in motion the other wheels inside her body. Tiny wheels. Millions of tiny wheels. She rubbed her right knee with her left hand. Then she rubbed the other knee. The wheels didn't stop. They went fast. "Did you know I have wheels in my knees?" she asked.

"It wouldn't surprise me," he said and reached for the rest of the cigarette. "You could have waited for me." He did not hand it back to her.

The wheels became faster. She leaned back and closed her eyes. Something was moving between her flesh and skin, a thin layer of something, separating her flesh from her skin. It was the smoke. Gray smoke. What if it didn't come together again? There'd always be this layer of gray threading under her skin. She wondered if anybody had ever died from smoking grass.

"Has anybody ever died from smoking grass?" she asked Nick.

He put his arm around her shoulders. "Not that I know of."

There was always a first time for everything. She'd be the first person in history to die from smoking one and a half marijuana cigarettes. Nick would wear his black suit to the wake. His mother would take the children to Lord & Taylor and buy a black velvet dress with a white lace collar for Nicole, a Little Lord Fauntleroy black velvet suit with short pants and white knee socks for Timmy. She did not want a wake. She did not want—

"How are you feeling?" Nick asked, massaging her shoulders.

Her fear dissolved. How could anyone be afraid of anything? She felt serene. She felt wise. She knew all the answers without having to recite them.

"How are you feeling?" His face was very close to hers and looked awfully fuzzy around the edges.

"Fine," she whispered. If only he'd leave her alone to let her absorb all this wisdom floating around her, just waiting to be absorbed. She'd open her pores, let it all in. Maybe this was the wisdom she'd been waiting for, the wisdom that was part of being an adult, the wisdom she was entitled to because she was turning thirty.

"I wish you hadn't started the second one," Nick said.

It was an incredibly funny statement, the funniest thing she had ever heard. She began to giggle. And it wasn't just what he had said, but also the fact that he wanted her to think she was only imagining the house was swinging. As if she didn't know he had rigged the house to the maple tree. He must have planned it for weeks, rigging it like one of those porch swings, the whole house hanging from that tree, swinging swinging swinging higher and forward and what if a car came down the street and the driver looked up and saw a house swinging across the street. What then?

"I know what you did." She giggled.

He patted her back.

"Why are you patting my back? I'm not choking. I can look right through you. I bet you think I don't know how you did it." Her hands began to tingle as though they'd been asleep for a long time.

He kept patting her back. "Relax."

The wheels in her knees. They started again. Then the other: in her arms and her breasts and her waist and under her tongue. Everywhere. Even faster than before. The wheels made the house slow down and stop and the tingling was the strongest behind her forehead. It tingled too fast. Because of the wheels. Like the inside of a watch. Only faster. *Stop.* Much faster. There had to be some way to disconnect . . . "I'm afraid."

"This wasn't one of my better ideas," Nick said.

"You feel it too?"

"I had less than you."

"If I die—"

"You won't die."

"Christ. Will you let me finish?" she cried. "I might not have much more time left and if I die I don't want a wake and I don't want the children to wear black and I don't want a wake and . . . Nick?"

He looked upset. You couldn't really blame him with a dying wife. "I'm sorry I brought the stuff home," he said.

She felt his arm around her back, the warmth of his body against her side. Maybe she wouldn't die, just end up retarded from the smoke inside her. It was winding its way into her head, up, pouring into her brain like waves, gray waves and Nick had married her for her brain and her brain would be smoke and—

"You'll be fine," he said. "It'll wear off soon."

His voice shut the wheels and the tingling right off.

She had always liked the coffee table. Its proportions were so . . . right. Yes. Right. So graceful. So symmetrical. And the wallpaper. So peaceful. She took a deep breath. Why did people worry about things? There was nothing to worry about. If one looked, all the answers were there. One just had to let them float in.

She looked at Nick and remembered all the times he had gotten up at night when the children were babies, so she could rest. He'd bring the baby to her, and she'd nurse it, sometimes remaining half asleep. Nick would lie on his side, both eyes wide open, watching her and the child. Afterwards, he'd get up, change the baby, and put it back to sleep. Serenely she wondered what it would be like to make love.

Nick's eyes were unnaturally large and she closed hers. She kissed him. He didn't respond. She kissed him again, sliding her hand under his shirt.

"Why don't you wait for it to wear off?" he said.

She kissed his ears, the side of his neck.

She opened her eyes.

His shirt buttons looked absurd. They were round. Round and off-white. Never before had she seen anything as funny as those shirt buttons. She began to laugh. They had four holes and white thread was holding the round buttons fastened to the blue material of the shirt. It was hilarious, even more hilarious than the Fruit-of-the-Loom commercial with the talking underwear, a whole bunch of fruits, scaring the daylights out of the man in the commercial when he opens the drawer to get his skivvies, laughing and jumping around the poor guy, when all he wanted was to get dressed.

"How are you feeling?" Nick asked.

"Let's fuck," she said. She couldn't believe she had actually come right out and said it. It was different from mumbling a quiet "fuck you" when another car cut her off or when Nick left his clothes all over the bedroom. Usually she waited for him to make the first move. Sometimes she hinted that she wanted to make love. He didn't always get the hints. She wondered what time it was. Probably close to morning. Soon the kids would be coming down the stairs. Hurry.

"Let's fuck," she repeated, feeling deliciously wicked.

"Are you all right?"

"I feel great. Why? Am I shocking you?"

"You?" He laughed and unbuttoned his shirt. "You can't shock me." He opened his belt, unzipped his pants.

"Right here?" she asked. "On the rug?"

The wheels in her body, what if they pushed her uterus out of place, pushed it down too far and Nick pierced it? They'd rush her to the hospital in an ambulance while she'd be bleeding, bleeding to death and . . .

Her jeans came off too fast.

Didn't he feel the wheels? Couldn't he see the smoke behind her eyes?

"Nick . . ."

His hands were unfastening her bra and her shirt was already off and then his mouth was against her breast and what if . . . what if one of her nipples came off and . . . She twisted free. She'd be found dead on the rug. Dead and naked. Cause of death: Pierced uterus and smoke in the brain. One of the corpse's nipples was missing. Which one?

"What time is it?" she asked quickly to stall him.

"Only nine-thirty," he said. "It's all right. We'll postpone it."

She wondered if serenity would be next, and it was, and then the giggles, just as before. And the next time, when the fear came in its fourth cycle, it was weaker and had no object. Fear without an object. Introduction to psychology. Multiple choice:

a. hydrophobia
b. alimentation
c. anxiety
d. Algonquian
e. all of the above

93

It did not hurt.

It felt strange to know she was actually thirty, but even that had worn off by 11:45 A.M. when she was standing at the Formica counter, preparing lunch for her children, spreading sprouted-wheat bread with crunchy peanut butter and blueberry jam, pouring milk for Nicole, cranberry juice for Timmy.

94

My oldest student, Hillary, a small-boned woman in her early fifties, who always sits in the middle of the second row in class, asks me what my novel is about.

I tell her it's called *Intrusions*, that not only the writer intrudes, but also the reader, the characters, even the writer's children. "It must have been like that for you when your children were small, Hillary. Constant interruptions, regardless of what you were doing."

"Yes." She nods. "There always were interruptions. But I didn't mind. Nothing I did was important enough." She looks down at her hands. On her right is an aquamarine ring, on her left a narrow wedding band. "Maybe it should have been," she says slowly. "I don't know."

95

Hillary would never have kept a door closed between herself and her children. Sometimes I sit at my desk and listen to the silence, wondering if my youngest son is breathing under the door. What if he's lying there, quietly, without sucking his finger? What if he has fallen asleep? Maybe I should get up and look to make sure he isn't there. And if he isn't there, where is he? Quiet play doesn't necessarily mean that everything is all right. Children can get hurt. Children might hurt each other. How can I concentrate on my writing? How is my writing affecting their lives? How guilty will I feel when my sons are grown, when they have left? Will I regret the times I

did not spend with them? Will our needs be reversed? Will
I want more of their time than they can give me?
How much time is enough time?
If only I could leave for two or three weeks, I'm sure I
could sort all kinds of things out. I could sit down and
really work on the novel without distractions. I could keep
intact the inner world I created for Megan and Nick to
exist in. I can't stand those constant interruptions any
longer: they fracture my inner world. Every time it
becomes more difficult to rebuild it. I need to spend time
with Aunt Judy; she has to be developed more. And I have
to get at Megan's motivation. Her relationship with Nick
isn't quite where I wanted it to be when I started this
book. I need to go back and make revisions.
What if I just left for a few weeks? My husband and
children would be all right. I have a wonderful baby-sitter
who'd take care of the boys while my husband was at work.
They'd be all right without me, I think. Why not just leave
without agonizing about the decision?
"I'm hungry." My oldest son is sticking his head into the
study.
"Not now. You had lunch less than an hour ago."
"When can we have a snack?" He comes in. His pants
are getting too short again; I only bought them a couple of
months ago. "When, Mommy?"
"About three o'clock." *A cabin by a lake, at the shore, or
on top of a mountain. Isolated. Secluded.*
"Can you bake cookies with us?"
Words I like: serenity, solitude, tranquillity.
"Can you, please?" Those brown, persistent eyes.
"Cookies?" His friend's mother bakes cookies. A bad
influence. "How about some cheese or nuts instead?"
"Okay."
*Weeds in a copper pitcher on a low table. An open fire. The
light changing. I'd write by the window until dusk.*
"Can you play a game with us? Please?"
"I'll be out in ten minutes."

96

Before Timmy was born, even before she met Nick, Megan had decided that she would tell her children the truth as soon as they began asking questions. There would be no stories about storks or doctors' bags. As a freshman she had heard an appalling story about a three-year-old girl in the Bronx who had watched her mother change her baby brother's diapers. Pointing to his penis, she had asked if she ever had one of those. Her mother nodded and said that hers had come off when she was a baby. After her mother left the room, the girl took a pair of scissors and cut off her brother's genitals. Frightened by his blood and screams, she ran out of the house and into the street where she was killed instantaneously by a truck. Her brother bled to death.

Although Megan refused to believe this gruesome story (after all, there'd been just too many coincidences: the mother leaving the room, the scissors being available, the truck, the timing), she occasionally remembered the story, almost against her will. Her children would learn to name their rectum, penis, or vagina as naturally as they would learn to say nose, ear, eye, or finger. She would never say: down there. She would tell them how babies were born and how they were conceived.

When Timmy was fourteen months old, she came across the perfect book in a Hartford store. Full of pastel drawings, it explained the process of conception and birth step by step. How she wished there'd been a book like that in Aunt Judy's house. It would have made it impossible for this writer to stick her with Chapter 21 about her imaginary pregnancy and subsequent enlightenment by Mrs. Chadwick.

She kept the book in the lower drawer of her night table, waiting for the proper time to show it to Timmy. When he turned two, she was in her eighth month of carrying Nicole. She let him lay one ear against her tight abdomen and listen to the baby's movements. When he felt it jump, he laughed, accepting without questions that somewhere inside his mother was a baby. It was somewhat disappointing, however, to hear him tell his grandparents: "Mommy ate the new baby."

"Don't push it," Nick said. "Wait till he asks the right questions."

At three, Timothy Stone, the most inquisitive child ever to walk through West Hartford, still had not asked the *right* questions. Megan decided it was time to bring up the subject. One afternoon, when Nicole was napping, she opened the lower drawer of her night table and brought out the sex book. On its cover was a drawing of a baby chick escaping the shell. Timmy liked the picture.

She opened the book. There were five different groups: flowers, chickens, cats, dogs, and people. Each group had four drawings:

1. before
2. during (early stage)
3. during (advanced stage)
4. after

First there were the flowers and the bees and the little seeds and all that. Then came the baby chicks. Tim recognized the same drawing he had seen on the cover. He made her go back to it. It pleased her to see how perceptive he was. It definitely was a sign that he was ready.

Then came the cats.

Timmy's favorite were the dogs. In the first drawing they were just standing there, nose to nose, sniffing around without doing a thing. The second drawing showed one doggy on top of the other doggy, piggyback style. Timmy said that was "wicked neat." Wicked neat was his highest praise for anything, including éclairs. The third drawing let him look inside the mother doggy from the side. He could see three puppies in a little bag *inside* the mother doggy. The fourth drawing showed the puppies standing *outside* the mother doggy. He asked where the father doggy was.

Finally it was time for the drawings toward which Megan had worked so cautiously. Number one showed a mommy and a daddy, looking at each other, smiling without doing a thing. Number two showed the daddy lying on top of the mommy underneath a black-and-white checkered blanket. Megan waited for her son's reaction.

There was no reaction.

Slowly, she turned the page to a drawing of a baby inside the mommy's tummy.

"I want to look at the doggy pictures," Timmy said, reaching for the book.

97

Let's insert a weather chapter. We don't have one yet. Imagine a warm day in March. Imagine puddles. Mud. Temperature in the upper sixties. I won't nauseate you with the description of a balmy breeze, although you would feel it against your skin if you turned your face toward the white-flecked sky.

On dirt roads and driveways tire tracks stay and fill with water. The snow is beginning to melt around trees, large rocks, and houses. Patches of brown, tangled and matted, show through the dirty white cover. Grayish mounds, left at the sides of the road by the snowplows, are getting dirtier and lower. The asphalt looks sandy.

It's the kind of day children love; they need a change of clothing every half hour. The only thing that can make this day worse for Megan is . . .

98

"Megan," Aunt Judy said, as Megan picked up the phone on the second ring, "I'd like you to come to Boston with me tomorrow to visit my mother."

"Tomorrow? I don't think I can, Aunt Judy. You see, my car is scheduled for a tune-up and taking off the snow tires. And I don't know if I could find a sitter on such short notice. It's too long a trip to take the children along, and—"

"You don't owe me any explanations, dear. After all, let's face it: my mother is my responsibility."

"I really would like to see her. Couldn't we go Friday instead?" Megan pictured her aunt sitting on the green antiqued phone bench in the hallway between the kitchen and the bathroom, both feet in sensible shoes planted firmly on the beige tweed runner.

"I want to go tomorrow. It'll also give me a chance to do some shopping in Boston. Your children's birthdays are coming up again. I would have appreciated some help in finding the right sizes."

"You don't have to get them anything." It was completely unreasonable to feel guilty because her children's birthdays were coming up again. However, she felt guilty.

"Nonsense. You know I never forget their birthdays. I want to get them something nice."

Something nice meant something durable. Aunt Judy only bought brand names approved by *Consumer Reports.* She also expected thank-you notes (phone calls didn't count) for her gifts. The proper time during which to send thank-you notes should not exceed ten days after the receipt of above gifts. A year ago Megan had exceeded the proper period of time. On day sixteen after Timmy's birthday a letter had arrived. It began: D.M.

"What's a D.M.?" Nick had asked when she showed him the letter.

"Dear Megan. Aunt Judy abbreviates when she wants me to know she's angry with me."

The letter was short:

D.M.

Althgh I realiz that yr chdr ar too yong to wrt to me in ord to thnk me fr thr gfts I wd hv expct that y hd th corts to rembr *yr* manners.

A.J.

"I wish you wouldn't go through the trouble of getting something for them," Megan insisted, remembering the D.M. letter.

"No trouble," Aunt Judy said.

"Will you tell Dagmar that I've been thinking of her and that we might bring the children to see her on Easter Sunday?"

"If she's still there."

"What do you mean?"

"If you ask me, they don't know what they're doing. At the rate they're charging her, they should be able to deal with something like that. And what I intend to do is straighten her out before she does anything foolish."

"What's the matter with Dagmar? What happened?"

"Nothing happened. At least not yet. So don't worry. I'll drive up by myself."

"Do I have to call the nursing home to find out what happened?"

Aunt Judy didn't answer.

"Please?"

"No need to waste money on a long-distance call. Mother's doctor called me half an hour ago and told me that she threatened suicide. He said—"

"Is she all right?"

"Yes. But I want to talk with her to find out why she'd say something irresponsible like that."

"I'll come with you."

"I thought you couldn't go."

"I might be able to work something out with Sara or Jill, to take care of the children. And I'll check with Nick and ask him if—"

"You have to get his permission? Now, if you ask me, that—"

"I do not have to get his permission," she replied very slowly. "But we usually inform each other of our plans if they are out of the ordinary, particularly if they involve each other's cooperation. He'll have to pick up the children after work, feed them, spend the evening with them, and put them to bed. I can't just leave without making arrangements."

"I could have told you that when you were in such a rush to get married. But no, you couldn't wait to be tied down."

"Please, Aunt Judy. Not again." She fought the urge to bite her fingernails. "I'm not tied down. Let me hang up and make some calls. I'll get back to you."

"You don't have to."

"I want to see Dagmar."

99

99. There, I actually typed it: 99. One more chapter and I'll be typing: 100. What an exhilarating feeling. What a high, even better than the one I get from pecan pie. And it won't show on the scale.

—You're being self-indulgent.

—So what? Go away, Megan. This is my celebration. Besides, it's good to be self-indulgent once in a while.

—Not if there are other things to do. I have to get to Boston to see my grandmother and you still have a lot of loose ends to tie up.

—Like what? I can't stand loose ends.

—Then what about Nick's reaction to my haircut?

—For Christ's sakes, Megan, that was resolved a long time ago.

—Not for me. You never said how he liked it.

—Why is that haircut so important to you? Isn't it enough that you like it? I thought you were getting away from approval seeking.

—I am. I don't need his approval. I just want to know his reaction.

—Why?

—Because you promised earlier that you would give it to me and because I have a right to know.

—The character's right-to-know law? Why not? Let's get to your husband's overdue reaction, including detailed descriptions of what he is wearing, his facial expression, whether he's reading *The Wall Street Journal* or watching the six o'—

"The buzzer just went off, Mommy."

"Just a minute. I'll be right out. Could you please turn the oven down to 200?"

—Quickly now, Megan. Pay attention. This is the way I see it: Nick doesn't react. He says something like:

"It looks all right."

Or: "I didn't notice it until now."

Or: "It's your hair."

Or: "As long as you're happy with it."

Or: "What's for dinner?"

—Pick one or all of them, Megan. By now you should know yourself well enough to imagine your reaction. Why don't you make up a page or two of dialogue, while I get dinner ready for my family. Do me a favor and give Nick enough lines to keep him occupied. I don't want him to intrude at our table. Last night he sat across from me during dinner, between my children, staring at my hands to make me nervous, you know, the way he does it to you during an argument. But it didn't work; I only dropped my fork once. If you run out of dialogue, Megan, make him chop wood or play a game of tennis with him. Anything. Just keep him away from our table. And if that doesn't work, you can always describe the room the two of you are sitting in. But make sure to—

"Something smells burned, Mommy!"

—Make sure to be selective. I don't want the whole damn room to come at me when I edit you.

100

101

—Excellent chapter, Megan. Thank you. Now that you're finished, we'll consider your haircutting episode completed: reactions, doubts, flashbacks, whatever.

102

"Why do you jump every time your aunt whistles?" Jill asked and reached for a generous piece of blueberry bread.

Megan was standing in Sara's kitchen by the window where she could see Nicole, who was peddling Timmy's old tricycle up the Henegans' driveway and down the Henegans' driveway and up the Henegans' driveway and down the Henegans' driveway and up the Henegans' driveway and down . . .

"I don't jump," Megan replied. "But I really would like to see my grandmother. Nick and I were planning to drive up over Easter. This way I'll—"

"Is your grandmother all right?" Sara asked, looking away from the blueberry bread.

"I'm not sure. I guess the doctor said she's been acting depressed."

"That's rather vague," Jill said.

"How about some coffee?" Sara got up.

"No. Thank you. I have to call my aunt back. Are you sure you won't mind if I leave the children with you tomorrow?"

"I told you I was planning to stay home anyhow. Don't worry about it."

"And I'll be glad to drive Timmy to nursery school." Jill looked up.

"You can call her from here," Sara offered and bent to take a roll of aluminum foil from under the double sink. Her navy slacks stretched dangerously across her buttocks.

Megan noticed that Jill was watching too. Maybe she should have continued to go food shopping with Sara in spite of that first miserable trip which had taken twice as long as usual. Talking Sara out of pretzels, mocha chip ice cream, Devil Dogs, and pecan pie, arguing with her across a bag of caramel corn, she had forgotten half the items on her own list. But perhaps she should have tried again; it might have helped Sara to lose weight. After all, Sara never turned her down when she asked a favor.

While Megan called Aunt Judy, she watched Sara cut four thick slices from the blueberry bread, wrap them in aluminum foil, and put the package on the table.

"For Nick and the children," Sara said when Megan hung up the phone.

Nearly half the blueberry loaf was still left on the plate. Would Sara eat it after she was alone? Would she close the curtains? Lock the door? Would Donald and the children ever see any of it?

"I just wish you wouldn't let her push you around," Jill said.

Megan frowned.

"Your aunt," Jill said.

"She doesn't push me around."

Jill shrugged.

"I do have some responsibilities toward her. After all, I lived with her after my parents died."

"And you owe her eternal gratitude?" Jill lifted her chin. Her blond braid slid off her right shoulder and fell down her back. "Listen, your only responsibility is toward yourself. It should be your decision with whom you want to spend your time. Why do you feel you have to do things for her? You obviously can't stand the woman. You don't owe her anything. It was her choice to take you in. But that's finished. Over. It does not mean you have to make yourself miserable for the rest of your life showing gratitude."

"But that's selfish," Sara said. "I don't believe you can only do what you want to do. It doesn't work that way, not if you have others to take care of. Someone has to do the work."

"Someone. Right." Jill nodded. "But does it have to be you? Why not Donald?"

"You don't know Don. He would suffer a severe shock if I announced I wanted him to help around the house."

Megan bit her lip from saying that it would be healthy for Donald to suffer that particular kind of shock, that it could only improve his personality.

Jill laughed. "That would be good for him. Just think of all the time you'd save if he polished your kitchen instead of waxing that damn car of his. Why shouldn't you take off for a day or two? Do what you feel like doing. Eat out. Don't clean the house. You'd feel less pressured if you gave yourself the option of skipping your work once in a while."

"Don hates to eat out," Sara said.

"I think I'll have that cup of coffee after all." Megan pulled a chair next to the window. She knocked against the glass, twice, and waved to her daughter.

Nicole took her left hand off the handlebars and waved back. She was heading toward a large puddle.

"Why don't you call her in?" Sara suggested.

"She's too muddy. The next time I change her clothes, she's going straight into the tub." She turned to Jill. "You really think you can just shrug off responsibilities?"

103

I want to make a confession.

Something has been bothering me since Chapter 61.

You see, the police did not follow me to the turnpike.

Actually, I did not almost get a ticket for stopping by the side of the road. There was no police car, no officer who looked at me over the rim of his glasses. The conversation about not being quite myself (remember?) did not take place.

It is true that while driving to the university I was writing jagged words on a pad which was lying on the passenger seat. But I did not find myself twice in the wrong lane, simply because I have years of practice scribbling furiously while driving. I could get lost in downtown Boston during rush hour and still scribble furiously.

There was a side of the road, logically, no question about that; but I did not stop.

I only imagined stopping.

I imagined stopping and having a conversation with a police officer.

I imagined everything he would say and everything I would say, and after I was finished imagining everything, my fantasy entered my memory and joined my other fantasies, my dreams, and the comparatively few things that happen in reality. Only when I wrote it down in Chapter 61 as having actually happened did my almost-getting-a-ticket fantasy begin to prod around, showing its elbows, nudging me into this confession.

Mea culpa . . .

104

"Look at it this way." Jill leaned forward and rested her elbows on the butcher-block table. "If you weren't related to your aunt, if, say, you met her at my house or if, God forbid, she moved into this neighborhood, would you want to spend a lot of time with her?"

"I'd probably stay away from her," Megan replied. "I never quite looked at it this way. Still, I can't help feeling that I owe her a certain amount of consideration."

"But do you like her?"

Megan hesitated.

"Do you share her opinions?"

"You know I don't."

"Do you enjoy being with her?"

"Do you enjoy everything you do?"

"I don't do anything I don't want to do," Jill declared.

"You enjoy cleaning windows and floors, folding laundry?"

"Not particularly. But most of the time I don't mind. And when I don't feel like it, I just put it off. I won't let myself or anyone else pressure me into things."

Putting something off might be easy enough for Jill, but whenever Megan tried it, things had a peculiar way of fastening themselves to her mind, attaching themselves to her awareness in such a persistent manner that she was always conscious of them. They became obstacles. And if she allowed them to accumulate, they grew out of proportion. Into mountains. She'd feel inert at the prospect of having to get across them, intimidated by their sheer mass. So much easier to do things immediately, to get them out of the way.

". . . and if I don't want to see someone, I just won't," Jill was saying. "It's better than pretending. I haven't seen my parents since I left home, and I'd be quite content if I never saw them again."

"How can you say that?" Sara asked.

"It's easy."

"But don't you think that sooner or later you'll have to accept your parents?"

"Why?"

"As part of your past."

Jill shook her head. "Maybe my past, but not my parents. It's better for me to cut away from them. My father is a bigoted bully who turns obnoxious when he drinks too much, which happens most evenings. My mother won't disagree with him. When I had arguments with him, she always took his side. The safe side. I don't owe them anything. Sure, they set me into the world and took care of my bodily needs; but if I hadn't moved away after high school, my father would still be pushing me around. They've done me at least as much harm as good. We're even. I don't like them. So why should I pretend to? Just because they're my parents?"

Outside, Nicole was building a mud castle. Sitting in the middle of a puddle, she was scooping muck from the bottom with both hands. Megan got up quickly.

"But what about your own children?" she asked Jill. "Don't you want them to be close to you even after they've grown up?"

Jill picked a speck of lint from her denim skirt. "I hope they will stay close to me," she said slowly. "But not out of obligation."

105

I've lost the momentum of the last months.
The characters have moved out.
Instead of coming to me, I have to search for them.
It's not the same.
It's slow.
Frustrating.

They don't let me get close enough.

To avoid facing my typewriter and all those still-empty pages, I rearrange my cabinets, read the labels on soup cans and cereal boxes. Did you know that an eight-ounce jar of tartar sauce contains soybean oil, cucumbers, distilled vinegar, corn syrup, cabbage, egg yolks, sugar, salt, spice, dehydrated onion, water, peppers, alum. polysorbate 80, natural flavors, emulsion gums, propylene glycol, and turmeric?

Fascinating reading.

What the hell are emulsion gums? *Funk & Wagnalls* defines *emulsion* as: "1. A liquid mixture in which a fatty or resinous substance is suspended in minute globules, as butter in milk. 2. Any milky liquid. 3. *Photog.* A lightsensitive coating for film, plates, papers, etc."

There are eight definitions of gum, including rubber overshoes.

I never was that wild about tartar sauce anyhow.

Maybe I've stayed in Sara's kitchen for too many pages. Kitchens can be depressing.

When I run out of excuses not to write, I force myself to sit at my desk. I sort index cards. I sharpen pencils. I get up and make another cup of coffee.

Sometimes I write.

Most of it I throw away.

I go to the movies a lot. What I see does not satisfy me. The answers are too easy. Last night I saw *The Turning Point*. It's about two women in their forties. Twenty years ago, when both were dancers, they made different choices: one chose her art, the other marriage and children. Their conversations all carry the same message: *You can't have both. You must make a choice.*

I don't want to believe that. It's too easy a solution, an excuse for anyone who doesn't want to try. I don't want to make that choice. I want both. Dammit, I do.

106

Elevated on a gentle hill across from a bottle factory, the Golden Acres nursing home, T-shaped, low-roofed, arch-windowed, had a peculiar streamlined Tudor/Spanish appearance with its white stuccoed facade and dark beams.

Walking down the long hallway past smiling nurses, past reproductions of van Gogh and Degas under glass, past gleaming white metal carts with thermometers and folded linen, Megan became aware of her steps echoing against the marble floor.

Muzak piped softly. Persistently.

It was almost like being inside an expensive hotel, except for the smell, clean and antiseptic, absorbing the odors from the outside and from freshly opened Kleenex boxes, the scent of perfumes and of urine, the aroma of boxed chocolates and of cut flowers destined to wilt.

Megan followed her aunt, who, briskly, announced their arrival at the nurses' station, where everybody was smiling and young-looking. The pastel uniforms didn't look like uniforms, but rather like dresses, pale blue or pink, identical in cut, a narrow fake belt and two fabric-covered buttons in back.

As they turned into the right wing, the women's wing of the T-shaped building, Megan began to notice that most of the doors were open, framing faces that turned at the sound of steps, faces that couldn't hide the sudden flicker of hope leaping into their eyes before it slid down the corners of their mouths. Some of the women were in beds behind low metal railings; others sat in chairs or wheelchairs, dressed as if expecting visitors.

Against the cold floor drummed Aunt Judy's heels.

Megan felt like taking off her shoes. If she carried them, the women wouldn't hear her steps; she wouldn't be the one responsible for their unavoidable disappointment.

Suddenly she resented all those relatives who were not visiting. To avoid looking into the large rooms with their arched windows, she concentrated on her aunt's back, on the classic cut of the beige Brooks Brothers suit. Aunt Judy always dressed well.

The door to her grandmother's room was open. From the stereo came the low, powerful sound of Beethoven's *Eroica*, mercifully eradicating the Muzak. Sitting in a straight chair by the open window, Dagmar was looking out, her profile prominently etched against the dismal March day. A large-boned woman, she had lost weight in the last years; the shape of her gray dress was defined by the angular lines of her body, so much more precisely than the body of a round-shaped woman could have defined it. Clasped, her hands rested in her lap. Her strong cheekbones appeared lifted by the hollows in her cheeks, making her face look elegant, almost unapproachable.

107

Aunt Judy briskly walked past the open rolltop desk toward her mother. She bent to embrace the still form. "You shouldn't frighten us like this. Megan and I dropped everything and rushed right up here. Everything is in a turmoil over you."

"It's good to see you, Judy." There still was a distinct trace of the Austrian accent in the clear voice. "Megan. How are you?"

"I'm—" Megan started.

"You're going to catch pneumonia," Aunt Judy said and firmly closed the window. "It's much too cold and damp outside."

Dagmar unclasped her right hand from her left wrist and extended it to Megan. Her fingers were cool and dry.

Megan kissed her. "I'm so glad to see you. I've missed—"

"Now will you please explain to me why you go around making statements about not wanting to live anymore?" Aunt Judy sat down on the carved wooden chest at the foot end of the bed.

"I do not go around making statements, Judy."

"When your doctor called me, he said you were talking about suicide."

"Things get pulled out of proportion in this place," Dagmar said calmly. "I never said I would kill myself. I was merely discussing a theory with Ilse Peters and she misinterpreted. The woman is an alarmist. Dr. Rogers thought he was doing me a favor when he put her next door to me. You know I don't like being thrown together with people merely because they come from Austria, people who wouldn't interest me if I had met them over there. She is constantly coming into my room to talk about the Old Country as she insists on calling it. She still orders her shoes and coats from Austria, convinced she can only get good quality from there. For forty years she has lived in Boston, but she still talks about it as though she were visiting. I wish she'd go back to her Old Country and stop bothering me. If she likes it so much better, why does she stay here?"

"But what did you say to her about suicide?" Aunt Judy asked.

"That, under certain circumstances, suicide is preferable to life."

"Circumstances like what?"

"Constant pain. Loss of dignity. Knowing there's nothing left to live for. It's a very personal decision, Judy."

"But it's a sin."

Dagmar nodded. "I'm not surprised you see it that way."

Megan laid one hand on her grandmother's shoulder. Through the thin material of the gray dress, the bones felt fragile. Too fragile. "Please, Aunt Judy," she said softly.

"But you can't take the ending of your life into your own hands," Aunt Judy said. "If you believe in any kind of life after death, you must realize you can't do that."

"Don't tell me what to do." Dagmar stood up and opened the window. Picking up a leather-bound book lying sideways on the upper shelf between the windows, she fitted it into an open space between the other Karl May volumes.

Without knowing why, Megan suddenly felt like crying. She crossed her arms and swallowed.

Leaning against the windowsill, Dagmar faced her daughter. "I have already told you that I consider it a very personal decision. I do not wish to discuss it any further."

"But I worry about you." Aunt Judy's upper lip began to tremble. "I don't want anything to happen to you."

"Would it help if I told you that, at the present time, I have no intention of killing myself?"

"Will you promise me that—"

"No." Dagmar's voice was firm. "I won't lie to you. If, in a month or a year or ten years, I wish to choose the time and place of my death, I shall do so. It's important for me to know I have that option. *Freitod,* the German translation, is so much more positive: free death. I have always been aware of that option, Judy, even when you and Barbara were children. And I chose to live. I might choose to live until I die naturally. But I can't know that yet. Don't feel threatened by it; it's not something I thought of recently. I've stayed alive with it for a long time."

108

Where do I go from here?

For a while I considered letting Megan and her aunt stay for lunch at the Golden Acres special dining room for visitors. Through different perspectives, you would have found out about the memories of other people in the home, seen the sadness that comes with their acceptance, that it's too late to achieve some of the dreams they once had.

You might have noticed flaky scalps under thinning hair. Brown spots on the backs of unsteady hands. Wrinkled cheeks. Pinched lips. The pale neck of an old man by the window. Can you feel the pain in his right arm as he reaches up to break a dry leaf from the Swedish ivy? Experience the brittle texture of the leaf between his thin fingers? As I select from a kaleidoscope of images and thoughts, I become aware how much has to be left out.

You want to know what's for lunch? I could easily picture soft food of light color, chicken breast perhaps, or poached flounder with creamed cauliflower, mashed pota- toes, and vanilla pudding. As you eat, you listen to the persistent Muzak and observe the birdlike woman at the next table as she lifts her white cup. Holding the saucer with one hand, the cup with the other, she doesn't move her eyes from the porous face of the heavy, middle-aged man in the chocolate brown suit, sitting across the table from her, chewing and talking. Her son, perhaps, or an insurance salesman. She does not drink from the cup; it is as though she supports herself by holding on to it with all her strength.

You don't want to stay for lunch?

All right. You think it would be better to invite Dagmar out to eat, to drive into Boston for the afternoon, to see a matinee, and shop at Jordan's and Filene's? Don't you think I've considered that? Dagmar wouldn't want it. Although she cares for her daughter, she does not particularly care about spending a lot of time with her. It becomes too strenuous to insist on keeping her bounda- ries intact, to prevent her daughter from intruding. Be honest, how would you feel about a daughter like Aunt Judy?

109

—I don't want to go shopping with Aunt Judy.

—But Megan, I'm planning this important confrontation between the two of you right in the middle of Filene's basement. First you'll have lunch in a nice downtown restaurant, and then . . .

—Do you have any idea what it's like to go shopping with her? It's the pits. She marches into stores and loudly demands immediate service. If she can't find something, she loudly complains. As a child I used to think all adults shopped like that. You should see how she treats salespeople: she drives them into bumbling confusion or polite hostility.

—She can't be that bad.

—You don't know her the way I do. When I got my first bra, she took me to the G. Fox lingerie department and loudly announced—

—Loudly again? Aren't you repetitious?

—Loudly. Believe me. She loudly announced she wanted to buy a training bra for me. It took her twenty-three minutes to decide on one. I timed it. It seemed like hours. She kept holding different bras up in front of me and then sent me into the dressing room to try them on. While I struggled with the hooks, I could hear her tell the saleswoman how important good support was for someone as tall as her niece. After she finally decided on a bra and paid for it, she took it out of the bag again and asked the saleswoman if it would hold up in the wash. It was humiliating. I still feel embarrassed in stores, almost apologetic, and I whisper when asking for assistance.

—It won't be like that in Filene's. I promise.

—I don't want to go.

—You could shop for a shirt and tie to go with the suit Nick bought last week at Sage-Allen.

—Don't talk to me about that. I had to drag him there to

buy the damn suit. First he told me he needed a new gray suit before the end of the month. All through February he kept postponing it. The last day of the month he finally decided he needed it. We got to the store half an hour before closing. He was so wishy-washy about what he wanted that I ended up talking to the salesman and picking out the suit. I felt like an overbearing mother when I asked him to try it on. The salesman kept smirking. Timmy was chasing Nicole around the coatrack. It was awful. You know, sometimes Nick gets me so furious that I can't imagine another year, even another hour, with him. And he doesn't believe me when I tell him that.

—But don't you remember last month, Megan, when you were sitting in the rocking chair by the fireplace? He said that thirty years from now you'll still be talking about leaving him while sitting in that same rocking chair, and you looked at each other for a long time and you believed him. He came over and laid his head in your lap. You stroked his hair and made love in front of the fire.

—I remember. Moments like those are good. They are. But they don't automatically make the rest good. Do you know how much affection can be killed by bathroom sounds and odors? I've asked him to close the door, to please close the door. He says he forgets.

—He'll try to remember, Megan. I'll make sure he will. I'll make a note on his index card.

—I don't think he realizes that I'm scared someday my feelings for him will be gone. There won't be any left. Just indifference. And he still won't understand when I tell him they wore off, a little at a time.

110

Location: downtown Boston.
An expensive restaurant (it doesn't matter which one).
White tablecloth; candles; red water goblets.

Waiters in tuxedos; one violinist.

Mirrors in ornate gold frames; a huge copper espresso machine.

One intimidating waiter with arrogant sideburns, half hidden by above espresso machine, pouring the unused portion of milk from a white porcelain creamer into an A&P cardboard half-gallon milk container.

Aunt Judy: talking; eating; dabbing her lips with the white linen napkin a waiter originally deposited on her lap; talking; eating; talking; eating; dabbing; eating; talking . . .

Megan: not listening; eating; watching her aunt's lips move around food and around words; feeling her attention drawn to a conversation at the next table.

"He had to take her away. She kept sifting through the ashes."

They got up, two women in their forties, letting the words of their conversation settle on Megan like an itchy blanket. Earlier, their talk had centered around their monthly trip to Boston, an X-rated movie, a white sale, the popovers, and meeting the ladies' guild bus in four hours by the Prudential Center. Confidences had been exchanged about the minister's salary, the weather, and somebody by the name of Martha (or was it Marcia?) who hadn't paid for the bus trip yet and was always behind in her dues, perhaps because of her weekly payments at the Weight Watcher meetings, even though it was worth it; she had already shed five pounds in three months, only eighty-two more to go . . .

Megan had lost them about there, forced by Aunt Judy into deciding between cheesecake and sherbet, coffee and espresso, committing Dagmar or making her talk to the Golden Acres psychiatrist. It made her shudder to remember that for fifteen years of her life she had been subject to her aunt's decisions.

"There is nothing wrong with feeling the way she does," Megan said, leaning forward. "No, just espresso, nothing else."

"Why don't you order at least a small piece?" Aunt Judy suggested.

"No, thank you."

Raising his thin blond eyebrows, the tuxedo-clad waiter departed.

It was just then that Megan missed the story which led to the ending: *He had to take her away. She kept sifting through the ashes.*

She? Who was she? Whose ashes? Megan could see hands, long smooth fingers, ashes magnifying the pores, crusting under the manicured fingernails. No face. Just the hands. Sensuously sifting through her lover's ashes after her husband killed him? Was he the kind of husband who encouraged her to make comparisons? The urn. She saw the urn, white and blue. Where did he take her afterwards? Away. On a vacation? Or did he have her committed, first destroying her lover and then her sanity?

"I only want what's best for her." Aunt Judy dabbed her lips and burped discreetly behind the white linen napkin. "But she never takes my advice. She always was much closer to your mother than to me. Even when we were children . . ."

Why did it have to be her lover's ashes? Why such a cliché? How many husbands kill their wives' lovers and then surprise them with an urn? A child's ashes, then. It didn't have to be that morbid. Did other women ever watch their children at play, aware that someday they would be dead? Brush their soft hair and know the shape of their skulls underneath?

Aunt Judy's lips were making words.

Megan swallowed. "Please, don't make Dagmar do anything against her will. For some reason she wants to live in the nursing home. Even if it doesn't make sense to you or to me, I think it's important that she does what she wants to do."

"Would you be willing to take the consequences if she kills herself? It's easy for you to say that."

Consequences plus responsibility divided by gratitude equals guilt. Why not ashes from a fireplace? But why would she sift them? And why would he take her away? A fire. Perhaps their house burned down. The house where their children were conceived and born, where they grew up and grew away to move to a town nine miles from there or to Sweden. It didn't make a difference: they seldom visited. And they wore chocolate brown suits. She sifted the ashes, trying to salvage her son's first pair of shoes. When he was eight months old, she had them bronzed. They stood on top of the TV, next to the yellow box her daughter painted in third grade, the box in which she kept her children's baby teeth. Her hands would have lines, yes, unsteady hands with blue veins and brown spots; they would sift the ashes for lost dreams. . . .

"Are you listening to me?" Aunt Judy asked.

Megan nodded, resisting the impulse of running from the restaurant to find the two women, asking them to please tell her who was sifting through whose ashes, and where she was taken by whom. But even if she found them, would she dare ask? She couldn't just walk up to them and admit she had been listening to their conversation. Perhaps it was completely harmless. What if part of their house burned down and she looked for the good silver she rarely used, the silver she had saved for that special occasion she kept waiting for. And maybe he helped her and found his gold watch, the one his company gave him after twenty-five years of devoted, unimaginative service? But then why would he take her away? Because he cared? Because he wanted to protect her from the fear of having lost her memories with her possessions? *He had to take her away. She kept sifting through the ashes.* Yes. He took her to Florida, where she sat on a gray stretch of cemented beach, where she could not even sift sand. So much more plausible than a lover, condensed to dust within a blue-and-white ceramic container and touched by desperate hands, young and slender hands, trying to recapture the feeling of his arms, his thighs, his—

"You think so too?" Aunt Judy asked.

Megan blinked.

"I wish you'd pay attention. I'm going to see my lawyer and find out what should be done."

"Nick and I have talked to her about moving to Connecticut. We've offered her the extra bedroom. But she doesn't want to live in our house. Maybe she's afraid she'd be giving up her independence."

"If you ask me," Aunt Judy said, "she doesn't know what she wants. If she liked the nursing home, she wouldn't be talking about suicide."

"Maybe she'd agree to move if we found an apartment for her in West Hartford. She'd be close by and she'd still have her privacy."

"It's a way out for people who can't face their responsibilities."

"Moving to an apartment?"

"Suicide," Aunt Judy said.

"You've never thought about that?"

"Of course not. I'm surprised you even ask. Don't tell me you . . ."

Megan stood up and reached for her handbag.

"The bathrooms are over there," Aunt Judy said. "To the left."

111

—Wait, Megan. The bathrooms are over there. To the left. Where are you going?

—

—Aunt Judy is going to wonder where—

—Leave me alone. I want to be by myself. Without you. Without Aunt Judy, or Nick, or the children.

—What do you think you're doing? You can't just walk away.

—Why not?

—Because . . . because you just can't.

—I notice you haven't left yet.

—You know I can't. I have my children, my—

—You only talk about it, right? A cabin by the lake . . . Remember?

—That's different, Megan.

—

—At least tell me why you're doing this.

—I don't want to talk about it. I need time to think.

—That's great. Just great. Anyone can walk away. You know that, don't you? Anyone. But it takes real strength to stay.

112

—Why now, Megan?

Why are you walking away now, when there were so many times that you stayed? Why did you stay that first Christmas when Nick gave you four aprons made by handicapped people? Why did you stay on all those off-days when everything looked gloomy and dark and alike, when you felt resentful of your surroundings because they were too familiar? Why did you stay when your first enchantment with motherhood wore off? Did you hope that, somehow, it would return, this feeling of being totally needed and accepted? There were moments when it came back, moments that made you hope for more, right? That warm feeling that is strongest when you feel the soft hair of a newborn against the side of your neck, can you ever recapture it? Why did you stay in the store last week when Nick made you pick out his suit? You felt like walking away from him and the discreetly smirking salesman. But you stayed. Why? Why did you stay when you discovered that your firstborn had the unfortunate tendency to urinate straight up at you whenever you took off his diaper? Because you learned to adapt, right? You learned to hold a diaper between him and you whenever you changed him. You stayed through five years of ass-wiping, 1972–77, one of them overlapping: 1972–75 for Timmy, 1974–77 for Nicole. Why are you leaving now after they have learned to wipe themselves? Why did you stay for hundreds of Sunday dinners with Nick's parents, listening to the same stories about the same people, most of whom you had never met, listening to the same statement from Nick's mother although you had promised yourself you'd walk out if she ever said again: "I don't know how you young mothers do it. I admire so much what you are doing." Why did you keep writing annual thank-you notes for the initialed shirts she gave Nick for Christmas? Why didn't you tell her how much you disliked them? Why did you stay at the last employee party? Nick offered to leave early, but you stayed and danced with your father-in-law, trying not to look at his sliding toupee.

You stayed as you did all the other times you imagined leaving.

Why?

Why are you walking out now?

What does it feel like to have actually left?

Do you want to go back?

Do you feel frightened?

Slightly ridiculous?

Are you worried about the consequences?

Have you considered calling Nick? Do you imagine what he might be thinking? What Aunt Judy is thinking? What Nick's parents will think when they find out? Are you worried about your children? About what they'll have for dinner tonight? For breakfast tomorrow? Who'll lay out Timmy's clothes for kindergarten? Put the tuition for Nicole's nursery school into an envelope? Are you worried about the laundry? About the roast you took out of the freezer this morning? Have you thought of calling the garage to postpone the tune-up for your car?

What are you thinking, Megan?

Are you stunned by the accumulation of all the times you stayed?

113

If I accept that Megan has left, I'd better make sure that she doesn't walk into a formula solution, such as:

Heroine walks away from a situation. Gradually losing or shedding her possessions, she sets out upon a mini-odyssey, say, a stop at Harvard for a quick Ph.D., a revolution in a Central American country, or even a job in a Hampstead laundry, during the course of which our heroine finds her roots, new relationships, new insights, and (last but not least) herself.

But all this has been done before. I refuse to let Megan lose her possessions. Her leather bag has a secure shoulder strap. It contains a wallet with eighty-seven dollars plus change, a checkbook with a balance of over two thousand dollars, two major credit cards, a handkerchief, peppermint Life Savers, two Matchbox cars, keys, a black comb, Chap Stick, everything she might or might not need, even two tampons, since I won't have any of my female characters bleed all over Boston, New York, Hartford, Portland, Dublin, London, Paris, or even Berlin, New Hampshire. That too has been exhausted by fiction, and I'm not about to stop the menstrual flow by sacrificing a freshly composed sonata, a five-page poem, or any other work of art. It would only support the worn falsehood that women have to sacrifice their art because they are women.

Haven't you heard? Sacrifices are out.

For now, just imagine Megan, wearing dark green slacks and a matching blazer, carrying above provisions in her shoulder bag, leaving the restaurant, crossing the street without looking back, and getting into a bus. Why? Because it happens to be there. You want to know what kind of weather to imagine? How about windy but mild, chance of precipitation: twenty percent today, ten percent tomorrow. The date? How does March 8 sound to you? Let me check my calendar. March 8 fell on Wednesday. We'll make it official: Wednesday, March 8, 1978.

114

Ten-fifteen P.M.

My husband is half asleep. I'm sitting in bed, editing Chapters 111, 112, and 113.

Opening one eye, my husband asks: "What are you doing?"

"Thinking."

"About what?"

"Solutions."

"Solutions to what?"

"What's the first thought that comes to your mind if I tell you about a woman who walks away?"

"Away from what?"

"I'm not really sure about that."

"Are you trying to tell me something?" He opens his other eye.

"It's only theoretical."

"What woman?" Now his dark eyes are focused on me, waiting.

"Megan."

"Oh." He yawns.

"You see, she leaves her aunt in a restaurant in Boston and walks out. I'm trying to figure out what happens next."

"That's easy. She gets flattened by a bus."

"I've already established that she gets safely on a bus." He closes his eyes.

"What would be the most interesting plot you could think of?"

"The bus turns over and flattens her," he mumbles.

"Kills her?"

"Mmhhh." With his eyes closed, he nods.

"I can't do that. I need her for the ending. Listen . . . Are you asleep?"

115

You really want to know what happened to Megan after she walked out of the restaurant and got on the first bus she saw?

So does Nick.

"What do you mean you lost her?" he asked when Aunt Judy called him and tried to explain that she had been looking for Megan for an hour without finding her.

"I waited for ten minutes. I thought she had only gone to the bathroom. Then I checked in there, but it was empty. I searched the lobby and talked to the waiter. Nobody had seen her leave. Then I gave a message to the waiter, in case she returned, and went out to look for her. I even asked a policeman, but of course he said he hadn't seen her, that he was busy directing traffic, and would I please get out of the road."

"Have you checked back at the restaurant?"

"Of course. That's where I'm calling from. Nothing. Absolutely nothing. I even called the nursing home to see if she had returned there. She could have taken a cab. But they haven't seen her. I don't understand what got into her."

"Did you say anything that might have upset her?"

"What do you mean?"

"Did you have an argument?"

"Of course not. Actually, she was rather quiet all day. But not more than usual. I'd never say anything to upset her. You should know me better than that. I'm surprised you even . . ." Her voice rose.

"Have you called the police?"

"Not yet. I wanted to talk with you first to see if she had called you. If you ask me, I don't understand this whole thing. It shows a complete lack of consideration. Why would she get up and leave without telling me where—"

"Would you please call the police? Ask them to check the hospitals. I'm sure there's an explanation for this, but I want to eliminate that possibility. I doubt they'll do anything about a missing adult in less than twenty-four hours. But find out about their policy anyhow. I'll stay in my office until I hear from you. Call collect."

"I can't say that you sound too upset," Aunt Judy said.

"Megan is thirty years old. She knows how to take care of herself. She might be trying to call me now. Falling apart is not going to change anything. So why don't you—"

"You don't have to repeat it. I'm not your secretary. I'll make the calls, don't worry, and I'll get back to you."

116

I'm beginning to wonder about my characters who are older than fifty, particularly Aunt Judy. Although I like Dagmar, I've not been very kind toward Nick's parents and have given you a rather bleak picture of Jill's parents. I'm not sure why.

Is Aunt Judy too one-sided? She took care of Megan as a child. But did she want to do it? Or did she consider it her Christian duty? Although I have mentioned that she dresses well and gives quality presents to Tim and Nicole, this might not particularly endear her to you. Something else is needed. Warmth? Concern? But the more I try, the less I'm able to show you her good sides. What if I left her the way she is? Don't we all know one-sided characters?

A solution would be to let you see Aunt Judy through other perspectives. Perhaps you could talk to her priest, who is familiar with the good deeds she does for the community. He would tell you that she never misses Sunday Mass, and that he can always depend on her. And if you interviewed the couple in the other half of the duplex, the elderly couple with the two cats that sit on the back of the green sofa all day and look out of the window, the arthritic couple who'd offer you M&M's from the silver pickle dish on their low living-room table, you might find out that, twice, when they were behind in their rent, Aunt Judy told them not to worry, that she hasn't raised their rent since 1961, that every Christmas she hand-decorates a receipt good toward any month of rent in the coming year, that she never forgets their anniversary and birthdays.

Perspectives.

They give you a more complex impression than the one Megan holds of her aunt, more complex than what Dagmar thinks of her daughter. You can get to know her much better in fiction than if you were related to her. What if we reeled in perspectives of half the population in Connecticut and made up touching stories about Aunt Judy's generosity, her gentleness, her goodness (the woman is a saint, etc.), the pleasures she has caused per UPS with her PPPs? Wouldn't the story get buried under statements from character witnesses?

You ask: What story?

All right, I'll get back to it before I lose you. Let's start with Aunt Judy's second phone call to Nick.
Collect.

117

"Nothing," Aunt Judy said. "Absolutely nothing. I called the police and asked them to check the hospitals. Nothing. At least we know she hasn't been in an accident. You know, I don't want to worry you, Nick, but could kidnapping be a possibility? After all, your father is quite wealthy."

"Kidnapping is usually planned well in advance. Your trip was something you decided on yesterday."

"Well, as I said before, I didn't want to worry you, but I thought it was important enough to mention. What are you going to do now?"

"I've talked to Sara. She offered to keep the children overnight. If I drive to Boston, I could meet you for dinner, and we could talk."

"Why don't you wait? I don't think there's anything you could do here. It would be much better if you stayed home in case Megan called. I'll find a hotel and check back with the police and the restaurant every couple of hours."

"Listen, thanks. But are you sure you don't want me to come?"

"You'd only be doing the same things I'm taking care of already. Why don't you wait until we know more?"

"It makes sense. Have you called the nursing home again?"

"I will. As soon as I hang up. Try to think if there's any other place she might have gone to. Does she know anyone in the Boston area?"

"Not that I know."

"I'll call you after I've found a room."

"I'm sure there must be a logical explanation."

"Of course," Aunt Judy said briskly. "There always is."

118

By the time the bus turned into the narrow street that led from the center of Boston, most of the other passengers had gotten off. Megan noticed that many of the streetlights were broken. Men in groups of three and four leaned against narrow, dark stone tenements. Some of the windows were crudely replaced by nailed plywood or covered with blind plastic or newspapers. The ones that were not broken showed tattered, faded curtains like the torn hem of a woman's cotton dress.

The bus stopped.

A black woman with a small girl got off.

On the sidewalk the men were looking at the bus. Talking. Smoking. One of them laughed, flashing shining teeth, as if inviting Megan to get up from her seat by the window and leave the bus before its doors closed. His right hand was halfway in the pocket of his tight, emerald trousers, except for the thumb which was moving up and down next to his zipper.

He stepped up to the bus.

Quickly, Megan looked away from the window. The back of the driver was wide. It was a wide, safe back with a pink neck that bulged just a little over the collar of his shirt.

119

—How did you really feel when Aunt Judy called you, Nick?

—That she must have said something to upset Megan.

—You never thought Megan might be leaving you?

—No. Why should she?

—But how do you feel about it? Are you worried? Upset? I need to know. I want to get your reaction right. Don't give me rational thoughts or explanations. Save those for Aunt Judy. Tell me what it feels like.

—I don't know. After all, you're making this whole thing up. If I were writing this novel—

—But you're not.

—If I were writing this novel, Megan and her aunt would finish lunch and come home in time for Megan to make dinner.

—You're avoiding my question, Nick. And stop jamming my stapler. Just leave it alone and listen. Pretend you're real.

—Thanks a lot.

—Pretend you're real. Pretend you are married to a very tall woman with red hair who also is real. Am I going too fast for you? Good. Pretend your wife went to Boston with her aunt. Pretend that this aunt called you and told you that your wife walked out of the restaurant where they were having lunch and didn't return. *How would you feel?*

—Don't shout at me. How would I feel? If she'd been nagging me for the past few days, I'd probably feel a little relieved.

—How can you—?

—Stop it. No need to get violent. You don't have to tear up my index card. I was just kidding. At first I might feel annoyed at her aunt for having caused this whole thing. Then I guess I'd expect to get a call from her, asking me to pick her up from the Greyhound station or the airport.

—But what if she didn't call you?

—You're really determined to make this a major crisis, aren't you?

—You don't seem too worried.

—Why? Would you like to see me frantic, tearing my hair, crying into my beard?

—You don't have a beard, Nick.

—How should I know? I don't have a reflection. I have to take your word for it. And you never wrote that I don't have a beard.

—Can't you be serious? At least for this chapter? I'm trying to figure out how Nick would react when he finds out his wife has left.

—Okay. As I see it, she has not left him. Me, that is. Sorry. She has not left me, but has walked away from a situation. I refuse to take that personally. I guess if she stayed away overnight and I didn't hear from her, I might get worried. I think I would. Actually, I might get quite upset.

—What if she doesn't come back at all?

—I thought this was supposed to be a positive book.

—What if she doesn't come back, Nick?

—Well, after feeling upset, I'd become very resentful after several days or a week, especially if I found out she just walked out on the children and me. But I don't think she would do that. She'd talk it out beforehand. It just isn't in her to do something sneaky; she'd want it out in the open. Besides, she usually plans things in advance. And if she had planned this, she would have wanted to tell me about it. She would have made arrangements for the children, left frozen casseroles . . . No. She probably would have taken the children with her, turned this whole damn thing into a family vacation. I don't know. It's so unlike her. This whole thing.

—You sound worried.

—I have every right to be. You have the nerve to make my wife walk away from a perfectly happy marriage, and you expect me to—

—A perfectly happy marriage? There is no such thing, Nick. There are strong marriages that can survive problems, but happiness is such a brief condition, interrupted by difficulties and plain, boring routine.

—Stop preaching. I want to know what you did with my

wife. Where is she? You're putting me through a lot of
theoretical bullshit while you play around with options.
Admit it, how many possibilities are you going to dangle in
front of me? You really must like to watch me squirm.

—I don't know how many. Not yet. That's why I refuse
to write an outline for this novel. I can picture several
directions it could go from here, three at least; but once I
start writing them, I might think of others. And I'm not
doing it to make you suffer, Nick. Really. It would be so
much easier to decide on the most dramatic option.

120

Someone sat down next to her.

She didn't even have to look out of the window to know
that the man with the green trousers was no longer
standing out there with the others. She didn't even have to
see the victory sign one of the men sitting on the chipped
stone steps sent with his left hand.

Her watch showed three-thirteen; the second hand was
on the four. She observed its slow, sweeping motion to the
five. The six. The seven. The man was looking at her. She
could feel his eyes and then she saw his face, turned fully
toward her, intense and not laughing anymore. It was a
serious face, a narrow, serious face with skin the color of
light olives, the kind of smooth skin Greek or Spanish
men sometimes have. If he said something to her, he'd
probably speak with an accent, the soft Mediterranean
accent of first-generation immigrants. He wore neither a
jacket nor a sweater, although it was less than fifty degrees,
just a very white shirt with long sleeves and those emerald
trousers without a belt. His right hand, no longer in his
pocket, held a large black bag firmly on top of his knees.
Across the back of his hand was a bright red cut. A recent
cut, it hadn't formed a scab yet. She—

121

"She bent and licked the throbbing slash."

"Get off the bus, Mr. Nelson. Please. You've already ruined one chapter, and I'm not going to let you intrude again. I can only imagine too well what you would make out of a situation like this. It would be thoroughly disgusting and nauseating."

"Let me just give you a general outline, something to keep the reader interested. All you do is fuck around with your characters' minds. What about their bodies? Why all this mental masturbation when you could be describing the real thing? If I hadn't come in, you probably would have made his black bag a doctor's bag and him an angel of mercy who has just delivered a baby in a fifth-floor walk-up, an intern, highly idealistic, too poor to afford a car. And you would even have found some way to explain those green pants and why he was rubbing his dick."

"He was not."

"Stop dreaming. Face up to the reality of this scene. The black bag is full of goodies, if you get my drift; shackles, a whip, spurs, a screwdriver, rope, you name it. They get to the end of the line. The bus line. They get off. Together. You can add more details later. He has her by the wrist. She follows him without questioning where he is taking her. She is in a sort of trance, if you know what I mean. When they get to a dingy alley and he pulls her into it, she finally begins to struggle. Nothing like a good struggle to titillate your readers. He slaps her—"

"I'm not going to—"

"Don't interrupt me. I said you could add the details later. He gets her into a back door and drags her up some stairs. You could put some good descriptions in here. Stop chewing that eraser and pay attention. You can learn a lot from this. He shoves her through the door and pushes her across the unmade bed, which reeks from the bodies of women he has taken there before. Beneath his powerful virility she thrashes. We'll save the black bag for the second rape scene. With his right knee he masterfully forces her thighs apart, savoring her struggle. Bruising her breasts with his strong mouth, he prepares to grind into her. He dominates her, consumed by inflaming lust. He feels the pulsating power of his penis, a loaded gun, as he masters her with a powerful thrust, pronging her shuddering cunt. She lies subdued, submitting etcetera etcetera. I'm glad you finally stopped interrupting because I'm going to let you in on a real clincher. Remember the first lesson I gave you?"

"How could I forget it?"

"Except for the reference to chess, everything else is there. It's your basic, everyday sex scene."

"I'm going to be sick."

"Once you memorize the basic rules and brush up on your vocabulary, there is no end to the possibilities. Wait. There's more. Hey, where are your manners? You can't just run out of here."

122

"Und dabei habe ich die Mädchen immer gewarnt, daß außerhalb dieser Klostermauern die Versuchungen der Welt auf sie lauerten," schluchzte Schwester Anneliese in ihr Taschentuch. "Ich kann doch nichts dafür wenn eine meiner Schülerinnen solch ein Buch schreibt."

"Aber regen Sie sich doch bloß nicht so auf," sagte Schwester Monika und legte ihre Hand beruhigend auf die zitternde Schulter der Schwester Anneliese. "Keiner kann Sie doch dafür verantwortlich machen."

"Die Ehrwürdige Mutter will eine Untersuchung in meine Lehrmethoden unternehmen, um festzustellen ob es mein Einfluß war, der Ursula zu diesem Buch getrieben hat."

"Ach Du lieber Himmel." Schwester Monika schlug beide Hände über ihrem Kopf zusammen. "Wie lange war die Schülerin denn bloß hier im Internat?"

"Nur ein paar Jahre. Eine typische Einzelgängerin. Mit Gruppen wollte sie überhaupt nichts zu tun haben. Dauernd hatte sie die Nase in Büchern. Erinnern Sie sich? Sie hatte viel Last mit dem Rotwerden." Schwester Anneliese schüttelte ihren Kopf.

"Dieses Buch sollte ihr mehr als genug Grund zum Rotwerden geben," sagte Schwester Monika mißbilligend. "Vielleicht hatte sie gehofft, daß es nicht übersetzt werden würde. Wie ist sie denn nach Amerika gekommen?"

"Ich weiß nicht genau," schluchzte die noch immer schluchzended Schwester Anneliese. "Sie hat irgendeinen Amerikaner geheiratet. Kinder hat sie sogar, zwei Jungen. Können Sie sich so etwas vorstellen? Eine Mutter die so etwas schreibt?" Sie trocknete ihre Nonnentränen. "Soviel ich weiß, hat sie sogar ihre Nationalität geändert. Und mich wollen die hier verantwortlich machen für was eine Amerikanerin geschrieben hat."

122

"And I was the one who always warned the girls that beyond these convent walls lurked the temptations of the world." Sister Anneliese sobbed into her handkerchief. "It isn't my fault if one of my students writes a book like this."

"Please, don't get so upset," said Sister Monika and laid a compassionate hand on the trembling shoulder of Sister Anneliese. "Nobody can hold you responsible for this."

"The Mother Superior is going to hold an investigation into my teaching methods to find out if it was my influence that drove Ursula to this book."

"Oh, dear heaven." Sister Monika clapped both hands above her head. "How long was the student here in boarding school?"

"Only a few years. A typical recluse. Refused to join groups. Always had her nose in books. Remember her? She used to blush a lot." Sister Anneliese shook her head.

"This book should give her more than enough reason for blushing," said Sister Monika disapprovingly. "Maybe she hoped it wouldn't be translated. How did she ever get to America?"

"I don't really know," sobbed the still-sobbing Sister Anneliese. "She married some American. She even has children, two boys. Can you imagine that? A mother who writes something like that?" She dried her nuntears. "As far as I know, she has even changed her nationality. And here they are trying to hold me responsible for something an American wrote."

123

There was no bus.

124

Or maybe there was a bus, but Megan didn't get on it.

She didn't get on it because she didn't leave the restaurant.

Let's say she went to the bathroom and returned to the table after seven minutes.

Aunt Judy did not call Nick.

There was no reason for Aunt Judy to call Nick, other than perhaps to discuss the weather with him, which would bore reader and writer to tears.

Therefore, as well as for any other reason you might like to make up, Aunt Judy did not call Nick.

This certainly exhausts the subject of the telephone call to Nick.

What if they drove back to Hartford?

And then what?

Why don't we just abandon this option?

125

The bus stopped at the airport.

Megan got up, following the elderly couple who had been sitting in front of her ever since she had left the restaurant and gotten on the bus. Instead of looking out of the window, she had kept her eyes on the backs of the people in front of her. The woman's hair was very short and gray with two cowlicks that made the ends of her hair stick out. The man was taller. His back was wide. It was a wide, safe back with a pink neck that bulged just a little over the collar of his shirt. It was a back that one could study for a very long time without having to think about anything but its safe width. It was the kind of back one could follow from a bus, follow safely from a bus and into an airport, follow past a gift shop and a flower shop and a coffee shop to a door with the sign: MEN.

But no farther than that.

Just up to that door.

Megan turned.

It felt strange to be walking toward an airline desk without a suitcase.

I dedicate this paragraph to one of my research assistants, a woman from Delta Airlines who just answered my phone call and kindly gave me the information that not Delta but New England Airlines flies to Nantucket, that she would be glad to look up their schedule for me, that a round trip costs sixty-two dollars, one way thirty-one, and that there are two flights that would fit the schedule of the friend I was inquiring for: four-thirty, arriving on Nantucket at five-thirty; or a later flight, leaving Boston at seven-ten. I told her I would get back to her after confirming my friend's itinerary.

Forgive me, my unknown, unaware assistant.

126

—Do you want to go back to Nantucket, Megan? It's only March, not the best time of the year for walking along a deserted beach. There won't be anyone waiting for you at Wauwinet House when you get back from your solitary walk, no one to give you an insufficient amount of sympathy about your blisters and your sunburn. Actually, you won't have to worry about sunburn.

127

Like smooth marble her knees jutted from the water.

Supporting herself with her elbows, Megan slid her body back and forth to distribute the steaming water rushing from the antique faucet into the lukewarm surroundings. Gertrude Stein might have written that a bathtub is a bathtub is a bathtub; but this was not your standard assembly-line production bathtub. It was a wonderful bathtub, a huge, white, porcelain-coated, high-rimmed bathtub on tarnished claw feet, a tub Megan could lie in with her legs only slightly bent, the first tub in which she didn't have to sit when taking a bath. She had always wondered what it would be like to submerge herself up to her neck in warm water.

You ask how she got into this tub. Whatever happened

to smooth transitions? Joseph Heller would have given
you a very specific description of the tub's location,
such as:

THE BATHTUB WAS IN NANTUCKET ON THE THIRD FLOOR
OF A WHITE CLAPBOARD HOUSE JUST FOUR BLOCKS AWAY
FROM THE FERRY STOP AND ONE BLOCK SOUTH OF A
SUPERMARKET, THREE BEAUTY PARLORS, AND TWO COR-
RUPT DRUGGISTS . . .

Cut two beauty parlors and scratch one corrupt drug-
gist.

As she moved her hips forward and back, Megan's
shoulders touched the cool rim of the tub. Like a river
breaking through an embankment, the water moved
between her thighs, rippling the strands of her pubic hair
like seaweed, rising and swaying under the gentle force of
the waves. When the warmth was spread evenly through-
out the tub, she turned off the faucet and leaned back.

How did she get into the tub?

You're quite persistent, aren't you? I'm getting there. Be
patient. You see, at this time of the year it was not difficult
at all to find a place to stay. The cabdriver had recommended a house right in town, four blocks from the ferry
stop etcetera. He said he knew the people who owned it;
they were year-round residents, teachers, both of them.

He did not ask how long she was planning to stay, and
where her luggage was. A young man with an intelligent
face and hazel eyes, he had large, uneven teeth. His neck
was not the kind of neck that kept thoughts dormant.

In front of a low, white fence the cab stopped. The
house had three stories and was square, built of white
clapboards. If it hadn't been quite dark, Megan would have
seen that it had a widow's walk on top, on which she would
stand the following morning and look out toward Wauwinet and the Great Point Light, remembering the opening

chapters of this novel. But her recollection would be different from what you would read, should you turn back to the first pages, different because recollections of the past change gradually as they are influenced by the present. It would be impossible for her to remember her stream of consciousness, although she might vaguely recall thoughts of "Jaws," the bathtub toy she had bought for her son. Quite likely she would remember walking ten miles along a deserted beach, that her feet were blistered, that she got a sunburn. She would not recall what she imagined the second Mrs. Stone to be like, unless, of course, I change my mind and put it within her reach. But I'm positive there won't be a single thought of Y.L., since she remains unaware of him; since he, as we have clearly established, is only a figment of *your* imagination.

128

But we're fourteen hours ahead of schedule, and while we are messing around with the future, Megan has met the owners of the house, Cal and Nina Marcus, both of them in their thirties, both short, overweight, with pale hair and glasses, jeans and velour shirts: Nina's a soft apricot color, Cal's dark green. If you are an intrusive reader, you can either close this book with a sigh of exasperation or cut out the chapters, fitting them together like a puzzle. You might like to sort them according to color, time, dialogue, images, weather—or tell me to go to hell and stop second-guessing you.

If you decide to read on in spite of everything that has happened between the two of us, in spite of all the times you have forgiven me for breaking the rules, then I'll confess to you how tempted I was to make this a house owned by two elderly eccentrics who dabble in devil worship and macrame. Consider the possibilities: human sacrifices, weird sounds, eerie smiles, black capes that rustle in the night . . .

You think you can manage the transition from cab to house to room on the third floor to tub all by yourself? I'm not about to write a detailed strip scene, not even for you. I blush too easily. I blush even more when I notice that people take my blushing personally, people who don't know that I blush talking to my children, the neighbor's cat, even to myself.

Let's assume Megan is in the tub now.

129

"You know what I'd like to do?" I ask my husband during dinner.

"What?" He stops eating.

"Go away by myself. Just for a few days, maybe even a week."

"Why don't you?" He pours more milk for our youngest son.

"You know I can't."

"Why not?"

"The children. They need me."

"They could go to the baby-sitter. I'd pick them up in the evening."

"It wouldn't work. The laundry would pile up. Who would clean the house? Do the shopping? The dishes?" I wait for him to assure me that he would take care of all that, but he is eating silently.

"Can I come with you?" my oldest son asks me.

"Where are you going, Mommy?" his brother wants to know.

"Nowhere."

"Why don't you go?" my husband asks. "Really. If that's what you want to do, we'll manage."

"You know I can't."
"You don't want to?"

130

"When I'm constipated I want relief overnight—"

Abruptly, Nick turned off the TV and the voice of the helmeted construction worker, extending a bottle of laxative with a constipated smile. He hadn't heard from Aunt Judy for three hours. Why hadn't she called? Surely she must have found a room by now. He sat down and, for the fifth time, picked up *The Wall Street Journal.* Looking at the headlines above the long, narrow columns, he tried to remember what he had read before. Nothing looked familiar.

"I want Mommy to tuck me in." Nicole was standing at the top of the stairs, clutching her patchwork dinosaur to which she had given the bizarre name Kingkongcinderella.

"I already told you your mother won't be home in time to tuck you in."

"But I can't sleep."

"Yes, you can," Nick assured her, wondering uncomfortably how he would react if someone assumed the authority of deciding whether he was able to sleep or not.

"I can't sleep with all the bats," she whined.

"Bats?"

"The bats for the bat trap."

"What are you talking about?"

"The bat trap for catching the bats. Mommy can cook them tomorrow."

"Nicole, there are no bats in this house." He dropped the paper on the low table and walked over to the stairs. "This is the last time I want to hear from you tonight. It's very late. Your brother is already asleep. Go to the bathroom once more and then get into bed."

"I'm all empty."

"If you get up again there'll be trouble." In a deeper voice, a voice which usually made his daughter giggle with a delicious mixture of fear and delight, he added: "Deep trouble."

She did not giggle. "I want Mommy to tuck me in."

"She isn't home yet. I've tucked you in three times already, and if you . . ."

She ran into her bedroom. He could hear the vinyl soles of her green blanket sleeper against the carpet. It used to be Timmy's sleeper before he outgrew it. On Nicole it somehow looked like a disguise, perhaps because she was slighter, perhaps because of the football appliqué. The first time she had worn it, Nick had felt an odd tug of something that wasn't quite sadness, but rather an awareness of time having passed. Timmy would never fit into that sleeper again. That part of their lives was irretrievable.

"Can I kiss you good night?" Nicole called from her room.

What if something really had happened to Megan? Slowly he walked up the stairs, feeling his nervousness like a damp growth at the bottom of his stomach. What if Megan, at this moment, was in pain? Helpless? Unable to defend herself against some maniac? But she wouldn't just let something happen to her; she'd fight, defend herself, she who had almost attacked a man with a bread knife two weeks before Christmas.

131

The water was getting cool.

Megan sat up and turned the faucet back on. Sliding her bottom back and forth, she felt the warmth spread and was reminded of seaweed. There was nobody to disturb her. Nicole would not come in, would not sit on the edge of the tub, would not tell her she made some good soup in the sink of the other bathroom, a surprise soup, which would turn out to consist of cloudy water in which floated her comb, toothpaste snakes, Q-tips, hand lotion, soap, an open perfume bottle, a hairbrush, Chap Stick, her watch, and a red Snoopy cookie cutter. She would not have to worry about stunting Nicole's creative growth by yelling at her.

It was quiet in the house.

Extremely quiet.

Only the tops of her knees protruded. The rest of her lay submerged in warmth, cradled in a comfortable limbo, relaxed, her mind subject to the slow passage of images drifting by, unwinding, not unlike film in a camera, moving after each click to a new frame. This was not the frantic clicking of the professional, but rather like the random accumulation of the amateur, adding to a loose string of seemingly unrelated images. And, like prints developed from an amateur's film, some of the images were hazy, their edges blurred, while others were focused clearly.

Scotch tape. Timmy using lots of Scotch tape to connect things in the house: chairs to the table, the sink to the toilet, sponges to the rim of the tub. Not this tub. Why? A strange desire for unity? And the drawings. Hieroglyphic drawings on jagged pieces of paper cut from shopping bags or construction paper and taped on walls, windows, doors. Pieces of Scotch tape that stick to his clothing and have to be peeled off. Why?

The water was getting too hot, uncomfortable, scalding her feet.

She turned it off.

The bathroom was filled with steam.

Aunt Judy, talking to a saleswoman: "I know. I usually have a problem finding clothes that fit her. Everything is too short. Good support is very important for a girl this tall."

And Nick: "If your hair feels comfortable this way, you should wear it short." Why was his approval so important? It shouldn't be. Why did it make a difference that he never said anymore her hair looked beautiful. When it was still down to her waist he often said it was beautiful. Why did she feel compelled to ask him how it looked short, although she swore to herself she would not ask him again every time he answered: "All right." Didn't he know that *all right* was not good enough?

Nicole, learning to tie her shoes: "I can't do this day."

Driving. The children in the backseat: "Are we halfway yet?" "How far is halfway?" "Can we have a snack? A drink?" "Mommy, I have to go weewee."

A journal entry in her mother's handwriting: "Megan started nursery school last month. Today she ran away from there for the third time. It worries me. In a few years she'll have to accept structure." Accept. Accept what?

A sound came from the door.

Megan looked up.

Through the haze of steam she could see the doorknob, turning, ever so lightly, but definitely turning . . .

132

"Daddy?" Nicole called from her room.

"I'm on my way."

He remembered Megan's initial confusion after she had realized that she was capable of violence. Again and again she needed to talk about it, to reason out what she had felt. That day, when she saw the man coming toward the house, it had been too late to lock the kitchen door. Jackets, snow pants, boots, hats, and mittens were lying on the floor between the door and the storm door where the children had taken them off just a few minutes ago. "I'm not sure what frightened me about him," she later told Nick.

"Maybe it was all that talk about the Peeping Tom the police were looking for in Farmington. Maybe it was because he wasn't wearing a coat or because I couldn't see his car. All I know is that I couldn't get the children's things out of the way in time to lock the door. Without thinking, I opened the drawer next to the stove, pulled out the bread knife, and hid it behind my back. I knew I would use it if I had to. He knocked once; without waiting for me to ask him in, he stepped right into the kitchen. He was as tall as I, in his fifties or late forties. I don't think I've ever been as certain about anything as I was at that moment about using the knife if I had to. I could hear the children's voices in the living room, and I could feel the wooden handle in my right hand."

The man, fortunately unaware of the danger, was the dog warden, checking on a complaint about a collie that had bitten the paperboy. He left after Megan, both hands behind her back, told him that although she had seen the dog in the neighborhood, she didn't know who he belonged to.

"I remember conversations in high school," she later told Nick. "We used to speculate if we could kill someone if we had to. Some of the girls said they were sure they could if they had to defend their lives. I wasn't sure. Not that I kept thinking about it a lot; but when I held the knife behind my back, I remembered those conversations."

But that day she had thought she was defending the children. Would she defend herself? Yes, Nick thought. Yes. She would. She had to. Whatever made him think her life was in danger? He was not going to give in to fantasies of horror stories, even if this writer was trying to lead him into them.

133

Remember Chapter 131 with Megan sitting in the bathtub?

Remember the sound by the door?

The haze of steam?

The doorknob?

If I hadn't promised you earlier that I was *not* going to make this a house owned by two eccentrics who dabble in devil worship etcetera, I could have really let my imagination take off with the turning doorknob, not stopping until I had told you all about the dungeons, the priest's skeleton, the shoe of the Avon lady, the black kettle under the bed, the porcupine, the torn veil, the coffin in the freezer, the photos nobody ever saw, the heroine's cry for help, the hero rushing to the rescue. . . .

What a solution! An ending for this book: Nick rescues Megan. And they live happily ever after. I could be finished with this novel in another couple of chapters. I'd have a satisfying ending. Have you ever noticed how many books end with death or marriage? Such final solutions. Unfortunately, I'm not even tempted.

So, cut the doorknob; cut the sound; cut the hero rushing to the rescue. This is a normal house, owned by a normal couple without particularly kinky habits, other than normal kinky habits, a couple wondering why their guest arrived without luggage, and why the bathwater has been running five times within the last two hours.

134

Nick stumbled.

"You ruined the bat trap," Nicole cried from her bed. "Look what you did."

He looked. Lined up a foot from the open door were most of the toys from the green toy chest: building blocks and dolls; plastic Indians and foam-rubber airplanes; Superwoman and Matchbox cars; used tennis balls and an ambulance; a wooden spoon and plastic eggs that once contained panty hose; coloring books and the Weebles marina; a stuffed giraffe and Bunty, the panda, its left ear missing; the rubber shark and the Cookie Monster. Together they formed an irregular semicircle blocking the way into Nicole's room.

"You ruined the bat trap."

"But there aren't any bats around here." Cautiously he stepped across the remainder of the peculiar construction.

"Yes there are."

He resisted falling into the predictable exchange of: No there aren't. Yes there are. Instead he asked: "Where?"

She nodded vigorously. "There is such a thing as real bats."

"I know. But not around here."

"Will you fix it?" She pointed to the trap.

"I don't think it's such a good idea to block the way into your room," he said. Before going to bed, he always made sure no toys were obstructing the pass into his children's rooms in case of fire. But this wasn't the time to add to Nicole's fears by talking about fire hazards. "I'll fix it," he said, kneeling to reconstruct the odd barricade. He'd have to ask Megan what this whole thing with the bats was about. He'd never heard Nicole say anything about bats, even though she acted as though *bat trap* were a totally accepted term.

"Can you tell me a story?"

"It's too late. You should be sleeping."

"Just a tiny one? Please, Daddy?"

The Moraney kids used to ask him the same question: Just a tiny story? As a thirteen-year-old he had gotten his first job baby-sitting for them. He took a box of instant chocolate pudding with him and made it for them after their parents left. From then on they asked for him; he was their regular sitter until he left for college.

"Just a tiny story?"

"A tiny one. All right. Once upon a time there was a little girl and her name was Nicole—"

"Daddy!"

"What's wrong?"

"I want the one with the two horses and the witch and the picnic and the toad."

"I don't know that one."

"Mommy does."

"How is this? Once upon a time there was a little girl who met a witch who was having a picnic with her favorite toad right next to a meadow with two horses and—"

"Daddy!"

"What now?"

"You got it all wrong."

"Why don't you go to sleep? You can tell me the story in the morning." He bent down to kiss her and pulled the gingham quilt up to her shoulders. "Good night."

The phone rang.

He flinched. Jumping across the bat trap, he barely avoided tearing it down. On the third ring he picked up the receiver in his bedroom.

135

You don't really want to listen to another phone conversation of questions and answers between Nick and Aunt Judy, or do you? Instead of giving you two additional pages of dialogue, let me summarize: Aunt Judy has found a hotel, has not heard from Megan, has an incredible case of heartburn, does not have any news from the police. There, a condensed version, just for you. This leaves space for two amendments:

1. The year of Timmy's birth. At the end of Chapter 40 Nick is driving Megan and her contractions to the hospital on March 27, 1971. Since Timmy is born on March 28, 1972, this would be the longest labor in fiction. Of course you know I could have gone back and sneakily changed the year in Chapter 40 to 1972; but I chose not to because you've been involved in this manuscript from the beginning.

2. My writing has brought the first positive results. Remember that little nail sticking out on the left side of the roll on my typewriter? The one that used to hurt my finger each time I pushed it in? Right, that's the one. After I read that section to my husband, he took a flat black screw, cut part of it off, and drilled a hole into it. He covered the little nail on my typewriter with glue and slipped the hollow screw over it. It took him less than ten minutes. My finger has healed, but writing is still painful, except for the times when I enjoy doing it. Sometimes I wish I could stop writing. But whenever I try, I feel guilty. And when I write too much, I feel guilty about not spending enough time with my children.

136

"What are you doing?—I'm feeding half my peanuts to the monkeys.—That's nice.—Yes. I'm giving them the shells.—Get it, Mommy?"

My oldest son is reading jokes to me, all ninety-six pages from a library book called *Going Bananas*. Lying trapped in the tub, I wonder if I should start closing the door when taking a bath. Although my children occasionally respect my wish for privacy when I'm writing, they interpret my baths as an invitation to communicate. Putting my head under water does not stop them from talking.

"I have a joke too," my youngest son insists, trying to make his voice heard over the running of the hot water I'm adding. "I want to tell a joke. I have a joke too. I want to tell a joke. It's my turn. I never get a turn. I have—"

My oldest son keeps reading loudly.

"Please, give your brother a turn," I say weakly.

"He always wants a turn when I'm doing something. It's not fair."

Of course it isn't fair. Not fair to me.

"What do you call a cuckoo bird with green feathers?" my youngest son shouts, jumping up and down.

"I give up," his brother replies impatiently.

"All crazy around the house. Hahahahaha."

I put my head under water (to rinse out the shampoo) and close my eyes. When I open them, only my oldest son is still there, sitting on the hamper. Maybe I should try going under again.

"How come you have your arm in a cast?—I broke my arm in two places last week.—If I were you I wouldn't go to those places anymore.—Get it, Mommy?" He pushes his hair back.

"I got it."

"You see, the other guy thinks he broke his arm in two places, not two places on the arm but two places he went to, like maybe climbing a mountain and then there was an avalanche and he broke his arm once and after that he went to another place and—"

"I got it."

"Look at the picture." He thrusts his book in front of my face.

I'm caught between the back of the fiberglass tub and black-and-white drawings of two men in suits, one of them with curls, the other bald with glasses and his right arm in a cast.

"Maybe he broke his arm when he fell out of a tree."

"Maybe."

He withdraws the book and continues reading.

I think of Megan Stone.

I think of Megan Stone every time I'm in the tub.

I think of Megan Stone every time I'm in the tub because I feel guilty about abandoning her in a tub three weeks ago. I need time to think. No, not about how to extract her from that tub. A short narrative would take care of that. But once she is out of the tub, she'll have to do something. But what? I need to think about options. Answers. Solutions. I don't want an open-ended situation that could lead anywhere, not excluding nowhere (if you'll permit me to quote the end of the first paragraph in Chapter 1). But all I've come up with so far is the certainty that Megan has to question herself to find out what she is trying to get away from. I don't want to call it self-discovery; that's too obvious, too much of a cliché. But there should be a move toward an acceptance of herself and toward a rejection of circumstances and roles that others expect to see her in.

How do I show that process? It has to be gradual. If I were a subtle writer, I'd demonstrate a gradual change through a balanced blend of thought, action, stream of consciousness, dialogue, plot, internal monologue, pace, etc. For special effect I'd throw in an occasional symbol or even toy with a metaphor or two.

But I'm not subtle. That's why Megan's two hours in the tub are taking weeks of my life. If I don't get her out soon, her skin will be pale and shriveled, particularly around the fingertips. Yet, as long as I keep her there, I don't have to make a decision about what she's going to do.

"Did you get it?" my son asks.

I resist the temptation to tell him I got it. "I'm sorry. I was thinking about someone."

"That's all right," he says cheerfully. "I'll read it again. —Why do you keep scratching yourself?"

"I'm not scratching myself."

"Not you, Mommy," he giggles. "It's the joke. One guy asks: Why do you keep scratching yourself? And the other guy, the one who is scratching himself all over, says: I'm the only one who knows where it itches. Get it?"

"Yes," I nod vigorously. "Yes."

Why can't I be content trying different brownie recipes and comparing the quality of floor waxes? Why am I haunted by characters who demand to be put on a blank page; characters who make me sit in front of this typewriter and, through an accumulation of letters, blank spaces, periods, and commas, coerce me into making sense of their imagined lives?

137

With the big toe of her right foot she flipped down the lever. In greedy circles the lukewarm water was sucked into the drain. Listening to the gurgling sound, Megan dried herself on the white towel. It was coarse; Nick wouldn't like it. He was particular about the towels she bought. He, who played tennis past exhaustion, whose physical endurance outlasted hers on hikes, who worked for hours in the garden until covered with sweat and dirt, wanted only the softest towels. Thick terry velour. At least he didn't care about the colors, as long as they were solids.

Vigorously she rubbed her arms, her legs. The towel was too small to fit around her. Nick liked towels to cover him. King-size towels. Towels he could wrap around his body. Nick liked . . .

Nick.

She dropped the towel. What time was it? She rushed into the bedroom. Her wristwatch was on the low stand next to the left side of the double bed. Ten-seventeen. She'd have to call. To let him know.

Let him know what?

Where she was.

But where was she? What was the address?

There was no phone in the room. Quickly she put her clothes back on, wishing for a change of underwear.

It was quiet in the house. She hadn't really noticed how

quiet until she walked down the stairs. On the second floor were no lights, but from beneath the door of one of the rooms on the first floor came a thin strip of yellow. Hoping it wasn't the Marcus bedroom, Megan knocked, once.

"Come in," a woman's voice called.

Nina Marcus was sitting on the floor next to a low table with three piles of papers. An open bottle of apple juice and a brown cup stood next to her on the floor. Her horn-rimmed glasses looked too big for her round face. Pushed back from her forehead, her fine blond hair stuck out over her ears, as if she had run her hands through it in exasperation. By the window was a single bed with a batik cover in various shades of blues. Two walls were covered with bookshelves, stacked beyond capacity with vertical and horizontal arrangements of hardcovers and paperbacks, magazines and papers.

"Come in," she said, taking off her glasses. "I was grading papers. But I need a break. Is everything all right with your room?"

Megan nodded.

"How about some apple juice?"

Megan's stomach drew together. "No, thank you. I really should make a phone call. To Connecticut. Collect." For an instant she wondered how Nina Marcus saw her.

"You can use the kitchen phone. Second door to the right." Nina motioned with her head.

"I'm sorry I interrupted you."

"No problem." Nina picked up a felt-tip pen and reached for her glasses.

138

The phone was black and hung on the wall next to the huge refrigerator, a bulky appliance speckled with someone's unsuccessful attempts at covering its dents and rust spots with white spray paint.

What was she going to tell Nick? How could she explain something to him that she didn't understand herself? He'd want to know why she was on Nantucket. She dialed "O." Maybe if she knew what she was doing here, she'd know what to say to him.

"Your name, please?" the operator asked after Megan had given her the number.

"Megan Stone." Her mouth felt dry. She found herself wishing Dagmar were with her.

"Just a moment, please."

She counted six brief, piercing signals before the voice of the operator came back: "I'm sorry, but the line is busy."

"Thank you," she whispered. "I'll try again later."

As she hung up, she felt relieved. At least she had tried. She could always tell Nick she had tried. Quite likely he'd be sitting on the bed by the oak decorator phone his parents had given him for his thirty-third birthday. She could easily picture him in the blue shirt without initials she had suggested this morning when he had asked his predictable: "What should I wear?"

Only this morning?

She could picture his back, the way he held his head, and the way he'd straighten after hanging up the phone. The children would be asleep: Timmy curled, Nicole on her back, her arms flung to her sides. How easy it was to imagine them in any position, three-dimensional: moving or sleeping; close or from a distance. Even friends and people she didn't know well, she could picture if she tried to, in motion or motionless. But then why did she only have a vague mental picture of herself? Flat and vague. Like remembering a photo. One perspective. She knew what her face looked like, yes, but her body? The way she walked? Moved? No. What did she look like standing by the phone, waiting to place her call again? She tried to see herself as others would. But all she perceived were isolated details: the color of her hair, her height, her rounded shoulders (stand up straight, child); she knew her eyes were gray, her hands long and slender. But how did it all fit together? She couldn't even remember the last reflection she'd seen of herself.

Did others experience the same?

Did Nick know what he looked like? From the back? The side? Did he ever attempt to catch his passing image in store windows? And, when seeing himself, did he know what the rest of him looked like at that moment?

Did he want to know?

Nick's and the children's movements she could recognize anywhere. Why couldn't she recognize her own? Once, at the tennis center, she had watched a videotape of Nick and herself playing singles. On film he moved just the way she knew him to move. But her own movements surprised her; not because they were particularly clumsy or graceful, but because they were unfamiliar. Like watching a stranger.

Again, she found herself wondering what she had looked like to Nina Marcus. Although she had only met her today, she could imagine Nina walking, stretching, bending over the papers she was grading.

139

Do you realize that you are at an advantage? That you know something I can't know yet?

You know the length of this book.

You can turn to the last page and say: Aha, there are xyz pages in this novel.

I wish I knew.

140

This time the line was not busy.

"Yes," he answered on the first ring, his voice sounding tight.

She had never heard him say yes on the phone. He always answered with a neutral hello.

"I have a collect call from Megan Stone. Will you—?"

"Yes," he interrupted the operator. "Megan? Megan?"

"Go ahead," the operator said and abandoned Megan to a faint crackling in the line and Nick's voice.

"Megan?" he said. "Megan? . . . Please . . ."

She swallowed, thinking she should say: I'm sorry; or: Please, don't be upset; or: I didn't mean to worry you; or: Don't be—

"We never play chess anymore," she heard herself say.

"Are you all right?"

"I'm sorry."

"Where are you?"

"I didn't mean to say that. About playing chess, I mean."

"Just tell me where you are. Please?" His voice sounded as though he were leaning over the phone, afraid she'd hang up without telling him where she was.

"Nantucket."

"Where?"

"I took a plane," she said, feeling terribly ineffective in trying to explain. "To Nantucket."

"Are you alone?"

She almost laughed. What a question.

"Are you?"

"Of course."

"What did the old bitch say to make you do this?"

"Aunt Judy?"

"Who else?"

"Nothing. I don't know. It's just that . . ."

"What?"

"I had to be by myself."

"But why?"

"I wish I knew," she said miserably. "Maybe if I understood it, I could tell you why."

He didn't answer.

"I'm sorry," she said. It seemed the only appropriate thing to say.

"Why didn't you call me sooner?"

"I tried. A little while ago. But the line was busy."

"Why are you doing this to me?"

"I'm not doing this to you." She leaned against the side of the refrigerator, felt its humming vibrations against her back. "It's something I need to do for myself."

"And it doesn't matter to you how it affects the children and me?"

"I'm sorry."

"Stop saying that. Don't you see . . ." He stopped. "Listen, I didn't mean to yell at you. It's just that . . . There's so much that could have happened to you. I didn't even know if you were still alive. Just tell me where you are staying."

"A guest house. I don't know the name of the street. But the people who own it are called Marcus. They're teachers and—"

"You have the phone number?"

"It's right here. 228-5847."

"You want me to come out there?"

"No," she said quickly.

He didn't say anything.

"Nick?"

"Yes."

"What if I stayed for a few days?"

"How long?" His voice sounded clipped.

"I don't know. A few days."

"But why? Did I do anything to hurt you?"

"No. I just need time to think."

"About what? Are you leaving me?"

"You sound so angry. I wish I could explain it better than this. It's not because of anything you did. But I need time to myself."

"Is there someone else?"

She shook her head and then realized he couldn't see that. "No," she said.

"You know, your aunt is still in Boston, trying to find out what happened to you. We've called the police and reported you missing."

"I'm sorry," she said miserably. Instead of simplifying her life, she was creating new conflicts, obstacles to overcome, explanations . . .

"I'll call her," Nick said quickly, his voice changing, becoming warmer, almost pleading. "Don't worry about her. And I promise not to give her your phone number. I'll also talk to the police. Only . . . Megan? Can't you tell me why you did this?"

"I will. As soon as I know."

"I love you," he said fiercely. "You know that, don't you?"

She cupped the receiver with her left hand. "Yes."

He didn't say anything, but she could hear him breathe as if he were waiting for her to say she loved him too.

"How are the children?" she asked.

"You mean to tell me you actually care?"

She felt a sudden stinging behind her eyes. She would not cry, even if—

"I didn't mean that. I'm sorry. But I feel so damn helpless. They're both fine. They kept asking for you. What do you want me to tell them?"

"That I'll see them soon."

"Will you?"

"I'll call you tomorrow."

"What's the area code there?"

"617."

"I might take a few days off and stay with the children."

"I'll call you tomorrow. Good night." She hung up before he could say another thing and took a deep breath.

When she got to the bottom of the stairs, the phone began to ring. It was a louder, shriller sound than her phone at home. Her left hand on the smooth wood of the worn banister, she stopped.

"I'll get it." Nina Marcus came from her room and walked into the kitchen. "Yes, she's right here," Megan heard her say. "Hold on." She extended the receiver to Megan as she came to the door. "For you."

"Thank you." Reluctantly, she took it.

"Megan?" Nick's voice sounded uncertain.

"Yes?"

"I thought maybe . . . I mean I could wire you some money. First thing in the morning, if you need it."

"I have my checkbook and credit cards. But thank you."

"At least I know I have the right number," he said, trying to make it sound funny by giving a little laugh. But it sounded forced. "Get some sleep. Okay? I love you."

"Good night, Nick."

141

—I don't think there's enough happening in this manuscript.

—Who asked you, Nick?

—It would speed up the pace if there were no interruptions. Just look at how Mr. Nelson handles plot.

—Don't tell me you'd prefer to have *him* write about you?

—Listen, he's called me twice this week, offering me a role in his latest novel.

—Nick, I'm surprised at you. Haven't I given you

strength of character? Values? Just name two valid reasons why you would want to switch to him.

—He has a publisher and I would get a lot of sex. Need any more reasons?

—No. But I'm disappointed you'd even consider it. I thought in you I had created a sensitive man, a man strong enough to reject the macho image, an intelligent man, a man—

—You really think I'm strong and intelligent?

—Of course I do. Besides, you've become rather special to me. I hate to admit this, but I look forward to your intrusions, regardless of how critical you are.

—And I always thought you considered me a pain in the ass. Really. Don't look so upset. I haven't given old Nelson a definite answer.

—But in Nelson's book you'd just be playing a role, Nick. No more than that, merely a role to fit the plot. In my novel the plot develops from you and the other characters. You have a tremendous influence upon what happens.

—Listen, I could use a break from all this mental agony you choose to put us through. With Megan in Nantucket, it looks as if sex is out of the picture. I definitely would not hold still for a masturbation chapter.

—What do you want? A major catastrophe? A flood? An earthquake?

—I'm not sure my homeowner's insurance covers earthquakes.

—How bourgeois.

—Whatever made me say that? Could you still cut that or change it to something witty?

—Maybe in the final revision. Whatever are your children doing upstairs? It sounds like they're both up, running around.

—Worry about your own children. I'll worry about mine. I'll check on them in a few minutes. But first I want to point something out to you. There is not enough of a distinction between you and Megan, even if she is a lot taller than you. Both of you have a relatively communicative marriage. You're about the same age. And you're both hung up on guilt.

—I don't think it's so unusual that we both feel guilty about things we shouldn't feel guilty about. That fits a lot of women who have children and want to do more than play house. It creates conflicts. But Megan and I are quite different. I don't have red hair. I'm seven inches shorter. I don't have an Aunt Judy (thank God). I'm not an orphan.

—You both have two children.

—What if I changed the number of children? I'd be afraid something terrible would happen if I wrote I had only one child. But what if I gave Megan and you another child or took one away?

—We don't really want another child. And it would be cruel to make us choose between Timmy and Nicole. Actually, it would be impossible—

—Don't get so excited.

—I just won't let you eliminate one of my children. I'd leave for good and take them with me.

—Calm down, Nick. It was only a thought. I didn't mean to upset you. What's that upstairs? Listen. Did you hear that?

—Quiet. That sounds like Nicole.

142

Two at a time, he rushed up the stairs toward the sound of the screaming.

"Daddy, Daddy, she's bleeding." Timmy came running from his sister's room.

Nick almost stumbled over him, trying to get into the room. Stepping across the bat trap, he saw Nicole, her face covered with blood. Her arms stiff against her body, she was standing next to the bed, her mouth open, her eyes huge with terror. Quickly he was by her side and lifted her, attempting to quiet her and to check the injury. Timmy was explaining what had happened, but Nicole's screams made it impossible to understand him.

"Hurry. Get some ice cubes from the freezer," Nick said. "First get me a towel. A clean one."

The blood was matting her tight curls to her skin and darkening them; it seemed to be pulsating from her forehead; since it was all over her face, it was hard to tell. Timmy came running with a light blue towel. When Nick tried to press it against her forehead, she began to thrash and scream even louder. Finally, he pulled her to the floor with him and sat her down across his legs. While he tried to stop the bleeding by pressure, he also cleaned the blood from her face with a corner of the towel.

"Go get the ice," he told Timmy, who was standing next to him and watching, his blue eyes wide, his lower lip indrawn.

He turned and ran from the room.

"Here, Nicole, I'll be very careful. You'll be all right. I know it hurts."

He tried to calm her, but she was panicky and would not let him wipe the blood from her eyes. He wondered what her world looked like, covered with this violent film of red. Carefully lifting the blood-soaked towel, he saw a gash in her forehead of at least two inches. Already the skin around it was beginning to swell, pushing the red wound forward like an obscene grin. For an instant he felt incredibly angry. This wouldn't have happened if Megan had stayed home instead of running off. This was what she deserved for shirking her responsibilities. He had a brief vision of her expression when he'd call to tell her about the accident. But as he saw Nicole's face, pale beneath the bright blood, he already felt uncomfortable at his thoughts. This would have happened regardless of who was taking care of the children. If anyone was responsible, it was he. He should have checked earlier when he heard the running and jumping.

It was frightening how much blood could well up from a head wound.

"How did it happen? Please, can't you tell me?"

She shook her head, sobbing wildly.

"Daddy. The ice." Timmy was back with the ice tray.

"I only need two pieces. Here, hold the towel for a minute. Like that. Good. Press against it, Timmy. Gently." With one hand Nick reached for his handkerchief. It was clean. Unfolding it, he took two pieces of ice from the tray and wrapped them into the handkerchief.

"Don't touch it," Nicole screamed when he applied the cold compress to the gash.

"Just for a little while. Please? It'll make it better."

"Is she gonna die?" Timmy asked fearfully.

"Of course not," Nick snapped.

Timmy's mouth began to quiver.

"I'm sorry," Nick said. "She'll be fine. Can you tell me now how this happened?"

"It was an accident, Daddy."

"But how did it happen?"

Nicole's crying was becoming more steady, and she stopped struggling against the ice.

"Nicole was jumping up and down on her bed. So I went in her room and jumped too. And then we were running from the door and jumping on her bed, and I got the farthest. And then we bounced some more and did it again. And then Nicole fell down and cried. And then I saw the blood." He pointed to an area in front of the bed.

Nick noticed some blood on the metal frame supporting the mattress. At the thought of Nicole falling and hitting her head against the hard metal, he flinched. Cautiously, he lifted the ice from her forehead. She sniffled and began to suck the middle finger of her left hand. At the thought of the ordeal awaiting her, he was overcome by a queer mixture of pity and nausea: the gash looked quite deep; it would require stitches.

Her body felt limp and heavy when he got up with her in his arms.

143

Five-forty-five A.M.
July. School vacation. Impossible to find a three-hour block of writing this time of year. Although I try to get up early, aiming for five and making it by six, my children usually are up within an hour, wanting attention and/or breakfast. My husband is home this week. He doesn't understand why my three hours must be consecutive. He asks me why I can't write one hour in the morning, one in the afternoon, and one at night. I tell him it takes half an hour or more to get back into my material, that every interruption sets me back.

Will I ever get this damn book finished?

144

—You will. Just listen.
—I wish I were as certain about it as you, Megan. Do you have any idea how difficult it even was to write you out of that bathtub?
—It certainly took you long enough.
—I had a feeling you were getting a little impatient when I left you sitting there in the lukewarm water, holding several loose ends in your hands. What I need now is a good ending. You know what I read once?
—Tell me.
—Wer schreibt mir einen guten Schluss?

—Very impressive. But what does it mean?

—Who'll write me a good ending? Günter Grass asked it in his novel *Katz Und Maus (Cat and Mouse)*. I wish I had written that sentence. I was thinking earlier of all the books that used to end in death or marriage. But you are already married, and I don't intend to kill you off to leave the reader with a feeling of completion.

145

Nick was driving too fast. He knew he was driving too fast. Strapped in the seat next to him with a seat belt, his daughter whimpered. Before rushing out of the house, he had pulled snowsuits over the children's sleepers.

"Is she gonna die?" asked Timmy from the back.

"I've already told you—"

"But what if all the blood comes out of her head?"

"That can't happen. Nicole will be fine. The doctors will make her head feel better." Perhaps he should have left Timmy next door with Sara. His questions could only upset Nicole more than she already was.

"Can I, Daddy?" she was asking.

"I'm sorry, love. I couldn't hear you." He leaned toward her, keeping his eyes on the road. A fine rain was falling.

"Can I get a lillipop, can I, Daddy?"

"She means lollipop," Tim interrupted from the back-seat.

"I know. Yes, you can, Nicole. We'll stop at the drugstore on the way home and buy you a lillipop."

"Lollipop," Timmy said. "Can I have one too?"

"Sure."

Nicole sniffled and slipped her finger into her mouth. Nick glanced at her forehead; it looked as though the bleeding had stopped. The three Band-Aids he had cut into butterflies were holding the gash together.

"How about lillipops *and* M&M's?" she mumbled.

"We'll see." He was going to buy her what she wanted, regardless of Megan's conviction that it was wrong to ease pain with food, that it formed bad habits because children learned to reach for food as consolation and ended up fat adults. Since he was the one taking care of the children, he would damn well buy them what he wanted to. What could be wrong with giving Nicole some candy after she got the stitches? It gave him an odd satisfaction to think of taking the children to the drugstore afterwards, to let each pick out three or four different candies. He'd call Megan from the hospital to tell her about the accident. Probably it was too late for her to get a plane out of Nantucket tonight; but there should be an early flight in the morning. She'd never take off like that again after seeing what could happen.

146

Through the double aluminum doors of the emergency room he carried his daughter, aware of Timmy following closely.

> ALL PATIENTS MUST
> SIGN IN HERE FIRST
> ———————————→

Following the direction of the arrow, he turned right and found other signs with arrows until, around the corner, he came upon a waist-high desk with an IBM typewriter and a black pigeonhole rack. Behind the desk sat a tired-looking woman with short blond hair and bony shoulders that showed through the material of her orange cardigan.

"Yes?" She looked up from a legal-size pad with a column of figures.

"My daughter had an accident and needs some stitches."

"Do you have hospitalization?"

"Blue Cross. Can't that wait? I really want someone to take a look at the cut on—"

"Who is the child's doctor?"

"Dr. Bogan."

She checked a typed schedule. "He's on call tonight."

"Can I watch TV, Daddy?" Timmy asked, pointing to a black-and-white set on a high corner shelf in the waiting room, which was empty, except for a pale, elderly man with a large bruise on his right cheek. Holding a red handbag against his buttoned corduroy jacket, he sat stiffly on a chair across from the TV, staring at the hazy screen.

"Yes," Nick said impatiently.

The receptionist hung up the phone. "Dr. Bogan is on his way," she said without looking at Nick. "You have your Blue Cross number?"

Shifting Nicole to his right arm, he pulled his wallet from his left back pocket, laid it down on the desk and opened the plastic credit card section, flipping past snapshots of Megan and the children to his hospitalization card.

Nicole began to cry. Her pale hair looked dark where it clung to her temples.

He kissed her wet cheek.

From the pigeonhole rack the woman pulled a blank form, inserted it in her typewriter, and, asking questions rapidly, began to type. She seemed to be possessed by an insatiable desire (an unacceptable cliché only in sex scenes) to fill each blank space on the form. Finally she pulled it out of the IBM and gave Nick a copy.

"Go down to the end of the hall and give it to one of the nurses at the station."

"Timmy, let's go," he called to his son, who had settled in the chair next to the gray-haired man and was watching Bette Davis light a cigarette.

"Do I have to?" Timmy's blue eyes didn't leave the screen. His hair covered his earlobes. He needs a haircut, Nick thought.

Bette Davis inhaled and tossed back her head.

Surprisingly, the receptionist lifted her head. "Why don't you leave him. I'll watch him."

"Thank you," Nick said, noticing that her eyes were an unusual shade of blue, almost violet.

Two nurses were sitting at the station, one of them drinking Energade from a can and working on a crossword puzzle, the other arranging small, pleated paper cups on a metal tray. To her he handed his copy of the form; she gave it to the nurse with the Energade.

"You want to come with me?" She got up and walked toward a door with a large "2" on it. Holding the door open, she let Nick pass her.

In the middle of the room stood a table, partially covered with a white sheet. He laid Nicole on it, and opened the drawstring of her hood.

"How did it happen?" the nurse asked and began filling out a new form.

While Nick gave her a brief account of how Nicole had hurt herself, he took off the snowsuit, careful not to touch her forehead.

"You're a very brave little girl." The nurse came over to the table and took a look at the cut.

"I'm not little." Nicole sat up.

"Of course not. I'm sorry. How old are you? You must be close to—"

"Three. But I'll be four soon. Will I be four soon, Daddy?"

Nick nodded.

"That's pretty old," the nurse said, taking two trays wrapped in green cotton towels from a white glass-front cabinet next to the window. She brought them over to the low table next to where Nicole was sitting, watching her.

When she opened them and Nicole saw the instruments, she began to cry.

"Dr. Bogan will be here shortly." The nurse left the room.

"I want to go home." Nicole tried to climb off the table, crying.

"I know. I know." Kneeling next to the table to block her way, Nick laid his face against the top of her head. Her fine curls were tangled and smelled salty. "You know what?"

"What?" she sobbed.

"I don't even know your favorite color lillipop."

"Lollipop." She sniffled, twice. "Purple," she said slowly. "And red too."

147

My youngest son has been up all night with what he calls the *throwups*. He pronounces it like a more productive case of hiccups. This morning I feel too tired to write. Still, I sit down at my desk.

—Why don't you go back to bed. Don't write for a day.

—If I don't write today, Megan, I might find a reason not to write tomorrow and the day after. Sometimes I wonder if perhaps there is some truth to films and books that say I can't have *both*, my family and my writing. What if someday I have to decide between them?

—Would it be as difficult as deciding which of your children you'd save if your boat turned over in the middle of a lake and you were the only adult with them?

—That's different. I'd never sacrifice one for the other. I'd find a way to save *both*. One could swim on my back, the other next to me. They'd take turns as they got tired. I taught them how to swim when they were babies.

—Can't you do that with your writing?

—How?

—Maybe if you stopped punishing yourself . . .

—For what?

—For *wanting* both.

148

"What do we have here?" Pink-skinned, short, and yellow-haired, Dr. Bogan rushed in, tiny beads of moisture on his smooth forehead and upper lip. Briefly nodding to Nick, he hurried to the sink. Over his left shoulder he winked at Nicole while briskly soaping his hands. "This is pretty late for you to be still up, young lady, isn't it?"

Her mouth quivered as though she were undecided between smiling and crying.

Nick placed his hands on her shoulders.

Dr. Bogan dried his hands and pulled on whitish rubber gloves, mumbling something about the last shipment being too tight. Stepping next to Nicole, he gently probed the wound with his fingertips. "Don't seem to be any bone chips in here."

She screamed.

Firmly, Nick held her shoulders.

The nurse returned with two young men in light blue shirts with patches on their left upper sleeves. They wore dark blue trousers with black belts and black, shined shoes. The one with the crew cut and the blond mustache had on white socks. The other was almost a head shorter, and his brown hair covered his ears.

Dr. Bogan said something, but Nick couldn't understand him.

"What?" he asked.

"Firemen," the doctor shouted. "They're doing their emergency training here." He looked up, shaking his head, and reached to adjust the angle of the two high-intensity lights above the table. They were round and chrome-plated with handles on both sides. From one of the trays he took a small clear bottle, shook it, and broke off the pulltop tab, exposing a reddish rubber diaphragm. He picked up a square piece of gauze and motioned to the nurse, who handed him an open bottle of alcohol. Setting the gauze on top of the bottle, he turned it upside down and saturated the gauze pad. Sweet and strong, the smell of alcohol tinged the air. With the gauze Dr. Bogan wiped off the diaphragm. The dark-haired fireman passed him a syringe from the tray, and the nurse closed the alcohol bottle, whispered something to Dr. Bogan, and left the room. Holding the small clear bottle upside down, the doctor shoved the needle into the rubber diaphragm and slowly filled the syringe. Nicole's crying had almost stopped. Fascinated, she watched. The blond fireman was rubbing his left wrist and looking at the floor.

"This isn't only a local. It also reduces the bleeding," Dr. Bogan explained to Nick as he set the needle down on the tray and unfolded a white cloth with a hole in its center.

"I can't see," Nicole complained as he set it over her face, the hole exposing the gash.

"You will. In a minute." Swiftly, he began to roll the cloth up from the bottom, uncovering her mouth, then her nose and right eye.

Nicole blinked.

"Nice job," he commented as he removed the three butterflies from the wound. Holding the cloth down with his left hand, he reached for the syringe and gently put the needle in the open wound, squirting and

149

I can't do this chapter. Dammit, I can't even watch someone getting a needle on TV without cringing and drawing my arms close to myself. How did I get into this mess? Why did Nicole have to get hurt? Why do I have to go through this detailed description of her getting sewn up? I don't want to. I'd rather clean the stove, fold laundry . . .

Why doesn't someone intrude? Anyone. Please? Even you, Mr. Nelson. Where are you? Nick? How come you're so quiet? Even my husband and sons aren't home. I don't want to do this. Someone . . . anyone . . . please interrupt.

Megan? Megan? Talk to me, please. I'd much rather write about you. What if I came to Nantucket and joined you and we both forgot about this book? Skinny Bogan is standing here with that damn needle, waiting for me to write how he sews up your daughter, and you aren't even listening to me. You don't even know what happened. And I feel too miserable to describe it in any more detail. I just want to get it over with. I still can't understand what you ever saw in Bogan. To me he looks sadistic, the way he stands there with that needle

150

squirting and drawing it from one end of the wound to the other as if he were gluing the wing of a model airplane.

Still holding the cloth in place with his left hand, he turned to Nick. "We'll let that sit for a minute so it can take effect."

"You want me to hold that, sir?" the short fireman asked.

Bogan nodded and let the fireman stand next to him. "A little more over here," he suggested, moving his hand.

The fireman grinned at Nicole. His partner walked over to the sink.

"How's that?" Carefully, Bogan probed the wound with his bony fingers.

Nicole's screams skipped a beat.

Nick held her down.

Reaching for the syringe, Dr. Bogan repeated the process so painfully described earlier. He opened a blister pack containing a curved needle with a thread already attached to it. Studying the writing on the page, he frowned. "I guess this is the right size," he finally said. "First I thought it looked a little big." From the tray he took forceps and gripped the needle with its jaw about midway. As he placed his left hand on the cloth, the fireman withdrew his hand. Using the forceps, the doctor inserted the needle into one side of the wound.

Nick could feel the muscles in his daughter's shoulders and arms as she struggled to get out from under the needle. He held her down. The fireman had her by the legs. From the sink came a thudding sound. Dr. Bogan was saying something, but Nicole's screeching was so loud that Nick couldn't hear him. He saw the point of the needle coming up on the opposite side as Dr. Bogan pulled it through.

"I'd better use some more anesthetic before we proceed," he said, tying a knot. "Look at that," he said to Nick, motioning with his chin toward the sink.

Over his shoulder Nick could see that the blond fireman with the white socks had fainted.

151

—What a cop-out. What a lousy, lousy cop-out.

—Who asked you, Dr. Bogan?

—You can't stand the sight of it, and you react by making one of the firemen faint. Just because you don't have the stomach for it.

—Why don't you take care of your patient instead of ranting at me?

—Classical case of transferring inability to cope with a

situation to another individual. Very interesting that you'd choose a man to faint. I'll have to mention this to my colleague. Have you met Dr. Buchheim? A devout Freudian. He's still looking for case studies to use in his book on transference. He'd be fascinated by your symptoms. They even show in other areas, especially when you let this poor child here get hurt.

—What are you talking about?

—You really don't know? Tell me, why do you think Nicole got hurt?

—Because she was jumping, of course, and hit her head.

—And because her parent wasn't watching her?

—I guess so.

—Don't you see? One parent's child gets hurt, while another parent's child, your child, does *not* get hurt. You really should talk to Dr. Buchheim about his theory on superstitious transference. It's fascinating.

152

He cut off the knot with surgical scissors and picked up the syringe again, lifting the flaps of skin on both sides of the wound as he drew it from one end to the other.

"You're being a very good little girl," he said to Nicole.

Nick felt helpless. He bent close to her ear. "It's almost over."

"I want to go home," she screamed. "I want Mommy."

Motioning to Nick to hold her down, Dr. Bogan picked up the forceps and finished sewing her up quickly, making seven more knots. After inspecting the skin closely, he turned to Nick. "I want to make sure it meets nicely so that it'll heal with a minimum of visibility." He reached for a white aerosol can and sprayed the cut. "This will seal it to keep it from getting infected. It also helps to heal."

It reminded Nick of the clear lacquer he used to spray

wooden models with as a boy. He never painted them; he liked the look of the natural wood; the clear lacquer always was the finishing touch.

"Calling Dr. Buchheim. Calling Dr. Buchheim," the tired voice of the receptionist came across the intercom.

Dr. Bogan nodded to the short fireman, who let go of Nicole's legs and rushed over to the sink. Pushing the white trash can with the chrome lid aside, he began shaking his partner's shoulder.

"Hey, Fred. Come on. Come on, Fred."

Dr. Bogan peeled the cloth off Nicole's forehead. There were a few bloodstains around the opening. "Give me both your hands. Good. Now swing your legs down here and sit up."

She followed his directions, letting herself be pulled into a sitting position.

"Christ." Fred was sitting up, shaking his head. "I didn't, did I? Tell me I only imagined—"

"Listen, it's all right," his partner said. "Really. Right, doctor?"

"Sure," Dr. Bogan said, pulling off the surgical gloves. One of them he dropped on a tray, the other he brought up against his lips. Gathering the opening with one hand, he began to blow into it. Its milky whiteness turned transparent as the rubber extended, the fingers sticking out stiffly like an engorged cow's udder. With a flat piece of white string he tied it and handed it to Nicole. "Can't let you leave here without a balloon."

"Christ," Fred groaned, trying to get up. "The second time this week. How can—"

"Don't worry about it, Fred," Dr. Bogan said. He turned to Nick. "She should be fine. Bring her back in seven days so I can take out the stitches. But come to the office"—he lowered his voice—"not to the emergency room. The rates are too high here."

153

Not until he was almost home did he realize that he had forgotten to call Megan from the hospital. Maybe it was better this way. Sure, she would have returned immediately, but would she have come back for the right reason? How long would it have taken before she felt again the need for time to sort things out?

Nicole, rapturous with the obscene-looking balloon, was quiet on the drive home. A quick stop at the drugstore supplied her and Tim with more candy than they usually got in a month.

In her room, he helped Nicole to take off her snowsuit and boots while Timmy took care of his own. Next to her bed, on the floor, was still the ice tray where he had left it; it was full of water.

"Time for bed. You two better sleep real fast so you can catch up on all the sleep you've missed."

"Where's Mommy?" Timmy asked.

"I don't want to sleep in my room," Nicole said. "Can I sleep in your bed, Daddy?"

"I want to sleep in your bed too. Can I? Can I?" Timmy was jumping around on one foot.

"Stop it," Nick said.

"Please, Daddy?" Nicole tried.

For a moment he hesitated. "All right," he finally said. "But only for tonight."

Timmy ran and jumped on the bed.

"No." Nick held his daughter's arm as she tried to follow her brother's example. "That's how your accident happened."

Timmy crawled under the blanket and pulled it over his face. Nick could hear him giggle, could see the small body wiggling under the covers.

"No jumping. Do you understand me?" He pulled the blanket back.

Timmy grinned and nodded. Nicole climbed in next to him on Megan's side of the bed, and Nick tucked them in.

"How are you feeling?" he asked Nicole.

"Can I have my balloon?"

"It might pop if you rolled over on it."

"You can tie it to the headboard," Timmy suggested.

Both watched as he fastened the string of the glove. It bobbed above their heads.

"I wish I had one," Timmy sighed.

"Maybe if you cut your head . . ." Nicole started helpfully.

"Good night, you two," Nick said. "I'll be back up in a little while."

"Can you leave the light on?" Nicole asked.

He pulled the string of the 40W closet bulb and closed the folding doors partly; only a narrow beam fell yellow across the carpet and bed.

154

Carrying the ice tray down the stairs, he realized how tired he was. Relief, apprehension, anger—they all had solidified into a heavy numbness that made him move slowly, indifferently. In the dark kitchen he dropped the tray into the sink. To turn on the light would require too much of an effort. He opened the refrigerator, staring at the contents. On the second shelf from the top were four cans of Pepsi; he reached for one of them, twisting it downward to free it from the plastic rings that held the cans together.

The phone rang.

"Where have you been?" Aunt Judy's voice bounced into his left ear before he had a chance to say hello. "I've been trying to get you all evening."

"I had to leave the house for a while."

"Do you have any idea how late it is?"

"No." He opened the Pepsi and took a drink.

"What if Megan had called? Do you know how often I've checked back with the police? If you ask me, they're just about the rudest, most incomp—"

"She's all right."

"Megan? Is she home with you?"

"No. She needs to be alone for a few days."

"What are you talking about?"

"She called. Earlier. There's nothing to be concerned about. Why don't you—"

"Do you have any idea how worried I've been?"

"Could you call the police and tell them that she's been found?"

"Yes. Just a minute." There was a pause. "I got my pen. What's her phone number?"

"I'm sorry. But I don't think that's such a good idea."

"You don't want me to talk with her? Where is she?"

He felt relieved at the distance between West Hartford and Boston.

"I insist you tell me."

"I can't. Why don't you check out tomorrow morning and drive back home? I really appreciate all you—"

"I want to talk to her. I insist."

"I'm sorry." He flinched as the receiver was slammed down on the other side.

155

Megan woke to the sound of rain against her window. Driven by the erratic wind in gusts, it whipped sharply against the glass, followed by sudden silence.

A shutter rattled.

She lay still. Her first memory was of her phone call, of the hurt in Nick's voice. Despite the strange bed, she had slept well, had slept through the night instead of waking intermittently as usual when in an unfamiliar bed. She couldn't even remember any dreams. Had Nick slept as deeply? And the children, were they up by now, asking Nick what they should wear, trying to charm him into making French toast?

She yawned. An entire bed to herself. Nobody climbing in with her, pulling the blanket from her, talking at her. Maybe she'd go back to sleep, think later. Much later . . . Clothes. She needed clothes. First of all underwear. Maybe some jeans and a T-shirt. A toothbrush and toothpaste. She could charge her purchases. Breakfast. One of the restaurants might be open for breakfast. If they accepted American Express, she wouldn't even have to cash a check. But maybe it would be better to stop at the bank and establish—

She sat up, shaking her head. There, she was doing it again: making plans. If she didn't stop it, she'd lose the day running errands. What she needed to do with her time was think. Once, years ago, Beth-Anne McCarthy, a friend of Aunt Judy's, had canceled a visit to their house. "I'm taking this morning to sort out my life," she had said on the phone.

To Megan it had sounded absurd, like an extended form of New Year's resolution. How could anyone choose a day to evaluate a life? According to Aunt Judy, Mrs. McCarthy did it twice a year and thought it necessary; she believed that everyone should take the time to sort out what was important from what wasn't, that people would be better adjusted if they did.

Listening to a shutter rattling from the same direction as earlier, Megan wondered if Mrs. McCarthy still chose mornings to evaluate her life. Did she mark the day ahead of time on her calendar? What did she write? Sorting-out day? Evaluation day? Or did she do it spontaneously and cancel all plans? How did she go about it? Itemize her life on a sheet of white paper with a red line down the center?

Assets and liabilities? Was there a total of both columns at the bottom of the page, indicating a profit or loss? And how about depreciation? Worn-down feelings, were they written off? Did Beth-Anne McCarthy cross out what she wanted to discard? Check off the items, one by one? Add new perspectives? Long-range goals?

If only it were this easy. It sounded too contrived to work for her. How much easier it would be to make a list for Nick. His noncommittal attitude would be No. 1 under liabilities, his reluctance to give advice even when asked for it. He'd probably place it under assets and label it tolerance.

156

It was not a pig's bladder. Neither was it a malignant growth, glob of suet, creative pillow, Midwestern-Chinese musical instrument, unusual soap carving, rare fungus, or lump of leftover foam insulation.

It was a glove.

A surgical glove.

Shriveled to handsize, it looked limp and waxen as it dangled ghostly above the heads of the sleeping children.

157

Softly, Megan's stomach rumbled. She sat up, propping the pillow against the headboard. How could she feel hungry at a time like this? Thinking about her life should be more important than thinking about food, although a cheese omelet certainly would be nice. Usually she didn't even like to eat anything until late in the morning. Why then did she feel so hungry? She had only eaten . . . When? At the restaurant with Aunt Judy? She must have eaten after that. But she hadn't. At least there was a reason for her hunger.

Furiously, the wind jabbed the rain, again and again, a thousand needles against the window. Not the best of mornings to climb up the stairs to the widow's walk and gaze toward Wauwinet and the Great Point Light as forecast in Chapter 127. Another expectation flattened.

Comfortable in the warm bed, she didn't feel terribly tempted to set out in search of clothing and food, those irritating necessities distracting her from the evaluation of her life.

158

"Maybe I *will* go away for a few days," I tell my husband at the dinner table.

"Where are you going?" My youngest son asks.

"Can I come along?" The other one wonders.

"You guys stay home with me," my husband says. "This is just for your mother." He looks at me. "Where are you thinking of going?"

"Maybe Maine. I might drive up the coast, find a place by the water. That isn't too far. I'd be back quickly in case of an emergency."

"What emergency?"

"I don't know, but just in case . . ."

"There won't be any emergency."

"Wonderful. Still . . ."

"Why don't you fly to Bermuda?"

"By myself?"

"You've wanted to go there for some time now; and I've been there already."

"I'll go," our oldest son says. He loves to travel.

I'd have to make sure enough food was in the house. The laundry should be done the day before I left.

Baby-sitting arrangements. Sheets and towels. A large bag of dog food. A list of—

"I could take a week off and stay home with the children," he says.

"You have this all planned out, haven't you?"

"Why don't you go to a travel agency? Look at some brochures."

159

It felt good to be walking through the cobblestone streets without anyone making demands on her time: there were no schedules to meet, no meals to prepare; although, feeling the damp rain cool on her face and hair made Megan wish for her beige hooded raincoat back in the hall closet at home. Breakfast she took in the almost empty dining room of an old hotel in the center of town. She ordered a cheese omelet with home fries, cranberry juice, coffee, and English muffins, which she spread generously with rosehip jam.

By the window two men in suits sat talking and eating. The younger had a black attaché case on the floor next to his chair; twice he bent to open it and pulled out papers which he showed to the other man. Like an insurance salesman he moved his hands with important and convincing gestures. The only other people in the dining room were a man and woman in their late fifties or early sixties, eating slowly, saying a word or two now and then, nodding occasionally in the manner of people who have sat across from one another so many times that each step of their daily ritual has become established, predictable, until nothing much needed to be said between them.

From the corner table she had chosen, Megan felt almost invisible as she observed them.

A man came into the dining room. His dark blue windbreaker—

160

". . . was open, revealing his broad chest. He had an intelligent face and hazel eyes. His teeth were large and uneven with a gap in front. Megan recognized him immediately, the cabdriver from the day before. Forcefully, he slid into the booth next to her. She swallowed, her heart throbbing with painful ecstasy, as he pressed his muscular thigh against hers. She shuddered when his strong hand masterfully—"

—No, Mr. Nelson. No more.

—Don't be so sensitive. You women writers—

—No more. This is my book. I won't listen to you.

161

—Congratulations. You actually did it, told the old goat to get off.

—Thank you, Megan. Does that mean you actually approve?

—Don't start looking for *my* approval. You'd be going in the wrong direction. But, yes, this time I do approve. I only wish you had kept him out all the other times. There are so many other voices you could have listened to instead, strong voices, voices of other women who write.

—But I didn't ask him to intrude. He forced his way into the novel.

—As long as you won't let him back in.

—I won't. Even if he tries. And I won't be polite about it. Tell me, that man with the blue windbreaker, who is he?

—You're asking me?

—Why not?

—Well, I think you have the usual options here. You can either develop him into a major character, examine his life through flashbacks and stream of consciousness, give him a few distinctive traits, have the reader identify with him, throw in a few complications that would connect him in some farfetched way to me, turn him into Y.L. with the only slightly callused soles (and you thought I wouldn't recall); or you could make him a walk-on, an old man, say, who just looks around the dining room as if searching for someone and then, with a shrug of his sagging shoulders —how's that: "sagging shoulders"?—leaves. The reader might feel a little sorry for him but will forget him by the end of the chapter.

—I'll go with the second option. I don't need any more characters. All I want is to get to the end of this novel. I might go away by myself when I'm finished.

—Where to?

—Maybe Bermuda. I don't know yet. I'm going to a travel agency this afternoon to look at some brochures.

—Won't you miss us when you're finished with this book?

—Miss you? I don't think so. I'll be very relieved. Last night I had an idea for my next novel, just the story; I haven't thought of the characters yet. Imagine, Megan, a story line I can hang on to like a rope. Writing this is too much like climbing the Eiger without a rope: too unpredictable. I'm so tired of constantly having to invent. What I want to write next is a book where I can *see* where I'm climbing, where I can set foot into crevices found by others.

—You'd be bored before you got to page 52.

—Maybe. But right now it sounds tempting. Safe. None of my new characters would interfere with *my* life. I might even know what happens at the end. What the hell am I going to do with you, Megan?

—What you usually do when you get stuck: work on a poem or a very short story to give you the illusion of actually finishing something.

162

She paid for her breakfast at the table.

The drugstore was only half a block away. Crossing the road, she noticed there was hardly any traffic. Two years ago, the summer week they had spent on Nantucket, the line of cars had been winding slowly—much slower than the hundreds of rental bicycles with wicker baskets in front of the handlebars—through the narrow streets, past the brick or clapboard houses with hydrangea bushes in their small front gardens. Now the island was almost deserted, the washed blue of the circle blossoms dormant until next summer. For almost a month after coming home from vacation, she had tried to find a nursery in Connecticut that carried hydrangea bushes. She would have liked to plant four of them between the shrubs in front of her house, had even pictured how they would look; but nobody carried them.

Entering the drugstore, she shook her hair and felt beads of rain run down her neck. On the left side of the middle aisle she found toothpaste, Crest, and a blue toothbrush. At the end of the same aisle she picked up a bottle of Johnson's Baby Shampoo. She always used the same bottle as the children. Nick probably would forget to wash their hair, and they certainly wouldn't remind him. Especially Timmy. He hated to get his hair washed every other night. And Nicole's hair needed to be combed out while still wet so it wouldn't tangle. Maybe she should call home and remind Nick. Or write a letter. But that would take too long. She should get some stationery though, just in case, a pad of white paper, linen finish. And envelopes. A pen she had in her handbag.

Next to the checkout counter was a shelf with foam-rubber animals, sponge puppets shaped like alligators, rabbits, frogs, and dinosaurs. A woman with a brown raincoat was paying for two packs of Silva Thins and a newspaper. Waiting by her side was a small girl whose hair was curly and blond, a shade darker than Nicole's. She almost stretched out her hand to touch the child's hair, and although she quickly pushed her hand into the pocket of her jacket, she felt she knew its texture as if she had brushed it every day.

163

—Why didn't you, Megan?

—How? Can you see me ask: May I please touch your daughter's hair?

—Strangers used to touch your children's hair without ever asking.

—I never liked it.

—Why didn't you tell them?

—I guess I didn't want to upset them. Saleswomen in department stores were the worst offenders. It always seemed like creating an unnecessary scene. Now I think I would. I'd just tell them, politely, not to touch my child's hair. You think I wouldn't?

—I wouldn't be surprised if you did.

164

In a clothing store a block away she bought a yellow rain poncho and a sweatshirt, orange, the only one in her size with long sleeves and without a map of the island printed across the front. She picked up underwear, two pair of socks, and almost—but she resisted—a dark blue Van Heusen shirt that would have gone beautifully with Nick's gray suit. She charged her purchases and wore the poncho out of the store.

The rain rolled off the slopes formed by her shoulders and arms circled around packages. After stopping at the post office to buy stamps, she passed an empty playground. The bright reds, yellows, and blues of the equipment glistened like wet paint. Timmy would like the monkey bars, while Nicole would head for the small merry-go-round.

Damn.

Why couldn't she see things through her own eyes?

Why was everything she saw filtered through the awareness that Nick and the children were not with her?

165

"I want to ask you something." My youngest son stands by the study door.

"Not now. I'll be finished in a little while." He knows he shouldn't interrupt me. I'm right in the middle of a first draft. *Megan, the next step would be to—*

"But I'm scared. About the house."

"What about the house?" I turn my swivel chair to face him.

He climbs on my lap. How heavy he's getting. "Is our house gonna sink?"

"Houses don't sink." Instantly I remember a documentary about West Coast mudslides. "At least not around here." *Next should be Megan's afternoon in her room, trying to—*

"But I'm afraid it's gonna sink through the hole in the rug."

A few days ago we had a minor accident. A high-intensity lamp burned a hole into the dining-room carpet.

"Like the ship." He puts one arm around my neck. His hand feels sticky.

"The *Titanic?*"

He nods. His brother read to him about the *Titanic* last week.

"Houses don't sink."

His nodding becomes vigorous. "There is such a thing of houses sinking like in quicksand."

"There is no quicksand under this house." *The things Megan notices, her awareness of—*

"But I think of it when it's dark."

"It won't sink. Believe me."

Silently, he slides off my knees.

"Close the door, please," I call to him as he leaves the room. *Megan, where were we? Walking past the playground, the bright colors of the play equipment like wet paint.* Does he really believe our house is sinking? Should I have taken more time to . . . *Megan, the rain rolling off her yellow poncho, her face damp.* The terrors of my own nightmares as a child, so much more vivid than my nightmares now, which I can rationalize. My father, sending me back to my bed: "It's only a dream. Go back to sleep." Back to my dark room, to the threatening shapes I know are waiting for me. *Is our house gonna sink?*

I turn off the desk lamp and get up to find my son.

166

—You know what has been greatly overrated?

—What, Megan?

—Solitude.

—How can you say that?

—Because I'm up to my neck in solitude. I feel smothered by solitude.

—Hey. What's the matter? What happened?

—Nothing happened. Absolutely nothing. All I've done is sit in this room all afternoon, trying to figure out *why* I'm sitting in this room. I've counted the ribs on that damn radiator over there at least twenty times; I could draw the design of the rug with my eyes closed; I've even tried to write a letter to Nick. But I don't know what to say. And even if I did, how would I know I still felt that way by the time he got the letter?

—Why don't you call him instead?

—I've tried. Twice. At five and then again half an hour ago. Nobody answers.

—Maybe they went out to eat.

—You know, all afternoon I've tried to think of *my* life, of what I want and don't want. And of what to do about it. But their faces keep getting in the way. I think of the warmth and softness of the children's skin when they're asleep; of the hurt in Nick's voice when I called him yesterday. I can't seem to separate thoughts about myself from thoughts about them. It's so frustrating.

—Why don't you try calling again?

167

His voice sounded calm, detached. "They're fine," he said. "They're asleep."

"Already? It's only seven."

"They were tired."

"What time did you put them to bed last night?"

"I didn't keep track. Is it important if they go to bed late one night and early the next?"

"I tried to call twice." She tried to untangle the long black phone cord. "Just a minute."

"We only got back half an hour ago. I took them to the Pancake House for dinner."

"I had hoped to talk with them." She wondered if she should ask him to wake the children. But maybe it would be better to wait until tomorrow to call again.

"How long are you going to stay there?"

"I'm not sure."

"Why don't you stay for a week or two?"

With her right forefinger she traced one of the rust spots on the refrigerator where the white spray paint was peeling off. "Are you trying to keep me away? What's the matter?"

"Nothing."

"You're telling me that I *need* one or two weeks?"

"Whatever."

"You're just putting more pressure on me by telling me how long to stay away."

"I'm not putting pressure on you. I want you to be sure you really want to come back."

She didn't answer.

"You know what your problem is?" His voice sounded angry. "That you even think there can be an ideal relationship. There is no such thing. So stop waiting for it. Don't worry if our relationship will be good in five or ten years. Look at it as it is now, not at your fantasies of it."

"Does that mean I have to accept it as it is? What's wrong with trying to make it better?"

"And running away is your idea of making it better?"

"I'm not—"

"I think we have a damn good marriage," he shouted.

"It's too damn predictable."

"And what's wrong with that? You expect your heart to start beating every time I walk into the room?"

"It doesn't."

"You learn what to expect from someone you live with for eight years."

"Nine years."

"Whatever."

"Stop saying 'whatever.' You really want to know what's wrong with being predictable? Every morning I know you'll ask: *What should I wear today?* Do you have any idea how angry I get, lying in bed and knowing you'll ask that again?"

"Maybe you shouldn't be lying in bed. Maybe you should be up, making my breakfast."

"We're back to that? I thought you had accepted by now that I'm not the breakfast-making type."

"Then maybe you should accept that I'm not the clothes-choosing type. Why don't you put them out at night for me? You usually plan everything else ahead of time."

"I only plan things ahead of time because you don't. You're so damn wishy-washy when it comes to making a decision that nothing would ever get done if I didn't plan ahead."

"You don't give me a chance to plan. You rush into decisions; you even make decisions where none are required. Most problems solve themselves if you leave them alone."

"No, they don't. That's another one of your convenient excuses."

"You know, this isn't solving anything. I don't put pressure on you. You do that all by yourself. I don't tell you to visit your aunt or send her thank-you letters; I don't—"

"What about those ghastly employee parties?"

"I've never insisted you come."

"But—" She stopped. He never had insisted. He always had left it up to her. Last time he had even offered to leave early. "All right, so you don't insist. But what about the dinners at your parents' house?"

"I like my parents."

"You make that sound like an accusation."

"I like having dinner with my parents occasionally. What's wrong with that?"

"And once a week is occasionally?"

"Whatever. It doesn't mean you have to come along."

Don't worry, she thought. *I won't.* "Have the children been asking for me?" she said quickly.

"Of course they have."

"I really wish I could talk with them. But I guess if they're asleep . . ."

"You want me to wake them up?"

He was probably asking that because he figured she wouldn't want to interrupt their sleep. Dumping the decision on her again. *You do what you think is right. Let it be upon your shoulders.*

"Well?" he asked.

"I'll call tomorrow," she said quickly.

"I'll be here." Suddenly, he sounded very tired. "Listen, maybe things haven't been perfect. But if there are problems—"

"If?"

"All right. We have problems. But I think they can be solved."

"How?"

"I don't know. But I want it to work. Maybe if we talked . . ."

"Yes, maybe."

"Tomorrow? You'll call?"

"We'll talk tomorrow."

168

—You think he was bluffing?

—About what, Megan?

—Telling me to stay a week or two. You think he really means it? Maybe he feels so sure I'll come back that he can risk bluffing like that.

—He must have a lot of confidence in your relationship. He said he wanted it to work. If he had insisted you come home, you might have resented it.

—I probably would feel pressured.

—At least you don't have to worry about his objections. The last thing you need is a lot of opposition.

—Still, he gets me so angry. Suggesting it so calmly. As if he didn't care.

—You know he cares.

—Stop taking his side.

—What do you expect him to do? Take the next flight to Nantucket and sweep you off your feet?

—You know I don't. Maybe I should stay here the two weeks.

—To see who holds out the longest? An endurance test? You want him to beg you to come home?

—All right. I admit it. I want to go home. I wish I were with Nick and the children right now. At least now I know how important they are to me. Don't you think I want things to work out too? I want to . . . What time's the next plane leaving?

—Why do you have to rush into everything? Even going back. You still don't know what you ran away from.

—From myself? From the pressures I put on myself? Maybe Nick wasn't all that wrong. I do put a lot of pressure on myself. Nobody tells me to do most of the things I feel obligated to do. If someone else demanded all that I ask of myself, I'd probably quit. What if I only did what I wanted to do?

—Do you have to jump from one extreme to the other? Why don't you give yourself some time? There is no need to go back so soon. Isn't it enough for you to know you *want* to be with Nick and your children? Why can't you stay for a few days and enjoy the solitude?

—You and your damn solitude. I'm drowning in it. Why do you want me to stay here? Because it fits into your plot? You have something planned for me for the next few days? I tell you one thing: I'm not going to walk on that wretched beach again. If you think you can—

—Don't get so hostile. The plot develops from you. I'm not forcing you.

—Why don't you go away? You've been talking about

it enough. Why are you still sitting at your desk?

—I am going. I've even made reservations for a week in Bermuda. I'm flying there two months from now. That'll give me plenty of time to finish this book. You know what's strange, though?

—What?

—Now that I know I *can* leave, the urgency is gone. It's almost as if I didn't have to go away, as if just knowing that it's all right to leave is enough. Does that make sense to you?

—I think so.

—And you know what's the hardest thing about it? Letting myself go away. Giving myself the . . . I don't know, permission isn't quite the right word, but it's something close to it. Let me look in the thesaurus. "PERMISSION: leave, allowance, . . . tolerance, . . . freedom, liberty, . . . indulgence, . . . favor, . . . release, . . . open door, . . . authorization, . . . sanction, . . ." All of them close, but not quite it. A mixture of all of them? Maybe it has to do with forgiving myself. Forgiving myself for wanting to leave my family and my writing, saying to myself: It's all right to leave and all right to come back.

—Without punishing yourself for it afterwards?

—I hope so. It might take practice. The first time I might feel a little guilty while I'm away. Who knows, I might even want to ask for a parachute after the plane takes off. But I won't. I'll go and I'll stay for a week.

—Is that why you want me to stick it out here for a whole week?

—No. But it is one of your options. What if you rushed back and in a month or a year you felt like running away again?

—But at least then I'll know that I'm not running from Nick and the children. I can remember that if I ever feel like leaving again. And maybe it won't happen again. Maybe I'll—

—Live happily ever after?

—How tacky. I didn't say that.

—You know, if you learned to accept yourself the way you are, you—

—I do. I've always accepted myself.

—Your height? The color of your hair?

—You want me to pretend I like red hair? That I'm not too tall?

—Too tall for what?

169

This cabdriver was older, quite heavy, with gray hair that struggled to cover his ears, and he didn't talk to her at all on the way to the airport. Taped to his dashboard were pictures cut from magazines: Charlie's Angels, The Fonz, a leopard, Superwoman; to the far right, on the passenger side, two faded color snapshots of family groups.

Carrying yesterday's purchases in the pink plastic bag from the clothing store, Megan was the first passenger to board the small plane. Inside it smelled, strangely enough, from peanuts and bouillon. Sitting down on the worn green vinyl seat, she looked out of the window. Things would be different from now on. They had to be; she'd do something about them. She would demand Nick's involvement, ask for it two or three times if he relied on her to make his decisions.

"Stop nagging," he'd probably say.

"I'm not nagging," she'd remind him. "If you ask me to do something, you consider it a question; if I do, you call it nagging."

She'd tell him to get his own clothes in the morning, and even if he left the house in plaid trousers, a striped shirt, and his old tweed jacket, she wouldn't interfere. One good thing about that combination: he couldn't go wrong in his choice of socks. Maybe she'd give him a crash course some evening in matching his clothes. It might take a week for him to learn, maybe two. But she wouldn't fall back into the convenient trap of making choices for him.

Fastening her seat belt, she leaned back. She thought of Dagmar, alone and content in her room at the nursing home, Dagmar who knew *why* she wanted to be there and felt no need to explain her reasons. Dagmar who could always retreat to the calm center within herself. How she wished she could talk with her. Maybe next week. She'd drive to Boston alone. And she'd wear shoes with rubber soles. The other women, waiting in their rooms for visitors, wouldn't hear her steps on the cold marble floor. The door to Dagmar's room would be open; she'd step behind the silent form, place her hands on the calm shoulders, look out of the window with her, in the same direction. Words would not be necessary; she'd wait until Dagmar wanted to speak.

How she wished she could see Dagmar more often. But Boston wasn't that far from West Hartford. She could easily visit at least once a month if Dagmar let her. And maybe, after some time, her grandmother would agree to move closer. Maybe if she knew how much she was wanted . . .

The engines started.

Megan felt a tight tickling at the bottom of her stomach, not unlike the sensation she sometimes had when returning for a duty visit to the duplex where she had grown up. Aunt Judy would insist on talking to her as soon as she found out she was back. Instead of dreading a confrontation with her aunt or feeling guilty, she suddenly found herself looking forward to the challenge.

She could imagine Aunt Judy's voice on the phone: "If you hadn't set it into your head to run off in Boston and leave me with the responsibility of choosing birthday presents for your children, I would have . . ."

She could hang up on the accusing voice, replace it with silence.

Or she could say: "I refuse to feel guilty."

But Aunt Judy probably wouldn't call; she'd come to the house instead, unannounced, her sensible shoes anchored to the braided doormat. "Don't you think you owe me an explanation about your abominable behavior in Boston?" Pushing her way into the living room.

"I don't want to talk about it."

"I demand an explanation."

"You can't demand anything from me."

"Is this the gratitude I get for all the years I took care of you?"

"Did you *want* to take care of me? Did you enjoy it?"

"I considered it my responsibility."

"But did you want to do it? Did you like me?"

"You always were a difficult child. I thought that once you grew up, you'd become more sensible. But I guess I was wrong."

"Do you know how much I tried to please you? To win your approval? I don't need your approval anymore." She'd leave the room, walk into the den and close the door; a few minutes later she would hear Aunt Judy's car back out of the driveway. Maybe someday they would be able to talk without demands and guilt. But not yet.

The plane lifted.

As she felt the wheels separate from the runway, the tickling in her stomach expanded into a moment of queasiness. She swallowed and it went away. This was always the worst part, taking off; once she was up, she was fine. She looked at her wristwatch. In Boston she'd have fifty minutes to catch the Delta flight to Connecticut. By the time she landed in Hartford, it would be five-thirty. Dusk. Instead of calling Nick from the airport, she'd rent a car and drive home. She'd see the lights in her house from the end of the street, lights in the living room and den, lights in the kitchen, where Nick and the children would be sitting at the table, eating dinner.

She'd knock, once, or maybe she'd walk to the front door, unlock it, quietly, and come in through the living room. There'd be a warm fire in the fireplace, toys on the rug in front of it. Standing in the kitchen door, she'd look at them for a few moments. Then Timmy would notice her. Jumping up from the table, he'd run to her, and she'd kneel down, catching him against herself with one arm, holding the other wide open for Nicole. Closing her eyes, she took a deep breath. She could almost smell their fine hair, feel their soft faces against hers. Nick would get up and . . .

She opened her eyes. There, she was doing it again, imagining things ahead of time, painting details of a homecoming that might never be matched by reality. She looked out of the small window. Beyond her reflection she could see, at a distance, a long curved stretch of sand and, at the end of it, the Great Point Light. Although it didn't seem deceptively close, it didn't look too far for someone determined to reach it, someone who'd ignore the faded signs threatening prospective intruders, someone who'd loosen the nails, one by one, and remove the weathered boards.